BRAIN IN A JAR

DAVID CHARLES SHAW

Publisher's note: This is a work of fiction. Names, characters, places,
and incidents either are the product of the author's imagination or are
used fictitiously. Any resemblance to actual events, locales, or
persons, living or dead, is entirely coincidental.

Edited, formatted, and book design by Kristen Corrects, Inc.
Cover art design by Charles Yu

Library of Congress Control Number: 2018904008

ISBN-13: 978-1-7321869-0-3 (paperback)
ISBN-13: 978-1-7321869-2-7 (ebook)

First edition published 2018

davidcharlesshaw.com

BRAIN IN A JAR

DAVID CHARLES SHAW

CONTENTS

It was January twentieth. That fateful evening began like any other but ended like none other—putting into motion the story of a man who wanted to be a machine and of something that was neither man nor machine but was trapped in between by a desperate idea of love.

CHAPTER ONE

- Outside -

I reached for the wet fire inside my head. Rapid, uneven breaths sending tremors through my arms and legs, I quivered on the cold floor. My fingertips feeling hair as they slid around something painful and hot. I held my breath then—a sigh of relief. *No blood.*

My eyes shot open. Beside me was a tiny spider fighting oily steel, light and shadow spinning around us. I fixated on the hopeless desperation of its flailing legs against a slick slope it could never climb, death at the bottom. I stared blankly until, finally, I pushed it up over the slope with a finger. It was gone. Rolling onto my back, I saw the nest of rapidly moving industrial robots several feet above me. *I'm under the assembly line... I was hit in the head.* A feeling of stupidity riding on a wave of pain washed over me. I watched the arm's shadows dancing across the sloped walls of the trench like spiders' legs as I collected my thoughts. *Did it reach for me? No that's crazy. This is my own fault. It could have been a lot worse, I guess.*

I sighed as I rolled and heaved myself up into a slumped over sitting position. I ran my fingers through my hair again, gently feeling up my wound before applying a light pressure to the area with my palm. *How long was I out?* I checked my phone. *It couldn't have been more than a few minutes ago, and nothing has found me yet.*

I haven't been down here since we installed this line for the new owner. I put my phone away. *First time I come back to it and this happens. Not like an assembly line can be grateful though, no matter how intelligent we make it. That still shouldn't have happened, but I don't know what I did wrong.*

I looked around. Everything was the same as it was then, aside from a thin layer of dust and some oil on the walls. I took a deep breath then rose to my feet.

Staying low, I made my way toward the access ramp at the end of the trench and emerged onto the open factory floor. Through the moving machinery surrounding me, I looked across the vast room. Not a person in sight, which wasn't surprising. There were only a few engineers and a few still un-automatable office workers in this pooled manufacturing plant. Few people were needed; almost everything was automated and highly modular. *I need to get back to my office then get out of here.* My hand still on my head, I made my way down the walkway, towering walls of moving machinery encased in shimmering crystal cases on either side. I passed an assistant, its stalk body turning atop its bush of short segmented legs to watch me. I heard a chirp of concern followed by the pitter patter of it coming after me.

I want to go home, I don't want to deal with this right now. I ignored it and walked faster, the door in sight. I slid into the gray office, knowing the machine wasn't allowed to follow me in without permission. With a sigh of relief, I made for my desk.

I gathered my few things then left the meager office. I waved goodbye to a distant person who didn't wave back, and I wondered if they had seen me or not as I walked down a long dimly lit hallway toward the parking lot outside.

At the end of the hall, I pushed through the heavy gray door, resenting it for not being automated like everything else. I stood for a moment, feeling the crisp evening air whipping at my face. Small snowflakes were beginning to fall from the overcast sky only to instantly melt as they hit my cheeks or the still-warm asphalt. An ambulance, its windows oddly dark, was parked in the far corner of the lot, near where transports picked up finished goods from the factory floor. Even from here, I could already hear the steady bass hum of the low flying transport ships over the old highway in the distance. I looked away.

I stepped out into the parking lot, letting the door slip away behind me as I briskly walked to my car. I opened the car door then sat down inside, dropping my dull black briefcase on the worn passenger seat beside me. Without pause, I activated the electronic key for the ignition and heard the car softly hum to life as I promptly turned on the heater and shivered. Satisfied, I leaned back and tried to relax as the car put itself into drive then began moving down the damp parking lot driveway, heading toward the new civilian highway that ran alongside the older, larger one that was now reserved solely for low altitude commercial and industrial transports.

Then, in my mirror, I saw the assistant from the factory floor standing alone in the parking lot, its spindle arms limp at its sides. The door to the office was still closing beside it. It seemed to make eye contact with me through my mirror. I averted my eyes then shut them. *I will report this tomorrow.*

My car pulled into an opening in a line of fast-moving vehicles, beginning the long trip back home. Everything was moving normally. I didn't have a worry in the world other than the slightly uncomfortable cold and that of possibly getting home a few meaningless seconds sooner—not that I had much to go home to anyway, at least not anymore. *What am I even going to do?* I sat up and opened my eyes, her face somehow refusing to leave me even after all this time.

From my place on the road, I could see the massive flying transports only a hundred yards to my right, plowing through the thick fog lingering above the asphalt like ghostly whitecaps on a sea of black. Driving so close to them still made me feel a little anxious even though they'd been using the old highway for several years. The transports and their high-speed travel were not only a source of slight and somewhat irrational anxiety. To me, they were also an occasional source of amazement or even awe at what humankind had been able to accomplish so fast.

Most of the transports I saw on my commute were like windowless metal skyscrapers turned on their sides and flying over 300 miles per hour toward their various destinations, most often into or out of the Northern Heavy Industrial District. Once there, they would unload their contents, likely raw materials, into one of the many factories or towers. The transports and factories were interesting to me, but the towers...they were the true wonders to be feared and marveled at.

Each tower was a privately owned company, almost a privately-owned city-state, most often in the form of a towering skyscraper-like building. Many reached miles into the sky while others remained entirely underground. Once great factories and industrial complexes, they could produce almost any tangible or intangible product on demand with unbelievable efficiency and speed, even whole other towers. Most often now, spaceships—if anything—were the sole product seen leaving them, birthed through gaping doors to disappear into the dark above us.

So complex and highly automated that they became more like giant organisms than buildings, the towers were incredibly self-sufficient and powered themselves mostly through what they could absorb from the air, sunlight, or from the earth beneath them. Some were even capable of moving.

I hunched over and squinted, struggling to see the top of the skyline through my fogged car window. I wondered how many towers were looking back at me right now, and if...she could see me through one of them. "No—no one will see me," I muttered, remembering a report I had recently read about how many of the areas of lowest population density on the planet were now thought to be at city centers.

Even though the towers were the largest part of many modern cities and densely packed relative to their enormous size, most of the towers were thought to have permanent populations ranging from a couple hundred people to just dozens or even single digits. Due to their reclusive nature and the vast lack of any information escaping them over the past few decades, it was difficult for anyone on the outside to know for sure. It used to be different.

The article continued by stating that most towers were once run like regular for-profit companies, except with large and permanent live-in workforces of throngs of scientists and engineers recruited to work alongside advanced AI. Talented people were still occasionally taken in today but, like those before them, they usually never returned to the outside. The towers were no longer regular businesses, though, and most were known to be simply controlled by individuals of a class of human owners called masters, who presided over them like kings. A typical master would control a single tower, but others might have many clustered together or scattered across the Earth and parts of our solar system.

The lack of contact with people led to a discussion of the numerous rumors that some of the towers were their own masters now, void of human workers and governed purely by the logic and protocol of their own machine minds— automated zombie computer systems continuing onward after the deaths of their users. Some people went so far as to call the towers "alive." It was likely nothing different from a person leaving a computer on when they're not in the room—or at least that's what I told myself.

Regardless of who or what controlled them, though, the towers and their highly secretive masters did what they wished, when they wished, and how they wished. What was left of our shell of a decentralized government did little to oppose them out of economic and military fears stemming from the advanced technologies developed and horded by towers, which their masters could easily wield if they were so inclined. Some still communicated with government diplomats assigned to them, but many refused.

Over the years, an increasing number of people and governments adopted the stance of treating the towers as foreign guests or as sovereign themselves, leaving them to do as they wished so long as they did no harm. Some people went so far as to even call the towers the "next step" in our development, comparing them to how the individual and independent cells of a slime mold will move as a whole to form spore-producing stalks that spread the organism in the wind. In many ways the towers had come to fulfill this reproductive role, and like the humble slime mold with its spores, send thousands of spaceships into the sky, presumably to seed and reproduce humanity in places unknown. However, many resented them for no longer sharing discoveries with the outside world as they once did for profit.

The towers, along with some communities, gained the technological means to produce nearly all goods locally and cheaper than ever before. This self-sufficiency caused the towers to no longer need or really care for money, and so most tower masters—who were often once scientists or business owners themselves—quickly realized their newfound sovereignty and became possessed by a technocratic and industrious desire for knowledge, physical growth, and sometimes even domination. Thousands of people had become kings of their own self-sustaining and self-made micro-nations then largely shut themselves off from the rest of the world. We transitioned to a post-global world of isolationism and inward perfection, because technology and automation made most trade obsolete.

Generally peaceful and introspective in nature, most towers still strove to keep their contact with the outside world minimal, usually concentrating entirely on their own internal goals, although there were more socially or economically motivated tower masters that shared with others or even fostered communities that built up around their foundations. Despite this general docile and reclusive nature, there had been a number of all-out wars fought between towers and occasionally even with the governments of host nations over questions of sovereignty and resource rights. These organism-like micro-nations had rules of their own and were now usually respected as such. Few nations could resist the influence of this new class and instead struggled to become more like them with little success.

It was all intimidating yet incredibly fascinating to me. Too often, I asked myself what my life would be like if I had been chosen and taken in by one, like she had… Again, I shook her eyes from my mind.

If only I had one, I thought wistfully. *To be truly sovereign and free…to be a master, my own master.*

My car continued to drive as I looked out and up into the graying sky. The clouds had cleared enough to reveal the golden lights of cities on the once-pale moon. *It looks more like the sun every year.* The thought pulled on a string of thoughts that together filled me with a melancholy, bittersweet feeling of nostalgia mixed with pride.

Like beads on a string, I was rolling over these thoughts when it happened.

A streak of light burned through my field of vision and impaled one of the transports behind me. The impact filled the air with an explosion of light and sound that shook my car and sent painful shockwaves through my body. With my ears ringing, I looked over my shoulder to see an eruption of flames through a small hole in the transport's side. The transport wobbled, then started losing altitude and began to drift in my direction. The massive vehicle loaded with countless tons of cargo was listing toward the civilian road.

I reeled around to take control of the steering wheel and slammed my foot on the pedal, forcing it to the floor. It was a desperate attempt to maneuver out of the way of the tumbling transport, but my sudden burst of speed caused my tires to hydroplane on the wet cement.

The front left corner of the transport landed center on the trunk of my car, instantly flattening it and partially crushing the front half of the vehicle. The steering wheel flew past me as my body was folded and pushed down onto the floor by the impact. Parts of the vehicle violently ripped away or were pulled under the transport, which continued to slide forward, smearing what was left of the car across the cruel pavement until jagged holes were worn through the floor beneath me. I had never heard such horrible sounds or felt such pain as I was forced down toward the road, sparks hitting my contorted face as pavement raced past the tip of my nose.

I blacked out after the first several seconds of the accident. I was sure that I would die, but somehow, I remembered first miraculously regaining some state of consciousness in the back of an ambulance some time later. I could hear people and their machines rushing about the scene, clearing debris from the wreck and tending to me, the transport somehow already flying away as if undamaged, before I slipped back into the dark.

I woke again sometime later. This time, any adrenaline I had before had worn off, and I was in incredible pain. I was disoriented, but aware enough of my surroundings to see that I was in a white room, with bright lights bearing down on me from all directions. Several men dressed in white uniforms and masks stood around me, all holding strange white tools or standing beside white robotic arms that did.

"He won't live long either way," someone said bluntly as a spinning, circular-bladed cutting tool on the end of a robotic arm started and began moving toward me.

"I know, but it still just doesn't seem quite right to me."

The first person proceeded to plunge their tool deep into my forehead. Without further hesitation, the others buried their tools in what was left of my chest or face. I felt the pain, and I tried to scream but I couldn't scream, and I couldn't move. I couldn't control my body at all. I could only sit in shock as they cut deeper into my already horribly mangled flesh.

I lost feeling in most of my body then felt my head separate from it. The white ceiling appeared to rip in half and fly away as my skull split into two halves in somebody's warm wet hands. My eyes and ears stopped working. I felt dizzy. I felt deprived of oxygen but couldn't breathe or even feel my lungs anymore. So in my mind alone, I desperately screeched.

Everything went black.

Nina…

CHAPTER TWO

- Incubation -

Everything was nothing, and nothing was everything until my consciousness slowly returned, my senses following it one by one to fill a segment of the black void I was in.

Through closed eyes, I could see a light that warmed my whole body inside and out. I heard wind through rustling tree branches then the occasional sweet calling of singing birds as sensation returned throughout my relaxed muscles. The fresh smell of pine filled my nose, my lungs expanding with delight. I felt warm and content here, but I felt I had to go further; I had to open my eyes.

I looked up into a blue sky framed by an elegant ring of the swaying green crowns of stately trees, tufts of white clouds spread across its beautiful expanse. I silently gazed upward for a long time before I lifted my head, propping myself up on my elbows.

I was lying naked on a soft grassy patch of earth at the center of a valley. *This is beautiful, but how did I—what...happened?*

The feeling of being crushed and a mental image of metal and plastic compacting around me flashed through my head. *The crash—and that room—with those men. Am I dead...or is this all in my head? Did I imagine it all, or was it a dream?*

"No, no, I couldn't have," I muttered.

The more I thought about it, though, the more I came to realize that I didn't know the answer to either of those questions. I tried to remember, but my memory felt cloudy and disorganized. I struggled to remember anything beyond fragments.

"What is happening?" I asked myself. Panic began to crawl in through the corners of my mind. *This is impossible!* My eyes darted from object to object as I stumbled to my feet. "Is this real?" The once dream-like memories of the operation room and of the crash grew in clarity alongside my mounting panic until it almost felt more real than my current surroundings. I began to shake.

Frantically, I spun around, searching for some unknown enemy or a clue to my situation. *I have to calm down, I have to calm down,* I repeated to myself while trying to concentrate on slowing my rapid breathing and racing mind. After several long, stressful moments, I was able to regain some of my composure. *I need to keep myself distracted and find some answers. I should look around.*

Still struggling to keep out the insanity, I turned and walked up the gradual slope of the clearing and into the forest. I could see the edge of an empty field of grass ahead, through the trees. Despite the stress, I couldn't help but to think what a beautiful place this was. The warm aura of its greenish-blue shade seemed to suppress my panic and fear with every step. Even the ground was soft and pleasant to walk on with my bare feet. It was almost as if this place, whether it be real or an illusion, was designed to calm me.

I walked until I began to feel a warmer, dry breeze coming in from the forest's outer edge where great golden columns of light poured in around the dark tree branches. I sped up until finally I walked out into the field, squinting in the direct sunlight.

The grass-covered expanse seemed to go on for miles in every direction until it disappeared at the distant feet of the tallest mountains I had ever seen, their sharp peaks reaching past the sparse clouds and scraping the heavens.

I stood for a moment in wonder then shouted into the expanse. "Hello! Can anybody hear me? Hello!" There was no reply, not even an echo, and I suddenly had a curious feeling that I was going to be here for a very long time—alone. "What is this place?"

I felt a knot constrict in my gut again, but there was something about this place that relaxed me. *I can't remember very much about anything right now anyway, so why not try to relax, at least until I know what's going on?* I didn't have or, at least, couldn't remember anything worth going back to, and that in itself made me shudder. *I might actually enjoy staying here for a short time—maybe even a long time.* This was the kind of place I had only dreamed of exploring. A small, nervous laugh escaped my mouth. Something still didn't feel right. I felt like I was here, but also like I wasn't at the same time. I tried to think through jumbled and fleeting memories of the crash and of what had happened in the white room.

Did that really happen? Could it have been a bad dream? Am I imagining this, or was everything else imagined? What if the room was real and this isn't, or the other way around, or neither or both?

"Stop!" I told myself, digging my heels into the ground as if I were holding back a boulder of insanity. I couldn't answer any of these questions, and part of me didn't really want to anyway. *I will figure this out.* I turned and began to walk back toward where I had come from.

"What should I do?" I mumbled as I returned to the clearing a few minutes later. I stood idly thinking. *Something is definitely very wrong.* Despite the incredible beauty of this place, there was something underlying it all that felt kind of…ominous. Or was it just lonely?

After several minutes of pacing I decided to lay down in an especially inviting grassy spot near the edge of the clearing. I closed my eyes, feeling the warm sun caress me as I turned incomplete thoughts and memories in my turbulent head. The mixture of warmth, forest sounds, and the wafting of soothing aromas gradually coddled me into a deep and comforting sleep. *I really like this place…*

***

I woke up. I wasn't in the forest anymore. Below my feet was a smooth plane so black that no light seemed to escape it. My eyes darted upward and spun over the horizon, finding only the plane that seemed to extend into eternity in every direction. My confusion and despair leaped up anew and tore into my mind as my body shuddered under a horrible new sensation that I couldn't fully grasp. I clawed at my head, falling to my knees, my mind screaming internally with distress and emotional pain so intense that it felt physical. I screeched as if I were being eaten alive, desperately grabbing at my face and chest with my hands. I didn't know what to do.

Something was inside me, some force I couldn't yet comprehend. This inexorably black plane seemed to watch me, to look into my very soul and devour me. I felt like it had just arrived yet like it had been there since before I could remember: watching me, controlling things around me, even caring for me in its own horrible way. It was taking something from me. It was with me, but I was alone.

Cut by recurring lapses in consciousness, time itself began to blur with the plane until all I had left was the knowledge of my isolation. It was like there was a cold fire burning me from the inside, the flames of which were a sensation in my gut like a long tongue licking my chest in long stokes from the inside. I quivered and felt more alone than I ever had before.

***

I existed in this place, shifting between the plane and forest until I nearly forgot about time. Depression worsened then became numbness, and my only form of escape was to try to suppress the emotions haunting me. I didn't want to feel, only to think, all the while feeling like I was being nudged along by a force intangible. I felt myself become more and more like a machine.

Very slowly, I gained control of myself and learned to manipulate the environments around me until I could see through them like thin curtains. Beyond them lay a seemingly impermeable emptiness. My universe became a tiny sphere of conscious control in a vacuum of nothing, a dark un-enterable ether.

Eventually I decided that this prison was my own mind.

As the illusions fell away I came to be increasingly tormented by the lack of movement their loss revealed, in addition to the numbing loneliness that already constantly threatened to drown me.

I came to accept the accident and the operating room as reality. I was now a tiny ball of pain and awareness, and in my waking hours—if it could even be called waking—I could not see, could not hear, smell, touch, feel, or move anything outside of the illusions I came to be able to control on a whim. I didn't know how I was subsisting or even existing; how could I possibly survive? I didn't know, and I didn't care anymore. I thought frequently of death and became indifferent to it.

I existed like this for time immeasurable.

Somehow, I barely avoided drowning in the endless black hole of insanity and despair that would have destroyed me, and my physical pain gradually yet steadily diminished until I was almost comfortable just floating there inside of nothing—not comfortable—numb. I gave up to the apparent reality that I could not escape this place even through death, and that I might float here in myself for eternity.

Then on what I now know to be sometime in November, years after my initial accident, something happened. Something that broke my timeless trance.

I was idly thinking up some sort of game, adventure, theory, or really anything I could to try to create an illusion to occupy myself with. Then I felt it. There was something from outside of any illusion, a small push or pressure on the edge of my sphere of existence. It was like a wave, almost like a wave of water or physical force washing over and into me, moving the bounds of my very universe. *Is this real?*

Before I could decide, I felt pain—a sharp stabbing pain that penetrated deep into my side. The same feeling appeared on my opposite side, then I felt it coming from everywhere all around me. Terror gripped me. I couldn't begin to identify the source of the pain or how to escape it. The pain only pierced deeper into my being; my reality seemed to split around it. Then as despair and ideas of death crept in, the pain ceased to increase, held its intensity, lessened, then stopped altogether. I lost consciousness.

CHAPTER THREE

- Waking Up -

When I awoke, I didn't know how long I had been out. I knew only that I was thinking again, that the pain had stopped, and that there was something new that had been forced inside of me. What felt like several spikes lay buried deep inside of my form, strange and alien. I wasn't really sure what to think of them, of what they were, where they came from. These spikes weren't the only new thing in my mind, though. There was something moving, and I couldn't see through it like I could the illusions.

In my mind I could "see" something flowing in and out of one of the spikes as if it were a tunnel. It was a continuously flowing stream of tiny, faintly glowing particles that would flow out of the spike then slowly circle around me, almost inside of me. The particles would gently touch my consciousness then circle back into the same spike. For some reason I felt like the particles were watching me. I tried to hide deeper inside of myself, and from there I peeked out at the stream of light invading my little realm of existence.

I waited for a long time, cautiously watching the flow until I began to feel something much larger inside one of the spikes. It was like a wall of light racing toward me at an alarming speed. I tried to pull away, but there was nowhere to pull away to. I could only be aware.

The object hit me like a crashing wave. I felt a surge of energy and information being injected, pounded into my mind like a sheet of freezing ice and, before I knew what was happening, for the first time in a seeming eternity—I COULD SEE!

***

An impenetrable wall of light, quickly followed by flashes of every color, blasted through me. Then the colors melted away into a dark and fuzzy haze before the world grew brighter and clearer until, eventually, I was able to make out shapes and even depth.

The world formed before me into an intensely lit, pure white room. The room filled my head as if I were looking at it normally with eyes, but no matter how hard I tried, I could not see through it like I had the illusions. Still, something felt a little off. A blurry gray column at the center of the room captured my attention, but as the image continued to grow clearer, I realized that the column was actually a tall, lean man with broad shoulders.

The man had short light brown, almost blond hair, blue-green eyes, and a hawk-like visage complemented by a sharp-looking white uniform. A dazzlingly gold pocket watch chain hung from it. He appeared to be middle-aged, and as my vision continued to increase in sharpness, I noticed hundreds of small hair-like golden pins and plugs protruding through the skin on his right side. The pins had a sort of functional and electrical look to them that reminded me of pin connectors on an old computer CPU or of tiny antennas, only these were anchored in his flesh.

Then I realized he wasn't alone.

To his right there stood a young and slender woman. She had long black hair, a flawless alabaster complexion, and striking blue eyes laced with brilliant purple markings like the facets of a gemstone. To the man's left there stood a young man with platinum hair and green eyes. Behind these three people in front, I could make out the still slightly blurred images of several other individuals standing close together.

Every one of the people in the room was unusually pale
skinned yet healthy-looking, tall, lean, and all were dressed in
flowing white uniforms, giving them a dignified and sterile
appearance. In fact, like the room, every part of everyone was
pure white or close to it except for the hair of the young
woman in front. The contrast of her smooth piano-black hair
caused her to stand out against the room and everything in it.
I could feel myself trying to shrink back, further into myself.
They were all incredibly beautiful yet terrifying and powerful
looking, like angels waiting to judge me. The sight of it all—
and the fact that I had sight at all, if I was really even seeing—
was more than scary and confusing.

Am I going more insane?

My train of confused thought disintegrated as the man
standing front and center began to speak, his voice firm and
commanding yet calm. "Hello, can you hear me?"

I thought of saying, "Yes I can," and as I spoke it in my mind I
felt something small burst from within me and fly toward the
same spike that the wave of particles had come from only
seconds before. Not a moment later, another stream of
particles flew out of the spike and into the mass of energy that
was still inside of and now almost a part of me.

As the clouds of particles combined and churned, the man
said, "Good, very good."

The two people standing beside him looked a little happier and
perhaps even a little excited too, or at least less solemn.

The man in the suit opened his mouth to speak again but
before he could get a word out, near bursting, I let loose a
torrent of questions all at once.

"What are you, who are you, and what and where am I? How
long have I been here? What is happening to me?"

The man and the rest of the group seemed to become a little
more excited; tiny grins appeared on a few of their placid faces.
The man in the suit, now wearing a minuscule grin and holding
a little sound of pride in his voice, answered me.

"I am a human just as you are, and you can call me Ward. I am
the master and sovereign of the tower we are both in. This is

my first and greatest tower of three, and you have been here for more than two and a half years. We are very pleased that you have survived this long and have all been working hard toward that goal. We have been calling you A-404 for the past year, ever since you survived the initial transplant and installment."

I wasn't quite sure what to make of that. Another question pushed to the surface, which I had to know the answer to. "What happened to me?"

"You were crushed by a material transport ship that was shot down by a missile. Fortunately, a team of my workers had been assigned to find situations similar to your own and happened to be in the area. They were there to abduct what was left of any bodies by posing as a group of emergency government medical workers.

"Fortunately for both of us, they found you and saved you from imminent death by pulling you from your destroyed body and taking you here to me. As for what is happening to you now…" Ward sighed. "All that is left of your body is a brain in a stasis vessel with a liter of synthetic blood being propelled through it by a mechanical pump."

He paused for a moment as if to let his words sink in then continued, "We are able to communicate with each other because we have connected your brain to hardware through cables that are connected to the sockets now planted inside of you. Right now you are seeing and hearing us through a small camera on top of a desk. Everything you try to say is being passed through an interface then drawn on a computer monitor as text. Do you understand so far?" Ward took a deep breath and looked at me coolly, patiently but expectantly.

I felt unable to answer. I wasn't sure how much time passed before finally I forced out the words, "Yes…yes I think so."

"Very good," Ward replied, stretching out the words in a pleased tone. "Only two of your connections are being used as of now, but I will have much more connected to you very soon. Try to get used to what you have now because within the next few days I plan on installing the next round of new hardware in you. Think of this all as a sort of a new body that I'm giving you."

I remained silent, listening carefully to everything he said. Ward continued, "I have great plans and expectations for you if everything goes well." Suddenly his cheerful demeanor changed and in an authoritative and matter-of-fact voice he said, "You will do everything I instruct you to how I instruct you to. You are mine now, and you live only because I allow you to live by my means for my ends. If you attempt anything malicious or refuse to comply with orders, then I will immediately terminate and dispose of you. I am your master and you are my servant." He paused, and leaning forward a little, silently looked deep into my camera's lens as if he could see my soul inside it. Then in his usual calm and stoic manner he amiably asked, "Do you understand?"

I quickly answered with a yes; I felt I had little of a choice anyway. A barely noticeable grin of approval appeared on Ward's face as he replied, "Good, I will be leaving you now. I will check in with you again soon but for now my assistants here will ask you some questions and perform a few simple tests. Goodbye now."

He began to turn to leave but before he could, I sent another word to the screen. "Goodbye."

I saw Ward glance down at a place below my line of sight then he looked back up into my camera, probing the empty lens with his inexpressive gaze. Then he turned and walked out of my field of view. One by one, everyone in the room turned and followed him. Everyone disappeared from my sight except for the pale young woman with black hair and purple-blue eyes. She stepped closer then sat in a chair that I couldn't see and revealed an electronic sheet of paper. She set it down on a desk that was in front of me but below my line of sight and brandished a shiny black pen. Then in a soft but poised voice, she spoke. "Hello."

"Hello," I replied, apprehensive. I could see the back end of the pen moving in her hand at the very bottom of my plane of view.

Without looking up from the desk she asked, "What is your name?"

I began to answer her question but was surprised when I struggled to do so. *What is my name?* I tried to think of a name; I knew that I had to give her a name. *How could I forget my name?* Then a word popped into my head. I wasn't sure if it was my name or not, but it was all I could think of at the time. So I hastily answered her, "Alder."

She glanced up from her writing. "Is that all?"

"Yes. I think so." It was a lie.

She looked at the monitor then the end of her pen began moving again. After that she asked me a number of questions about the camera they had given me: if and how I could "feel it" with my mind. She also asked me my age. I told her I was twenty, but it was a guess; I truly didn't know and that scared me. It was another lie—a lie I told out of fear of not being able to answer her questions and of what they might do to me if I failed. She wrote down a lot after that, and I feared that she already somehow knew my answer to be wrong. *What has happened to me?*

She also had me do some simple tests and puzzles that I would watch her perform on the electric paper. I answered all of the questions as carefully as I could and, partially out of fear, tried to answer them as quickly as I could too, but she was always patient, regardless of my mistakes and pauses. When she was finally finished, she said goodbye then sighed deeply as she reached her arm around to the side of my camera and pressed a small button I could not see.

With a click, everything disappeared, and once again, I was alone in the dark with only myself for company. The shock of darkness wore off, and everything that had just happened played over and over in my mind, the magnitude of it slowly sinking in under the weight of years of isolation. *This is real—I'm in a tower…and—this really happened. They own me… What should I do? What can I even do?*

The deep sense of loneliness that I had grown so numb to gained a renewed sharpness. I tried to remember the faces of all the people who I saw: the scientists, Ward, the man standing beside him, and the woman—the woman beside him who had stayed behind with me. She stood out from the rest because of her hair, but there was something else about her, something more than that. *She seemed kind of sad, maybe even a little lonely—like me. What a strange thing to pick up on.* I felt sick.

***

The night was long and stressful, but I was able to feel something that I hadn't before. I was able to move, in a way. My physical body was immobile but parts of my mind, or its influence and awareness at least, could move into and out of the wires, metal spikes, and plugs stuck into me. When I moved, I felt as if I were made of water or air flowing through long constrictive canals.

I also never lost sight of the stream of little bright lights flowing between me and the wires. I still felt like they were watching me—and now I knew that they probably were. *Maybe it's like a computer program.*

I reached out with my mind, following the lights up through the cable they came from until I ran into a membrane-like wall. I tested the wall by pressing against it with my mind, but only the particle stream could pass through. *It must be another type of computer program.* I withdrew from the wire.

Finally, I had an explanation and some closure for what had happened, but I felt sick thinking about it—and of what they might be planning to do to me. I was terrified by all this new hardware and by the people I had met today, but somehow, I was also excited about it. *I've been numb and alone for so long.*

I thought about the name that I had given the woman. *Alder.* I couldn't remember where I had heard it before, if at all. Then I remembered that most people had two or three names: a first, middle, and last.

Just how much did I lose? In my isolation, I hadn't really even realized what I was missing, and it scared me. Eventually, I passed into a sort of idle state of mind that, over time, I had come to call sleep.

CHAPTER FOUR

- Germination -

There was a bright flash of light and a loud scratching static noise as an explosion of particles slammed into me. Instantly ripped from my restful state, I startled awake, shocked and confused until I realized that my camera had just been turned back on. I accepted the information coming from it, happy for some stimulation, and saw the black-haired woman come into focus. She stood centered in the view of my camera, calmly looking down into it.

"Hello, good morning," I said.

She saw the message on the monitor then flashed me a small smile. "Good morning to you too. I don't know if I'd call this morning though."

She walked out of my field of view, and I heard what I assumed was a door slide open then, a moment later, close. I was alone for a few minutes before I heard the soft *swoosh* of the door as she returned with a young man I recognized. *He stood to the left of Ward yesterday.*

The man carried a heavy-looking box in his arms with a small bundle of tools on top of it. His face was expressionless as he looked into my camera and set his box down in front of it on the desk. He opened the box and began to remove things from it.

"This is the one that was made in the lower factory last week," he said to the dark-haired woman.

"Thank you for bringing them."

The man lifted an elongated oval-shaped camera out of the box. It reminded me of a big metal football, considerably larger than a human head. Two separate lenses were positioned side by side, one of which was much deeper set than the other. The front of the camera curved back into multiple long, elegant points of varying length on the back side. The base of the camera connected to a long coiled arm made of some sort of stretchy, synthetic, black material. It reminded me of a huge black snake.

The man set the tools and the camera down on the desk. He opened the bundle of tools, took one in his hand, and looked into my camera. "We are going to remove this camera and install the new one." He moved his hands around its base. "This new unit has two separate cameras and integrated microphones. This should give you much better depth perception; ideally you will have better sight and hearing than any living non-enhanced human. Its neck is controlled mostly by a network of synthetic muscles and a few small electric motors. If you can control this, you will be able to maneuver the camera to look in any direction."

I listened and thought as he spoke.

"There is also an embedded system that will read aloud the data that would normally become the text sent to the monitor. So, you should be able to audibly speak to us now." He paused after he removed the last thing fastening down my camera. My camera wobbled slightly now, and it made the room appear to be shaking back and forth.

"Okay," he exhaled. "Now I'm going to turn your camera off." I saw his hand move to some place above me then in an instant everything fell into total darkness and silence again. *What will the new camera be like?* I anxiously thought about being able to move outside of this dark world, where I only had myself and the faint glow of the computer programs monitoring me as company. *And will I really speak again?* The prospect was a nervous thrill.

The minutes passed, feeling like hours, until I felt a burst of energy and the flow of information return like a wave crashing against me. The white light of the room and the pale faces of the man and woman returned to me in an explosion of light.

"Is it working?" I heard the man ask, noticeably more clearly than I had before.

Suddenly everything in the room began to fly away from me. The room rushed past my eyes. I was falling forward—the desk filled my vision—then I heard a loud smack as I hit the dense wooden surface. I felt nothing. The woman stepped forward and lifted the camera, so I could see her.

"Can you feel the insides of the camera or its controls?" she asked, looking down to the computer monitor for an answer.

"I think so." I froze—I had just heard myself speak for the first time in years and could hardly believe the voice was mine. It was metallic and monotone, almost like the default male voice of the text reader on old computers. I was forced to wonder if the horrible sound was caused by the hardware or by my mental state influencing the software. *I haven't spoken in so long. I can't even clearly remember my old voice.*

"Good," the woman responded, unfazed by the sound.

"Well, that works," the man added as he stepped back into view.

"Now try to move it," the woman instructed.

I felt around inside the different plugs stuck in my brain until I found one with a new stream of particles. *That must be the muscles and motors of the camera's neck.* I followed the stream up the entire length of the camera neck, and one by one, I found the few dozen control points that meshed with the synthetic muscles. I felt my way into the control nodes and grabbed on to them with my mind.

I would start by giving what I thought felt like a firm squeeze to all of them at once, but the instant I did, the room began to fly before me again. I launched up from the desk, out of the woman's hands, and slammed against something hard behind me. With a loud bang, I stopped moving.

The man and woman leaped toward me, grabbing the neck of the camera, trying to pull me down and away from whatever it was that I had just hit while both gasping with fear and surprise.

I panicked, and, clumsily trying to wrestle out of the man's grip, I began thrashing like a worm.

"Make sure it's not broken," I heard him forcefully shout to the woman, a slight quiver of fear in his voice. He struggled to hold on to the powerful anaconda of a neck with his arms then with his whole body as he was lifted off the ground.

The woman jumped up onto the edge of the desk and leaned forward, out of my field of vision, to inspect whatever was behind me. I could hear her hurriedly running her hands across it as if searching for something. She stopped and sighed. "There's barely a scratch on it."

"Good," the man ground out, still hanging from the thrashing snake-like neck of my camera. The woman began climbing off the desk but before she could, I unintentionally knocked her off. Then with one last thrust of my neck, the man couldn't hold on any longer and was flung across the room. His body smacked against the wall with a sickening thud before he slumped into a pile on the ground.

He looked back up at my camera with a pained look of shock on his face and gulped for the air. "We aren't trying to hurt you," he gasped angrily. "Please, calm down and relax!"

In my mind, I saw myself plunging my hard metal camera through his face and chest from above—like a striking bird or snake—but then I realized what was happening, what I had just done. I had lost control. A sinking feeling and fear came over me as the pent-up panic melted away. I clumsily released my death grip on the artificial muscles. The man staggered to his feet, and, with a firm grip, he slowly moved my camera back into a low upright position.

I squeezed the controls again, this time with more control and experience, just enough and in the right way to hold myself upright.

Finding and feeling the insides of the neck reminded me of controlling a muscle on a human body, although these synthetic muscles were simpler and gave a considerably smaller amount of feedback sensations. *I'll have to get used to this neck.*

"I don't know why Ward had us give this to him," the man grumbled. "It's too dangerous in my opinion."

"You have to be more careful," the woman told me seriously.

"You could have broken it," the man added, anger still in his voice.

"Broken what?" I asked. *This new voice will take time to get used to.* I still cringed at the sound of it.

"Do you know what would happen to us, and not to mention to you, if you break that?"

"Break what?" I asked louder and more forcefully this time. Without fully realizing it, I had raised my head upward and was now looking down at them from near the ceiling. I was still scared and confused, but felt oddly empowered by this new appendage. *He's right; this is too dangerous.*

"You," the man replied exasperatedly. He took a wary step back.

"It's behind you. Well, I guess it *is* you," the woman added, pointing at something unseen behind my camera.

I turned, not knowing what I would find. Shock and surprise overtook me as an enormous, clear orb several feet in diameter and filled with a clear liquid came into view.

I gazed through the faint, distorted reflection of my new camera at a lone fleshy mass suspended at the center of the orb, a pincushion of cold metallic spikes and tubes protruding from it in every direction. Plugged into the end of each spike were snow-white cables that connected the construct of flesh and metal to sockets in the walls of the orb. U-shaped tubes at the top and bottom of the chamber pumped fluid through them as red lines traced around their exteriors faintly glowed, presumably heating and filtering the fluid to maintain my homeostasis.

I stared at the whole of the apparatus, unable to pull myself away from the scene. Then the realization hit me: *I was the pink mass. That pinkish mass was my brain.*

The memories of the operation and the crash plowed into the forefront of my mind all at once. I relived everything and was left shocked and unsure of what to do. My very existence was inside that tiny ball of misshapen flesh. *This is me...*

The man's voice interrupted my melancholy daze. "I don't want to take any chances this time. I will make an order for more armor to be made and put on the orb."

I heard him put his bundle of tools and the old camera into the empty box. Lastly, I heard him pick up the monitor, and with it under his arm, his footsteps moved toward the door to my right where they disappeared into silence in the hallway. The door closed behind him.

"You have to be more careful," the woman said to the back of my new camera. She paused to take a breath then added, "I will be back." She picked up her electronic notebook and began for the door.

"Wait." I turned my camera away from the orb to face her.

She turned and looked back up into the lenses of my camera.

"Yes, what is it?" The sound of her voice almost gave me the insane impression that she was eager to answer me.

"What is your name—or...who are you?"

"My name is Nikaya, and I'm going to be taking care of you for now."

"Wh-what happens now?"

She looked at me understandingly. "Most likely, nothing will happen to you because of today. It was an understandable mistake."

"I'm sorry."

"It's all right; I'm not injured, just relieved that you didn't kill yourself."

She waited a moment for me to say something else, but when I didn't speak, she walked out of the room. The white metal door softly closed behind her. A few moments later the lights in the room dimmed to a faint glow but my camera remained on.

Nikaya… Nikaya… I rolled the word over in my head. Once again, I was alone in the room—only this time I was able to look around. I had an entire day left to examine my room in its entirety.

I began at the floor and worked my way up, looking in every direction at everything I could. The room was octagonal in shape with beveled corners; the floor, ceiling, and every wall was of the same bright white. Eight small, white bumps marked the locations of the cameras hidden in the ceiling, one in each corner of the room.

The room had three doorways, two of which were on the walls adjacent to the wall in front of me; the third was directly behind me on the other side of my orb.

The orb rested a few feet above the ground at the absolute center of the room, held by a white metal column extending up from the floor and down from the ceiling. Looking closely, I noticed white metal sockets, similar to those I had seen in the walls of my orb, on the ceiling, floor, and columns connecting to the orb. I assumed these were for connecting the orb, and me, to the rest of the tower.

My camera was positioned atop a rounded white pedestal reaching out from below the orb. In front of this pedestal stood a small, worn wooden desk that blatantly stood out against the shining and sterile-looking metal room.

That night I further explored the inside of my camera as well. I found that I was able to turn it on and off myself and that there was no other way it could be turned off except for from the inside. That tiny bit of power I had thrilled me. It gave me a very small but much-needed sense of control, knowing that only I could control this one little thing. After seeing what I had accidently done to the man earlier today with the camera, and realizing what I could have done, I knew that if the need came, I could probably kill him or anyone else with it.

Still, I couldn't help but wonder the same thing that the man had before he left. *Why would they give me this? It seems like a real risk on their part.*

My gaze eventually returned to the glasslike orb behind me. I looked deeply into it, examining every detail as I circled the orb as far as I could reach with my camera's neck. I noticed a second smaller pump next to the one that I had already decided was circulating the liquid in the orb. Multiple thin transparent tubes filled with crimson-red liquid connected the pump to my brain. The pump must be acting as my new heart, I realized, pondering how I didn't have a heartbeat anymore. I didn't breathe either; I hadn't ever since I arrived here.

Only one of the sockets on the outside of the orb had anything plugged into it—a thick white cable that connected to one of the sockets on the column beneath the orb. *It's probably what connects me to the camera.*

When I finally tired of looking around the room, I left my camera on and sat idly staring at the wall. *I think I've been awake in this place for three days now, but I don't know… I don't feel tired. I don't feel anything.*

Gradually, I drifted back into small but scary ideas and questions I couldn't answer, paranoia and distrust revealing themselves and blossoming. I had acquired an underlying distrust of nearly everything—of my captors and of the environment they placed me in. I was aware of everything in my room in incredible detail now, but still, I couldn't help but wonder sometimes. Perhaps a result of being trapped in my mind for years, I still found myself on occasion questioning my surroundings. *How depressing and stupid… As far as I know, I'm just a brain in a jar—maybe I've always been… No—whatever I experience must be treated as real.*

With a little difficulty, I eventually pushed away these destabilizing thoughts and eagerly escaped into my idle state.

CHAPTER FIVE

- Growth -

Flash—the lights in the room were turned on, jolting me out of my idle state. I glanced to my right and saw Nikaya standing in the doorway looking at me.

"Good morning Nikaya," I said as politely as I could, trying to show off how I had modified my new voice last night. I had tried to make it sound more natural and refined but wasn't able to completely remove the metallic and machine-like sound of it. I found myself sort of liking the effect, though—something about it felt fitting to me, to my numbed mind and synthetic body.

"Hello," Nikaya replied, sounding a little surprised and maybe even slightly impressed by the new voice. "How did you do that with your voice?"

"Last night I was able to sort of um…reorganize it until I had it where I wanted it. I didn't like the old one too much."

"Well, those are excellent results."

"Thank you. So what do you have for me today?" I was mostly over the initial shock of reuniting with the outside world and found myself wanting them to give me more. After all, I had been rotting in a prison of myself and nothingness, doing virtually nothing for years.

"More hardware." Nikaya stepped away from the door and it opened, revealing a metallic man pushing a cart that hovered above the floor, a large box on top of it.

The robot entered the room, followed by several other identical machines moving smoothly and soundlessly across the floor with an almost eerie perfection. They were about the same size as a man but taller and thinner with entirely white metal bodies and three eyes. The third eye—crimson in color—was smaller, and placed near the center of the machine's neck.

The lead robot, pushing the cart, stopped near the middle of the empty area in front of me. Nikaya leaned forward and opened the box on the cart.

"Where are the other people, and the man from yesterday?" I asked, a little worried that I may have injured him.

"Smit will be here later."

"Okay," I replied plainly. *So his name is Smit.*

When she was finished, I watched her tell the robot with the cart something that I couldn't understand, then together the machines began to move. They walked over to the cart and, one at a time, carefully lifted long white cables out of the open box. The cables were a few inches thick and on either end was a gold and white metal spike the length of a human hand.

"What are they for?" I asked, looking down into the box.

"We are going to connect you to more of the tower."

The robots began carrying the cables toward my orb.

"What will that do?"

"You will be connected to the tower's main systems. We are going to start giving you more control, tests and possibly even eventual work assignments," Nikaya said. "You will also be able to access and learn to control machines by going through an interface." As she spoke, the robots began plugging their cables into the sockets around my orb.

As each cable locked into place, I felt the space inside of it open up around me—almost as if the very universe were expanding. I became aware of the new areas as my mind's feelers expanded into the inside of each cable that connected my brain to a socket in the ceiling or floor.

I explored the new area until I was stopped by a wall of particles at the end of each cable, like the one that I had found two days ago. I examined the walls, experimentally pushing and pulling on them with my mind as the robots continued to work until there was a cable connected to every socket on my orb. When the crew of machines had finished, all but one joined a single file line then, like ghosts, silently left the room through the door to my right. The one remaining walked to the cart, grabbed the handle, then stood completely still, waiting for Nikaya's command. She stood in front of the desk, holding her electronic notebook and looking up at my camera.

"Can you feel them?"

"Yes," I replied, knowing she meant the cables.

"Good."

"What are the walls of light?" I asked, puzzled.

"What do you mean?" She looked happy that I had asked the question, like she was expecting it. I felt like she knew the answer to this too but still wanted me to explain myself, perhaps as a sort of test. This was all part of the experiment.

"There are glowing walls at the ends of the cables, and one of the walls has something coming in and out of it."

"What's coming in and out of it?"

"It's like a little stream, and I feel almost like it's watching me. What is it?"

Nikaya looked pleased. "Do you know much about computers?"

"Yes…" I answered, although my voice belied my uncertainty.

"Well, the walls are a type of computer program created by the tower's computer and put in place to prevent you from entering or interacting with other parts of the tower—sort of like a firewall, for your protection. As for what you called a 'stream' coming in and out of you, it's another program that's monitoring your health. It's nothing to worry about," she added reassuringly.

Apprehensively, I pulled away from the walls a little. "So I'm inside of a computer then, or a part of one?"

"Yes and no. We can install hardware and some software in you, and your life is maintained by that hardware," Nikaya explained. "However, you aren't a part of the tower computer, just inside it. We both are, really."

"What do you mean we both are?"

"The whole tower is connected, everything, and it doesn't differentiate between the insides of its wires and the insides of its halls." I wondered what she meant by that, but she continued, "The area we've given you so far is yours to move freely and safely through and we plan on giving you more soon, once you to learn how to create your own programs and walls."

How am I supposed to do that? I don't even understand how I'm able to move through or feel the insides of the cables, or even how I feel myself. Nikaya seemed to detect my confusion. "It's all part of the experiment, and I will do my best to explain it. It will be different from anything you've done before, inside or outside the tower, and it's something that you will have to figure out for yourself, but the fact that you've already found out how to move through the cables and find the walls shows me that you're already using the taline interface."

"Taline?"

Nikaya smiled. "Taline is what we call the substance that almost everything in the tower is made of, including the cables and spikes connected to you. The crystalline structure of the metal can be modified and shaped into circuits by applying varying voltages in specific ways using an interface, and those 'walls' are circuits, or programs, created by the tower computer using interfaces similar to the one connected to you.

"I don't personally know what it is like to experience it, or how consciously or subconsciously you do it," she continued, "but I know that when you say you 'look' at the walls or the programs that are watching you, what is really happening is your brain is using the interface to create a circuit in the taline. Your awareness of these things is through physical points of contact between the circuits. Technically the feeling is the result of tiny voltages leaking from the computer's circuits into yours, or inducing a current in them, then being interpreted by your brain." She paused. "Do you understand all of this?"

"I'm trying to," I answered tentatively. "And I can't move through the walls because the circuit is so dense there?"

"Yes, sort of. It's also a result of the way that circuit is charged, though. Any virtual computation can be done using taline circuits and they can be formed into physical and semi-physical structures like the walls. Sort of like if you had a body made entirely out of brains that can be reshaped and organized however you want—or at least that's the goal. The taline circuits can even measure touch and temperature through tiny changes in the resistance and capacitance of the metal."

I tried and failed to remember anything I could compare this to. "It's—it's incredible…"

"It is, and your learning to use this human-taline interface is key. As I already said, it's also something you have to do mostly on your own." Smiling, she said, "I will be back." Nikaya turned and walked toward the door. Letting the robot leave before her, she then turned to face me again. "Just remember that while we may treat you like a piece of hardware, you aren't a machine unless you want to be. You're still human." Then she turned and left.

Her advice left me feeling unsettled, a mixture of pure amazement and trepidation. I thought about what she had said about the circuits being both physical and virtual objects. Knowing about the taline circuits made many of my experiences make more sense—which was comforting—but the realization that the tower computer I was inside of was not only a computer in a traditional sense but also a real-world behemoth that physically engulfed everything and everyone I saw scared me.

I need to figure out how to make walls.

Quickly, I found what I thought would be a nice place to try inside one of my new cables, and I tried to move as much of my conscious attention to the area as I could. I struggled to feel the individual circuits that Nikaya said were connected to me, feeling more like I was the inside of the cables than not. I tried to push against the walls of the cable, to shake things up, but nothing happened. I knew the circuits were here because I was here and moving through them, but I couldn't see the individual circuits or manually make changes to them. *Maybe my circuit is too disorganized for me to feel it, or I'm just missing something. I need to think about walls. What is the logic behind a wall?* I concentrated on the function and basic concept of a wall, pushing and pulling on the metal with my mind for a long time. Still nothing. *I need to try something else.* A little discouraged, I stopped and backed away. Then I noticed something new. Tiny glowing specs of light were left behind, scattered across the inside of the metal wire where I felt like I had been applying pressure. I felt over the specks with my mind, but I didn't know what they were, nor could I fully understand how they had gotten there. *Did I change the metal there somehow?* I withdrew most of my concentration to my brain and made a mental note to return to the specs later.

I was starting to feel a little frustrated when I noticed the stream of particles that made up the program that, as I was told, was only monitoring my health. Somehow, I doubted that it did only that.

I watched the stream for a while, trying to imagine what the physical circuit behind it might look like. I imagined it as a long and complex tree of wires or microscopic channels in the taline, shaped and made conductive by some force unknown, the little lights being the energy moving through them representing information. *I wonder if I can catch one.* I tried to get in front of the stream with my mind, wrap myself around it, and squeeze it…but nothing I did seemed to affect the flow. It just continued along its regular path. After another fruitless try, I resigned to just watching the stream again.

I concentrated on the cable the stream flowed through, mulling over how I interacted with the camera and if it might relate. I thought until, frustrated at my continued lack of success, I angrily punched at the surrounding cables. *I need to do this! What am I doing wrong?* Then I noticed that I had left behind particles just like I had the first time I tried to push against the cables. Intrigued, I looked closer, realizing that this time some of them seemed to be sticking together. *Well at least this is something.* Still not quite knowing what I was doing, I pushed out on every part of all of the cables until everything was covered with the little specks and strands of light. Then, with some mental effort, I moved some of the strands of particles and tied them together into a matrix of rings, lines, and shapes, all crisscrossing through the inside of the solid metal of the cables. Then I found a way to make patterns that I could move. I tried to force my thoughts of logical operations into them to transform them into increasingly complex shapes that did more complex tasks until finally, I could talk with my little creations.

We didn't communicate with words but instead with incredibly simple subconscious ideas passed through a sort of feedback loop I built into them. In the simplest of ways, they were asking me what to do and I could tell them as if they were extensions of myself. Figuratively, I jumped with joy.

With my thoughts, I moved the structures up and down the length of the cable and channeled energy through them to create more structures. The little machines would move in unison, rearranging themselves and growing into ever greater coded patterns of my design. Somehow, I understood exactly what all of my patterns and systems meant just by 'looking' at or feeling them.

I'm doing it…I'm using the interface!

I didn't completely understand how it worked but I didn't need to. The circuits themselves were being created subconsciously using the interface; I had just needed to learn to modify them. Now I could mold them and create virtual machines to move through the physical networks.

Filled with excitement, I moved quickly to create more machines, and more complex designs. I molded circuits into virtual factories that could replicate themselves or any machine I wanted, and I surrounded myself with them: paths and storage. Thrilled, I filled everything I could with machines, and I started to feel energy flowing from me outward.

I wove a wall of densely intertwined circuitry structured in such a way that only what I allowed could pass through—simpler than I had anticipated. I built a wall in each cable then raced onward. Emboldened, I even blocked off the program that was monitoring me.

My once mostly dark and still domain was now filled with light and racing with movement and energy. My little world buzzed as if I were at the center of a beehive, everything working hard yet effortlessly. I felt empowered, speeding up production until everything and anything made of taline metal connected to me was filled with glowing light that only I could see. Hundreds of thousands of machines and hundreds of layers of walls resided in every cable and spike around my brain.

With everything around me growing exponentially and mostly autonomously, I realized that I was starting to feel something that I hadn't felt in an incredibly long time, so long that it felt almost alien. I felt…hungry—*very* hungry and tired as well. The feeling confused me at first then I realized that everything I created and all of my still-growing swarming masses of machines were being powered by energy made solely by the cells in my brain.

I can't remember ever feeling like this before. I felt myself becoming more drained, and a sense of worry grew. Finally, I had to stop it. I shouted out a command with my mind: *STOP!*

Everything ground to a halt, and I felt like I deflated like a popped balloon. The increasingly intense feeling of exhaustion didn't stop, however.

Desperately, I began destroying virtual machines as quickly as I could, preserving only a small number of each type and a single intact wall in each of the cables. Those that were destroyed left nothing but trace amounts of heat lingering in their places.

I felt the strain on me lessen. The threat was gone, but my exhaustion still lay heavy on my mind. I felt short of breath; I wanted to breathe harder but I couldn't—I was allowed only a constant amount of oxygen by the machinery that sustained my brain.

I lay idly, trying to rest for a few minutes until I noticed the monitoring program doing something strange. The stream of particles had built up into a glowing sheet that covered the outside of the wall that I had made to block it. I watched it lazily from my side of the wall, not remembering until later what the particles were supposed to be doing: They were meant to gather information on me to bring back with them, and if the tower computer didn't get that information then it would clearly realize that something was wrong. *Perhaps blocking them was a mistake.*

Immediately, I regretted my little act of defiance, and didn't want to know how my captors might react to me stopping their spying. I was afraid of them and paranoid about just how much information their program was really collecting from me. I didn't want to be watched; I didn't want them to know about my newfound abilities. *I'm going to have to let them come back in. Surely they've noticed already, though, and saw everything up until I built the walls. I have to fake it. I'll make a machine to fake the information they're collecting.*

I struggled through my exhaustion to try to make a virtual copy of my brain from behind the safety of my walls, growing more frustrated as the monitoring program continued to pile up. I feared it was trying to find a way through. *I'll finish this then move it to the outside of the wall so the tower computer can reach it.*

Physically, it in no way resembled a brain, but the structure of it was designed in a way that might just confuse the monitoring computer. One last time, I tried to set it up to match the real thing as closely as I could. *I hope this works.*

As I pushed the tangled mess of a circuit that I had patched together to the outside of the wall, I watched the particles of the monitoring program flock to it, enter the model, then flow back out through the tower's virtual wall until the pile of machines had disappeared. It appeared to be working—as far as I could tell, at least—so I went back to trying to rest despite my still-racing thoughts.

This is horrible, I thought. *I need to get more energy somehow. If I could get the life support system to put more nutrients into whatever is being circulated through me, that would probably help...or maybe I could attach an electrical wire to one of the cables. Would that work, or could it kill me? I could ask someone to help, but they would wonder why I needed more energy.* I felt apprehensive about telling anyone why I wanted more energy, so I trashed the idea.

I will get back to normal if I rest for long enough. However, I needed more energy if I was to create more, and I desperately wanted to. I relished the feeling of the power from making and controlling so much so effortlessly—it was beautiful. I wanted more of that power and beauty—and feared I would need it to survive as well. I didn't entirely trust anything in the tower, and I wanted to be able to defend myself if the need came. How could I possibly sneak energy from or even fight the tower for it? I was too scared and far too weak to try anything remotely like that. The tower would undoubtedly overpower me or just have a person or robot simply destroy my brain or the machines keeping me alive. As far as I knew, they could just flip a switch to kill me.

After what felt like hours, Nikaya finally returned with her entourage of robots, Smit, and a large machine that I hadn't seen before. They followed a bulky cart stacked high with convex slabs of mostly clear plating.

Nikaya walked ahead of the procession to a place in front of my camera. "Hello Alder."

"Hello," I replied.

Smit stepped forward and, looking directly into my camera from a place behind Nikaya, began, "We are going to install this armor plating today. We don't want you killing yourself." He spoke in the dry, emotionless tone that I felt I was going to get used to in here.

I turned my attention away from him to watch as four robots loaded one of the slabs onto the arms of the larger machine. It had a single, huge red eye and walked on a sheet of short piston-like legs that looked incredibly strong and softly hissed as it did its work. One section at a time, the humanlike robots removed the cables, allowing the larger machine, with its many arms, to line up the plugs in each slab, spinning them in the air like nothing. Once in place, a clear liquid was injected in-between the two layers to bind them together. Finished, the lifting machine moved on to the next section as the other robots reattached the cables.

Everyone waited silently as the machines did their work. Nikaya stood in a corner doing something on a small handheld computer cradled by one of her arms as the fingers of her other hand danced across it.

I extended my neck, moving my head closer in attempt to see what she was doing, but she quickly turned the screen away. I retracted my neck to stay out of the way.

I watched the machines working, Nikaya typing, and Smit staring blankly until the work was finished. The machines returned to standing around the now empty cart. Seeing that the work was done, Smit led the group out of the room through the hallway to my right.

It seems like everyone always uses the door on the right. I wonder why.

Again, only Nikaya remained with me. Having set her device aside, she looked up at me. She seemed tired but had a nearly imperceptible grin on her face. I felt like I could almost see a weight pressing down on her as she looked into my camera lens, my unloving and non-living glass camera lenses. She stood close, but for a moment felt miles away, looking out from deep inside a distant prison of a body: lonely, secluded, and cold. I saw something familiar and painful in her eyes that I couldn't name or even remember.

She broke eye contact; the apparent weight on her disappeared, instantly replaced by her usual professional composure. *What was that?*

Nikaya walked toward me and stopped at the edge of my desk. "We are going to give you control over all of the lights in the room and we are going to let you change your orbs' internal parameters by a slight amount whenever you want to."

"Okay." *This is good news.*

"We also want to try to give you access to the surveillance cameras in the room to see how you handle that much visual input. We're also going to give you some wireless and long-distance control tests next session."

"What do you mean?" I asked, hiding my increasing excitement.

"You will find out then. The tower computer will move its walls back so that you can reach the lights." Nikaya paused momentarily then asked, "Have you found out how to make walls yet?"

"No not yet," I lied.

Nikaya let out a little sigh as if she were disappointed. "Oh well…" She took a few steps toward the door but stopped and turned back. "You should be able to find your way to the lights within a few minutes. Goodbye Alder." She turned and her back to me again and headed for the right door.

"Good night, Nikaya."

Nikaya glanced over her shoulder and gave a sort of half wave before finally leaving. *Why did I lie to her about the walls?* I was still afraid of this place and the people in it, but something about her seemed not as threatening, and they likely already knew the truth. Surely, they had been monitoring me as I made the walls and now they knew I lied to them. The thought made me anxious.

A few minutes later I felt the tower's walls inside of the cables move away from me. *This is a lot of new space to work with.* I moved out into the new lengths of cable to quickly build a new wall inside each of them, being careful not to do too much work too fast this time. I also liked the idea of keeping my creations closer to me, something comforting about it.

It wasn't until I had fully permeated the area that I found something inside the walls of my room. Small wire-like tubes branched off from the sides of most of the main cables. I sent some virtual machines in first then quickly frisked the insides of all the wires, where I found an interface to a physical device. I squeezed the interface with my mind; the outside world instantly went black. When I squeezed the switch again, the lights turned back on.

I turned the lights off, on and off, on until I felt used to the feeling of the new hardware. Still I couldn't pinpoint exactly where the light was coming from. *Maybe the walls themselves glow?* Later that day, I felt my way along another new wire, which traversed from inside my orb to the heating and circulation control units. I tried turning the temperature up and down a little, barely able to adjust it by a whole degree. I was a little disappointed, really. I was kind of hoping to feel something other than the regular cool nothingness of my world, but the device was undoubtedly set to prevent me from killing myself. *I'm not sure if that should bother me or not.* It would only take a few degrees to under or overheat the life-sustaining liquid that bathed my cells.

I continued building and organizing pathways until more new areas were opened up. When they did, I went into them all at once and was dazzled by an amazing 3-D image of the likes I had never imagined. I could see every corner and crevice in the room in fine detail all at the same time.

The image's incredible complexity and detail made it painful and confusing to look at, and only after hours of tumbling through the mess of information did I begin to adjust to seeing everything in the room simultaneously from nine different angles and locations. I no longer had a single image in my head of what was in front of me but an intricate three-dimensional map of myself and everything around me.

I fully extended my black snake of a neck, posing for myself and admiring the way light danced across the sparkling silver curves of my head from above. I moved to look directly into my new eyes one by one. *There's something sort of strange about having your own eyes turned on yourself…like watching and living in a movie.*

That night I continued experimenting with the taline circuits, devising a way to store excess electrical energy made by my brain inside the cables' taline metal. I stored what little energy I could to make an emergency supply in pockets of circuits close to my brain. It wasn't much, but it would come in handy and ease the construction of new circuits since not all energy had to come directly from my flesh.

I made another discovery—more significant than the energy storage: I found a way to store my memories. Visual or audio input from my cameras, even thoughts—I could store any piece of information that I wished inside of specialized circuits in the taline metal. I grew a dense and twisted forest of these circuits around my brain and with it gave myself a flawlessly photographic memory. I could store anything I wanted to outside of my brain, including commands and designs for my creations that could be used by my machines and factories as a sort of AI.

Later, at what I presumed to be night time, I finally drifted into an idle state of mind. I felt satisfied with my work and happily surprised by my eagerness for what the next day might bring.

CHAPTER SIX

- Outside the Wires -

Nikaya entered my room from the right door, holding her handheld computer against her chest with one arm and a small black box by her side in the other, white gloves now gracing her long fingers. There were dark shadows beneath her eyes, but I could still see her same underlying energy inside.

I was glad to see her. Somehow, I felt like I could somewhat trust her in this alien place—at least her more so than anyone else. When I looked in her eyes I thought I saw some real concern or at least real interest in me, in contrast to Ward and Smit. I realized, at that moment, that I thought she was fairly pretty too—in fact, she was beautiful. Her gloved hands emphasized a sort of beauty that I hadn't noticed before, and the curves of her flowing white garments created an appearance of stately height and form. She had an unusual, elegant, and almost otherworldly beauty, something that had remained unnoticed by me in my extreme stress until now. Maybe it was because of her black hair against the all-white world around her, but she seemed almost like she didn't belong.

Suddenly I found myself feeling that I needed to know more about her. I needed to know more about this place to survive—and oddly, I wanted to talk to her too. My creations and imagination were not company enough to support the weight of my isolation and the loneliness it inflicted.

I'm going to start a conversation.

I lowered my camera to her height to greet her. "Good morning," I said in what felt like the most casual and friendly tone I could manage through my inorganic body and depressed, industrialized mind.

Nikaya looked up and answered, "Hello."

"How are you doing?" I was expecting a quick reply, but she paused, staring into space. *What is she thinking?*

"I'm all right." She sighed then set the black box down on the wooden desk in front of me.

"That's good." I picked an item from the list of conversation topics I had hurriedly put together, but before I could say anything, she asked me a question.

"How are you?"

I was a little surprised and pleased. *She's wants to continue the conversation.* "I'm doing fine, better."

"Good." Nikaya opened the box.

There was a bit of a pause then I asked, "Is that the wireless equipment that you said you'd be bringing?"

"Yeah this is some of it."

"What is that?"

"This is a transmitter. The machine that will be installing it should be here soon."

Nikaya started to unload the contents of the black box. I watched from a couple feet above the desk with my main camera, even though I could already see everything with my new security cameras, each of which had at least a partial view of the desk.

The box was mostly filled with a fluffy, white packaging material, but resting on top of the cushion were two objects: One was a white and gold spike, about five inches long, with a one-inch wide socket on its thick end; the second object was a three-by-three-inch white metal cube covered in thousands of short golden needles protruding from every part of the cube—

like on an old CPU—except for an inch-wide socket on one side. *Are those antennas?* I wondered.

With her gloved hands, Nikaya carefully lifted the object and gently set it socket side down so none of the needles touched the desk. After placing the spike beside the cube, she moved the empty box to the side then looked up into my camera's unblinking eyes. "They should be here any minute now." She faintly smiled at me, but I couldn't do any equivalent gesture in return, so I simply gazed at her until she looked away.

Then with a little bit of apprehension, I asked another one of the questions I had prepared. "What's on the other side of the doors?"

She stopped and looked up at the ceiling in thought. "These doors?" she asked, motioning toward the white doors to her left and right sides.

"Yes and the third one behind me too."

"I don't know what's on the other side of those doors." She pointed at the door behind me and at the one to my left. "I've never been past the door behind you and I've only been through the door to your left a few times but…" She trailed off, then began again. "I can't tell you what's behind the left door, because every time I've been there it's been different."

"What do you mean different?"

"Everything inside the tower can be rearranged and we don't keep rooms that aren't being used for long. You will get to find out what's behind this door very soon, though." She pointed to the right door.

"How will I do that?"

"You'll find out soon." Nikaya smiled.

Her answers only left me more confused, but I didn't mull over them for long. The right door opened and Smit entered the room accompanied by a single humanoid robot. The machine had a jointless arm shaped like a mix between a drill and a small cannon.

Smit greeted Nikaya then led the machine to my desk. As they came closer, I pulled my neck away and upward to its full height, looking down at everyone from at least five feet above their heads. Through my auxiliary cameras, I could see my head shining brilliantly in the light from the ceiling.

Nikaya picked up the spike from my desk and inserted it into a round hole at the end of the robot's arm. She gave the spike a twist before looking up at me. "We are going to implant this in one of your cables now."

I nodded.

Smit stepped to the side as the robot moved toward the area between my orb and camera. Planting its feet firmly on the ground, it pressed the spike against the hard metal surface of the cable connecting the two pedestals.

With a quiet voice Smit ordered, "Now."

There was a bang like lighting and the arm kicked back hard as a puff of hot air and a sound of screeching metal filled the room.

I felt the presence of the spike appear as it was forced through the surrounding metal—painless. With my many eyes, I could see where the cable metal had been compressed and bulged up slightly around the protruding plug. The instant I finished feeling up the spike with my mind, I began constructing a large pathway between it and brain. I knew that I would want it later.

The robot silently retreated back to its place by the door. First Nikaya, then Smit stooped low over the column to inspect the freshly implanted spike and the metal around it.

"It looks perfect," Nikaya said.

"Good—" I said.

"Good—" Smit said simultaneously.

Smit looked up at me. For a fraction of a second we locked gazes then he turned away. What I saw in the man's eyes—a feeling I couldn't explain—made me uncomfortable.

"Can you feel it?" Nikaya asked.

I looked down at her. "Yes, I can feel it perfectly."

She looked pleased as she walked around to the front end of the desk and carefully picked up the cube covered in gold needles.

Smit and the robot left the room through the right door without a word. He only glanced back at Nikaya for a second as the door closed behind him. With them gone, I coiled my neck on my desk like a snake, putting my head at Nikaya's level.

I watched her carefully align the cube until it snapped into place as if being pulled there by magnets. Instantly, I felt the vast insides of the device open up. A maze of countless tiny, interconnecting canals branched off from a central channel that went through the plug and connected to the spike. Inside, I found a sort of on-off switch that, like the one in my camera, could only be controlled from the inside. My new pathway through the cable was nearly complete, and I finished it off by connecting the end of the path to the central canal inside of the cube.

"Can you feel it?" Nikaya asked.

"I feel it."

"Excellent." Nikaya stepped back as she pulled a rectangular device from a pocket and looked down at its tiny screen. "Now let's see if you can use it. When you're ready."

I gently squeezed on the virtual switch inside of the cube, and its insides began to churn and glow. Through a camera in the wall I saw a line appear on the screen of Nikaya's handheld device. *She can't hide things from me in here now*, I realized. *No one can. Surely, she knows this though.*

The line was nearly flat but oscillating ever so slightly. I felt my way through the canals in the cube, my mind's circuit feelers getting squeezed as they approached the golden needles. Externally the needles were fixed but on the inside they seemed to be vibrating. I forced my way into them, then immediately felt whatever entered the needles vibrate, compress, and begin to rip apart. I pulled back, alarmed.

Of course I can't build circuits in the air, and I can't reach outside the cables with my mind. I'm going to have to approach this differently.

Nikaya still held her sensor, waiting. I wondered if she knew what was going on inside the metal world around my mind, that I was rapidly iterating through and testing designs using my mind and clouds of virtual factories and tools. *She asks so few questions… I know I'm not the first to go through this, but I wonder if they have a way to see what I'm doing, or if she just knows from experience.* The thought was unnerving that all this work—which was so profound to me—might be mundane and expected to her. *I could also be the first to get this far and survive. This could even be a test to see if I lied earlier.* I stopped working, too busy rolling over fears and elaborate scenarios in my head. *No...I need to go forward with this.*

A cloud of simple machines was ready, and when I gave the order, the machines shot into the maze of needles, creating a sort of steady stream in all directions. I felt them enter the needles then completely disappear to my senses. *They've been destroyed.*

Over Nikaya's shoulder, I saw something on the screen of the device in her hands—a second, faster-moving line above the first.

Nikaya nodded. "Good job."

I had successfully sent something out—but nothing came back. Disappointed, I then realized that that was probably to be expected since I didn't have a second antenna to receive the signal and respond from.

Nikaya looked up at me and with one of her tiny smiles on her face. "Want to try to control something now?"

"Yes," I answered, probably faster than I should have. "What can I control?"

"This," Nikaya announced as she reached into her pocket and pulled out a tiny black and blue plastic car. A tiny antenna bobbed on top of it. She took two big steps back, pushed a small plastic switch on the bottom of the car, and set the little thing down on the floor at her feet. "Try to move it."

I may've been wrong, but I thought I heard a barely noticeable but playful tone hidden in her voice.

"Okay," I answered tentatively, lowering my head to scrutinize the thing. I had begun to feel a faint sensation coming in through the needles of the cube the moment Nikaya had flipped the switch on. It was unlike anything I had experienced before, and I felt certain it was coming from the car. The squirming signal passed through the channels and pathways of the cube, where it finally solidified near the center. It began asking me for commands, nearly identically to how my virtual machines would.

I'm just dealing with another machine. A simple mechanical machine controlled by a simple electrical control. The simplicity made me want to smile. This was going to be a test of communication, I realized.

I mashed together a command formatted in a way that I hoped would work and fed it into the cube. The virtual mass that had been installed in the cube by the car twisted the information around slightly, then I felt my commands disappear through the needles and into the air. A few moments passed—nothing happened. Then Nikaya spoke.

"I saw something new, but it didn't work."

I looked up at Nikaya as if she might give me some sort of tip or advice.

"Try again," Nikaya instructed in a reassuring voice, her eyes never leaving the screen in her hands. I changed the coding of the signal slightly, trying twice more, still nothing.

"Try again."

I thought for a moment then realized that the mass' twisting of my signal was likely formatting it for me. My previous two changes may have been useless. *What am I doing wrong?* Then it hit me. *I need a more consistent signal.* I began building a small city of factories inside of the spike and surrounding cable that began to churn out a constant stream of the commands.

I watched square waves appear on Nikaya's screen as I sent out a few short but high intensity bursts as a test, and unlike before I could feel weaker beams of the same signal bouncing back to me through the cube, likely from off the floor and walls. I set up a simple system to automatically filter out this feedback then finally projected my commands into the room at full force.

The car shot forward with an electric wiz. I watched it speed across the floor to where it hit the wall across from my desk and tipped over into a spin. I figuratively grinned then stopped broadcasting the signal.

"That's it." Nikaya walked to the car and put it back on its wheels. "I have to go now, but I'll leave this with you so you can practice for what we're bringing you later. Goodbye for now."

"Goodbye, and good night," I responded.

She turned and left the room through the usual door on the right. I was alone again.

Determined to master using the wireless before she returned, I strengthened my signal and optimized the machines I had built up around and in the antenna. I made some slight changes to the formatting of the signal itself then sent out a command for the car to reverse. In a slow, more controlled way, it drove backward a few feet then stopped just like I had told it to. I repeated the movement a few times, then, feeling satisfied, I moved on to turning.

At first, I had some trouble telling the car to turn and go forward or backward at the same time, but pretty soon I was able to drive the car in circles around the room. Once I was confident with my controls, I built structures and interfaces to hold copies of the command signals, making it easier to simply will the commands then let my virtual machines do the rest of the work.

After driving several laps around the room, I parallel parked the toy next to my desk. I could control it with ease now, but I still didn't entirely know *how* since I couldn't enter it with my mind. I was only broadcasting instructions that were being picked up by the electric machine governing the little toy. *I wish there was more feedback.*

My full attention returned to the cube. I had a feeling that it was hiding something from me, because surely there were more signals in the tower than my own. After hours of tinkering, I felt something alien: a range of faint but complex signals that weren't mine yet coming from all around me. I tried to interpret them, but I didn't even know which signals were communication and which might just be noise. *This is hopeless.*

Then I felt something: a bandwidth of signals that seemed to stand out from the mess. It came at the cube from every direction and seemed to saturate and almost resonate inside it. *What is this?* I felt its slow oscillations until it reminded me of the feeling of thoughts being passed around and turned over in my head. I felt increasingly uneasy as I struggled to try to understand it. Then I shrunk away from the antenna, feeling smaller than I ever had before, as if there were something living all around me, an immeasurable presence that I couldn't see but a speck of through a dark pinhole.

I shut the signal out. I didn't want to feel it anymore, and tried to push my fearful thoughts about it to the side. Then I turned out the light and continued working inside myself. I was in a tiny submersible stranded in the depths of the ocean, and I could do nothing but look away from the one black window that might reveal what was circling my prison, to pretend I wasn't there.

CHAPTER SEVEN

- Acceleration -

The right door opened, and a blinding flood of white light poured into my room from the hallway, carrying with it the silhouette of a slender figure.

Everything returned to darkness.

I turned on the lights, revealing the figure as Nikaya. I felt happy to see her.

I guided my little car up to her greet her and drove circles around her feet. As she looked down at it, I saw a tiny smile creep onto her face. She hummed a small half-hearted laugh to herself. *She looks tired.*

"Good morning," I said to her.

"Good morning," Nikaya answered in a bright but weary tone. She was trying to hide how tired she really was, I realized. "I see that you've been practicing."

"I have. So what is the new thing you have for me today?" I asked, moving my head out on its long black neck to greet her.

"We actually have a lot planned for this session, ahead of schedule."

"That's great." This sounded like it would be interesting. I was eager to explore and hoping for a new and better power source. I longed for the feeling that I had felt when I first discovered how to build in and rearrange energy in the cables.

Nikaya continued, "Also, Ward will be visiting you again soon. He seems to be very pleased with your progress."

I looked at her curiously then coolly responded, "Okay." Secretly, knowing that I would have to confront Ward again made me nervous. While I didn't think he or anyone else would hurt me for the sake of harming me, rooted deep inside me there was still a fear and distrust of the tower, its master and everything in it. The only thing that I felt I could trust here was Nikaya, but still I wasn't entirely confident in that either.

"Just a tip," Nikaya said, interrupting my thoughts. "When Ward comes, try to appear as powerful and healthy as you can. He is aware of all of the data already, but it's important that you show him in person that you are healthy and successful."

"Okay, I will." I assured her then before changing the subject. "So what are the plans for today?"

"First, there is a small but complex tower machine that is going to be given to you. If you can prove that you can wirelessly operate actual taline tower machinery then there is a second, more complex machine waiting for you."

"What is the machine like?"

"Well, it can fly, it will add a portable eye to your visual network and a few new senses as well," Nikaya said, rattling off a list of its benefits. "You will likely feel things that you haven't really felt since before you came here. So be ready for that, it may be a shock. You'll be able to freely move about some of the nearby hallways as well."

My attention had piqued at *new senses*, but I was excited now. "Did you say I will be allowed into the hallways?" The prospect of going outside this room and into the tower made me a little anxious—but thrilled.

"Yes, you will be allowed past this doorway." Nikaya motioned toward the door on my right. "I'm also going to give you control of the right door and one of the security cameras outside of it. The tower will still control everything in the hall and will also be able to open and close your door if you are for some reason unable—or unwilling."

It really wasn't much, but it gave me the feeling that they might trust me more than I had thought.

Nikaya continued, "There is also going to be a small charging station installed in your room for the machines that you're going to be given control over. Most of our machines hold a charge long enough that you may never need to use it, though." I was already excited, but this last sentence made my mind jump with joy—of course on the outside I appeared as lifeless and empty as ever. *This is it, just what I need, and it's being given to me here, right in my room!*

"When do I get all of this?" I asked, keeping my voice calm.

"Very soon. I will be back in just a few minutes with everything," Nikaya said, then turned and left the room.

When Nikaya returned she was carrying what I assumed was the machine that she had said I would be given. It looked like an elongated metal teardrop, about a yard long. The whole thing was a metallic silvery color, and on the larger end was a single dark crimson circle. I assumed it to be an eye.

"Is this it?" I asked, already knowing the answer.

"Yeah, ready to try it now?" Nikaya set the metal teardrop down at her feet and exhaled. It looked like it was heavy.

"Of course I am." I could already feel the device's presence seeping into the antenna cube. I had never felt anything quite like it, and it was totally different from the remote-control car. It felt almost like it was actively reaching out and pushing on, begging for a master.

Excited, I sent out into the air a flood of the strongest signal that I could produce. Almost in the same instant, I felt a sharp *snap* inside myself—then the machine felt like it was a part of me. The separate signals passing between myself and the device seemed to merge into an organized flowing structure unlike any I had felt prior.

I filled the machine with myself and felt invigorated as the insides of the seemingly solid taline teardrop started to wriggle and writhe. There was a flash of light—in my mind and suddenly I could see a new panoramic view of the floor, one of

Nikaya's feet, and the wall in the background as the machine's eye became mine.

To my further delight, I felt and watched as the machine righted itself then began hovering in the air. What had looked like a solid, hard surface from the outside of the machine moved and wriggled rhythmically, like smooth waves on water or a swimming eel. The white silver teardrop rose, its crimson eye now faintly glowing and growing brighter as it flew higher. In near shock at the staggering complexity and beauty of this thing, I stared at and felt this incredible new body part for several moments, its inner mechanisms filling me with a tingling sensation that reverberated through my being. It seemed to nearly be a natural part of me, like an arm or a leg. Communicating felt unbelievably natural compared to communication with the toy car.

It was all controlled by a non-centralized virtual computer integrated into the metal body of the machine, much like the virtual machines that I had created. There was a sort of built-in operating system that had programmed reflexes to help stabilize and protect the body. It felt almost scarily similar to how a human body would balance without the owner consciously telling it to. In the absence of my old body this hovering machine…was almost like a new one.

This is incredible.

"Do you like it?" Nikaya asked, breaking my trance.

How long have I been floating here? The machine hovered at eye level, facing the wall. I moved my camera head back into its upright position to give my new machine more room, then I turned it to face Nikaya. Watching and feeling the machine move made me shiver in awe. Its great red eye stopped about a foot from Nikaya's face.

Through my head I said, "It's amazing." *If this is only one of the lesser machines—that they are giving me just to see if I can control their stuff—then I can't even imagine what else Ward has in his tower. I need more.*

"Good." Nikaya nodded nonchalantly.

Time seemed to freeze—I was stunned. I had just felt something very special. Something that I hadn't felt in a very, very, long time—warmth. When Nikaya spoke, I had felt her warm breath on the cold face of this new metal body of mine. As quickly as it had appeared, the heat dissipated, and once again I felt coolness.

I hadn't felt any sort of warmth in such a long time. I tried to cherish the memory of the feeling and found myself being flooded with a wave of melancholy, loneliness, and grief. I tried to hold back the upspring of emotion. *I need to concentrate now.* The left door opened for the first time and standing in the doorway was one of the humanoid machines. It stepped over the threshold, pushing a tiny white cart with a gray metal cube on top of it. Nikaya turned around and looked down at the cube then back up at me.

"This is the charger that I mentioned earlier," she said. "It's going to be tap into an energy stream in the wall." She pointed to one of the walls on the right side of my room, but I didn't see any sort of plugs or attachments there for anything to connect to.

Nikaya stepped to the side to allow the robot and its cart to fully enter the room; the door closed behind it. The humanoid machine stopped and picked up the metallic cube then set it down where Nikaya had instructed. It promptly turned and left the room, pushing the cart ahead of it.

My full attention shifted back to Nikaya as she walked to the charger, her hand gliding across a keypad on her handheld device. Then she touched the back of the device to a side of the cube, and as it touched, from inside came an unnerving scratching noise. Then with a bang, three long metal spikes shot out from the smooth sides of the cube and buried themselves deep into the metal of the wall; a fourth penetrated the floor. Then the spikes constricted, pulling the charger toward the wall so that it was pressed tightly against it. Nikaya stood and backed a few steps away.

I watched as the cube began to open like a flower, unfolding into numerous interconnected and roughly rectangular segments. The upward-facing surfaces of each segment were blanketed with dozens of small spikes and projections that were angled toward the center of the device in a swirling pattern. Lightly colored stripes and designs graced the inside of the charger's petals.

"Try to hover above it." Nikaya looked up at my new machine. I watched my metallic teardrop elegantly swim through the air silently and smoothly, moving like a soft-bodied sea animal through water. I brought my new body part to a stop directly above the charger.

"Good. Now lower yourself toward the charger and stop just above it. Be careful not to touch it, though," Nikaya instructed. I hovered closer to the metal flower as Nikaya had instructed, and as the gap closed, I picked up on a strange tingling sensation. It was like the touch of an electrically charged piece of metal or a static shock. The sensation grew stronger as I moved closer until I stopped, just an inch away. I no longer felt like I was being shocked—I just felt a strangely comforting and enveloping warmth in my new body.

I closed off my many eyes from my mind and silently enjoyed the feeling for a few moments. After being in my cool liquid filled orb for so long, I welcomed it. I couldn't send any of the excess energy to the rest of my body, although it was tantalizingly close. It was like I was holding a freezing hand under hot water, unable to warm the rest of my cold body. Fragments of warm and fond memories of things I had experienced years ago, when I had a body, surfaced from the abyss of things I had forgotten. Things that I would probably never truly be able to experience again.

I was reluctantly pulled back to reality by the sound of Nikaya's voice.

"Can you feel anything?"

"Yes."

Good, it shouldn't take long for it to fully charge."

Nikaya certainly had an idea of what was going on but never appeared surprised by anything. *It's probably nothing special compared to the things that she's seen deeper in the tower. I need to get to these things.*

"What is this thing's name?" I asked.

"Oh, I nearly forgot to tell you." She sounded a little amused by herself. "It is called an SCU, more specifically the SCU-M14. The S, the C, and the U form an acronym for Scouting and Cleansing Unit. The M14 means that it is the fourteenth model. You can speak through it too—try it."

So this is just like a janitor.

I felt around with my mind for a second then things clicked into place. "Okay," I replied through the SCU. "How does this work? It feels like solid metal, and I can't see any speakers on it."

"Excellent, and good question," Nikaya answered. "It's hypersonic sound, there's a piece of hardware inside that emits high-frequency sound waves to the outside in a way that lets you decide where the sound enters the audible range. Your camera head works the same way; if you learn to control these systems, you can speak so that you're only heard in specific areas in air or even directly into someone's head so that only they can hear you."

"Wow." I had to think about that for a moment. "What would happen if I were to make the SCU touch the charger?"

Nikaya thought. "I'm not really sure what would happen. You could probably damage or even destroy either or both pieces of equipment by directly touching them together while the current is on."

"Am I able to turn the current off?"

"No, not yet, but maybe you can once you're given control over the door and the hall camera. No guarantees, though."

"Can I charge anything with it?"

"Probably." Nikaya shrugged. "It uses an electrical field of a specific frequency. I know that it can charge any of the machines in Ward's towers made of taline, which is pretty much everything."

I'll test it. My remote control car came to life, the tiny electric motor whizzing as the toy turned around my desk and drove to the base of the charger.

"That might work," Nikaya commented as she watched the toy.

I knew I wasn't going to be able to feel the energy with the car like I was able to with the SCU. Regardless, I inched the car forward, but before I could confirm if it was working or not there was a pop and a puff of smoke.

"I've lost control, Nikaya."

She bent over and picked up the smoking piece of plastic.

"Well it looks like it may have worked, but you overcharged it; it's small." She slipped the car into a pocket. "The SCU should be charged by now. There are some important things that we still need to do this session. Now follow me."

I did as she said, a little reluctantly. I felt the warm comfort of the charger dissipate as my SCU swam upward toward the airspace in front of my desk. "I'm ready."

Nikaya turned and walked toward the door on the left side of the room, and as she neared it, for the first time, I noticed something. She opened the doors by gently blowing on them when she was less than a stride away, and the part of the door that her breath had made contact with faintly glowed before the door folded open. She walked through the door and into the hall without breaking her swift stride.

I followed a short distance behind Nikaya, a little surprised that we were in the left hall because I had only ever seen people use the right. *This is the one that she said frequently changes.* I tried to stay close as she walked down the center of the long and blindingly white hall that seemed void of windows or doors. Blinding white light seemed to emanate from every surface, similarly to in my room, but here it somehow felt more intense. The hall seemed to continue on forever, fading into a white haze in the distance. I couldn't see its end. It was slightly disorienting, yet eerily beautiful and surreal, amplified by the fact that I was still seeing and hearing everything inside of my room through all of my cameras and sensors. I was also fully aware of the insides of my cables and of the tens of thousands of busy virtual machines inside them. I was sending a part of myself out into another place away from the rest of my body, a collection of disconnected parts through which my mind freely flowed between as if they were one. *I've transcended my body, or at least what I thought one was.*

Some time passed before the first turn finally came into view. We turned to the left at a ninety-degree angle and continued on our way. It wasn't long before something new appeared in the distance, a glowing red speck. I looked up at Nikaya—she seemed calm and was continuing normally. *It must be another SCU.* Still, I fixed my eye on it and edged closer to her. Cautiously, I watched the machine until it flew past us, just a few feet to my left. I waited for us to put some distance between us and it before speaking. "What was that SCU doing, Nikaya?"

"Most likely, it was scouting and possibly cleaning," she replied plainly. "There are hundreds of them systematically moving through the tower to find imperfections, intruders, or internal damage to the tower, but I've never seen any of those things here before. For the most part, they are just an extra set of mobile eyes and appendages for Ward and the computer."

"How do they clean things?"

I heard Nikaya stifle a small laugh, as if I had just said something mildly amusing.

"I'm...actually not sure. I've never seen one of them have to do anything before. I know that the last model, the SCU-M13, was able to remove dust and sanitize surfaces with UV light and electrostatic fields, but I've never seen them used. You can learn how to operate those tools soon—that is if you have them in that model." Nikaya took a long breath. "We are almost there."

I answered her with an accepting humming noise that I made by vibrating something deep inside of my SCU.

I found her answer unsettling, with her not knowing all the details. There were just too many secrets, too much unknown to me. I wanted this scientist to be a rock, something consistent in this place for me to trust. *I guess she can't know everything about this huge place*, I reassured myself. I looked up at her again and for the first time wondered how much she really knew.

"Nikaya, how long have you been in the tower?"

The corners of her mouth twitched then slowly her facial expression seemed to slightly deflate. "I—I'm…not entirely sure. A long time…" Then she sighed, obviously bothered by the question. "Almost as long as I can remember, really. It's sort of all become a bit of a…a white haze." She blankly looked down at one of her hands, turning it over as if inspecting it might somehow give her a clue.

"Oh…" I only felt more uncomfortable and uncertain than I did before asking the question.

We came to another turn, this time to the right, and with it came a stark change in scenery. The new part of the hall was only about a hundred feet long, the ceiling was higher, and it was considerably wider. It led up to and ended at a towering white door with a faintly glowing basketball-size orb embedded at its center, giving off a pallid and translucent blue light. Framing the door, pitch-black lines covered the entire length and height of the wall in a complex branching geometric pattern. The lines starkly cut through the white haze, intensely sharp and solid against all else around them. A memory of my years on top of the black plane flashed through my mind and a small but terrible sinking feeling came over me.

Nervously, I followed Nikaya toward the door. I looked up at the faint blue orb at the door's center in wonder then realized that Nikaya had fallen behind me. I stopped and turned to look back at her. "What is it?" I asked.

"Let's wait here. We can't go in yet." Her pressing but calm voice was followed by a complete and almost eerie silence. An uncomfortable feeling came over me as I looked back into her still eyes. It became so quiet that I could hear her heart beating. The silence was shattered by a deep hum that seemed to come from within the walls themselves, resonating through the hall like a torrent of rushing water through a cave, seemingly ripping apart the very air around us.

I inched closer to Nikaya's side. Hurriedly looking around, I expected something horrible to happen, but Nikaya remained frozen, her trancelike gaze nailed to the door. I couldn't decide if Nikaya's lack of reaction was more comforting or unsettling, but I didn't have time to decide. As suddenly as the noise had begun it stopped, leaving us with nothing but another uneasy silence.

"Nikaya," I said through my SCU.

No answer.

"Nikaya!"

Silence.

"Nikay—"

"Yes! I know." Her voice cracked under a strain I couldn't sense. Her whole body shivered as she looked up at the ceiling and clutched at the back of her neck. For a moment, I felt abashed, but then I realized that she wasn't talking to me. She didn't seem to even acknowledge that I was here at all. I spun around, scanning the hall again to see if we were still alone—nothing.

I thought to shout again, but before I could Nikaya's gaze broke from the ceiling and slowly twisted to lock on to me. She blinked, then, with a slight quiver in her voice, spoke.

"We…can go in now."

A sickly feeling of panic came over me. *She's terrified, but trying to hide it from me. What does she have to be afraid of in here? I have to say something.*

"What was that?" I asked, not moving.

A nervous look crept over her face. "I wasn't yelling at you. I'm sorry, but I—I'm not… You shouldn't worry about it. We can go in now." She faintly smiled at me then looked away, appearing to be fine once more.

Before I could respond, Nikaya strode off toward the door. She gently blew toward it just as she did with the door in my room, and I saw the blue orb at its center vibrate and there was a sound like a muffled gunshot. Then the two great white halves of the gate soundlessly folded open.

For a moment I was unable to move, confused by what had just happened. I looked around once more then collected my thoughts as I followed Nikaya through the door, hurrying to catch up.

A vast, bright white room opened up before me, and immediately I knew we were there for the object standing alone at its center. A machine very similar to—if not identical to—the ones that I had seen working in my room over the past few days.

Nikaya continued toward the machine until she stopped just a few feet from it. I cautiously did the same. "This is it," Nikaya informed me, motioning toward the humanoid machine at her side.

It was made of taline metal, the same metallic white as the SCU. Thin and several feet tall, it lacked a mouth and had two deeply set, jet-black eyes. A third smaller eye, red like the one on the SCU, sat at the center of the machine's neck. Overall, it had sharp facial features and a somewhat masculine build accented by translucent cloth-like membranes that loosely hung from the sides of the statuesque body.

I circled the machine then looked at Nikaya. She gazed back at me seriously. "Your final test is to learn to control this. This machine is considerably more complex than the SCU. If you can control it, you will be named a success." She seemed to choke on the word *success* a little—or maybe I just imagined it. I stared at the machine and pondered what she meant. *Named a success? As what? Success as an experiment?* It made me anxious, but I had few remaining qualms with taking part in and continuing their experiment now. *After all, they sort of saved me, and I love what they're giving me now. And what other choice do I have?*

"Well—try to do it," Nikaya urged gently.

"Okay." Despite my hesitancy, I really wanted to take it as my own; as soon as I had entered the room I felt the machine's operating system hungrily begging for a master through the SCU. I only hesitated because of Nikaya's strange behavior, just moments ago. I looked the machine over again, and finally gave in. My mind slammed into it through the wireless signals, engulfing its insides and filling it with myself. A connection was made, and I instantly took total control of the machine. I felt my newest body come to life. I could already feel its speed, power, and razor-sharp senses become a part of me, and I recognized the insides of the new body pulsating with energy just as the insides of my SCU did.

I looked out through the three eyes and saw my SCU floating below my newest head; simultaneously, I gazed back at myself in my new, shiny body through my SCU's eye. With the new body I looked up at the ceiling and around the room. Nikaya stood beside me, watching me. She seemed happy, but I couldn't tell for sure.

I looked away from Nikaya and held my new arms out in front of me, examining my fingers as I rolled them into a fist; they were long, thin, and felt incredibly strong. I rolled my shoulders and looked down at my new body. My legs were long and thin, and the torso was smooth and well formed. The translucent membranes conformed to the body along a curved line from the armpits to waist and hung behind me. I felt air flow through them and was able to smell it. I turned to face Nikaya again with the new machine. With a regal yet still metallic voice I said, "This is beautiful."

I sauntered around the room's perimeter, feeling the cold hard metal of the floor beneath my new feet and the wall as I ran my fingers down its smooth surface. I felt the cool air slide across my sleek form and waft through the membranes. The sensations and sights from the new body brought back to light forgotten memories of living. Years ago, they would have seemed insignificant and mundane to me…but now—now they were precious.

This is incredible… I felt almost as if I were in my old body, but this was better in so many ways. This machine was like a piece of art, like an idealized statue come to life. *It's beautiful…* "What is it called?" I asked through my SCU, still watching from Nikaya's side.

"We call it a Basic Inorganic Humanoid Unit, or a BIHU for short."

"A BIHU... So what do we do next?"

"We will go back to your room when you're ready, and that will be all for today," Nikaya answered. She too turned with my SCU to watch the BIHU do its lap. As she finished speaking to my SCU, I made my new body stop and look at her. I strode to her and stopped beside her and my SCU.

"I'm ready to go," I said through both machines simultaneously. *Whoa...there's something about speaking through multiple mouths that makes one feel powerful.* Inside, I grinned.

"All right, follow me." Nikaya turned toward the open door, and I trailed close behind, my bodies on either side of her. As we crossed the threshold of the doorframe, I heard what sounded like a faint electrical snap. I looked over my BIHU's shoulder to see that the door had completely closed behind us. In less than a second it looked just as it had the first time I had seen it.

We turned into the main hall and continued the long, plain walk back to my room. Eventually, my door came into view in the distance, and when we were close enough, Nikaya opened it with her breath as usual and we entered together. As the door silently closed behind us, I instructed my two new bodies to walk to the center of the room where they then turned to face Nikaya, who had stopped by the door. I had also stretched out my main head to greet her as we came in. Now in my room, I felt safe enough to speak.

"Nikaya, are you all right?"

She looked back into my head's unmoving glass eyes. "I'm okay."

"What happened back there? I'm worried about you."

"Something happened then someone was talking to me." She paused, then her next words came out in a rush. "I shouldn't tell you much more and I need to go now but will see you again soon, and don't worry about it, please." She glanced over at my SCU and BIHU then gave my head a last fleeting glance as she turned and exited.

"Goodbye." I watched the right door fold shut behind her as she disappeared into the blinding, empty whiteness of the hall. I didn't move for a long time. I couldn't help but wonder about what was going on with Nikaya, but it was futile. Eventually, I moved my head back to its upright position and my attention turned away from Nikaya toward my new body parts.

I messed with the SCU and BIHU on and off for a long time: The SCU flew laps around my room, looping and rolling through the air along the way. My BIHU walked, jogged, jumped, rolled, and picked at everything within reach. I experimented with the new noises I could make, and even tried to ride on top of my SCU with the BIHU, the attempt humorously failing.

As time passed and I felt increasingly confident and comfortable in my new bodies, my thoughts gradually returned to the problem of getting more energy for my brain and internal machinery. I circled the charger, examining it with every eye that could see it. I could faintly feel the flow of energy from it in both my new bodies but my brain was left in the cold. It was tantalizing.

I tried to come up with a way to somehow move energy from the charger to myself. The empty sockets and antenna were the only known physical entrances into my orb...but I discarded every new idea of connecting to them—they were bad or too dangerous. I exhausted the idea of using the charger altogether. Luckily, after quite some time I had something new to do, though: A new eye had just been connected to my body.

I felt like I should be more surprised by the bright flash and sudden new field of awareness it brought, but almost mechanically, I simply accepted the new input into the fold of my many others. I was now looking down into the right hall from the camera that Nikaya had said would be made available to me. The wires connecting me to the camera also branched off into an interface connected to the door. I built new walls and pathways to protect and improve the area then decided to test it.

I felt over the interface for the door then squeezed it, and with a snap the right door folded open at my command. Then, holding it open, I hesitantly walked to stand in the doorway with my BIHU. The hall seemed to go on forever like the other. *This is the first time I've been in the right hall. Alone too… This is the way Nikaya went.* She was nowhere in sight, though. Nothing was.

I stood and turned to look back at my room through the BIHU. I faintly saw the camouflaged eye above the door now that I knew its location. I looked at my main head looking back out at me looking in. Then I glanced over at the orb that I really was inside of, focusing on the tiny pink mass suspended by spikes and cables at its center. I stood still…then slammed the door in my face.

Tonight, I'm going to explore.

I turned around, cautiously looked out into the endless tunnel of blinding white. Then not fully knowing the risk I was taking or even where I was going, I set off down the hall. I walked slowly at first, then broke into a run, exhilarated at the feeling of cool air rushing past my new face.

I ran down the hall in my new body. I felt a sense of freedom and excitement, yet I still saw the inside of my prison through a multitude of eyes—one of which, the hallway camera, watched my newest body disappear into the distance. Before me lay a path with only one direction and no visible end, but, in this little way, I was in control.

I ran for what felt like several minutes, my long, untiring legs moving rhythmically across the floor. *This body is amazing.* It felt relaxed, calm, and like it could do anything or go anywhere I wanted to. I almost forgot about my reality for a moment. Eventually I came to a turn and stopped. With my right hand I leaned against the wall, looking around. Blissfully, I chuckled at myself then continued on my dangerous little adventure, trailing my hand along the wall.

As I walked, I felt an inconsistency in the wall with my fingers. When I looked, I saw a door—I had only been able to feel or see it because it was slightly open. Looking down, I saw that there was a piece of metal stuck in it, holding it open just enough that I might be able to force my fingertips into the gap. *This is odd.*

I stared for a long moment, wondering if the metal had been put there intentionally. *I'm doing it.*

It was much easier than I expected to force open the door. Once inside, I scanned the room. The narrow entryway led up to a spherical capsule that filled most of the room and merged with the back walls. Facing me was a wide open circular door into the sphere. Through the opening, I saw a white bed surrounded by shelves and delicate machinery curved to fit the round interior walls. Cautiously I stepped closer and ducked inside the capsule. *So this is how they live.*

I looked around. There was no decoration, little color, and few visible personal possessions. It was far cozier than my room…but it too felt like a sterile cage.

I saw a long strand of black hair on the bed. *Nikaya…is this hers?* With intensified interest, I looked around the room again, then quickly turned back toward the entryway, not wanting to be caught in here.

Then I saw something that I hadn't noticed before.

Hanging on the wall was a single drawing of a small, gray bird. I stood, wondering what it might mean to her, the only personal touch in the room.

I should move on.

I stepped out of the capsule then rushed out of the room, leaving the piece of metal stuck in the door where I'd found it. I turned then froze, finding myself looking into the eyes of another BIHU standing like a statue, not a dozen strides from me. *Of course something like this was going to happen, you idiot.* Our gazes locked in a seemingly unbreakable stare, but there was something splattered on its face. My eyes traveled along the trail of red specks down its side, over a crimson hand, and their journey finally came to an end on the floor—brought there by a bloody drip from a silver finger. My mind raced.

Then it moved. It took a single mechanical step toward me without breaking eye contact then stopped, as if it were testing if I would flinch and run. Then it spoke.

"Don't follow her, Alder."

"What?" *Don't follow Nikaya?*

Abruptly, the BIHU began walking toward me again. "Don't follow her."

I backed up, tasting venom in its voice and seeing purpose in its stride. *It's not stopping.*

I turned and ran in a sprint toward my room, not halting until I slammed the door behind myself as I leapt through. I slid to a stop at the base of my orb and spun around to face the door, expecting something horrible to happen, glued to the image of the hall through my eye above the door.

Did it follow me? Several tense seconds passed before I began to let down my guard. *Who was speaking through that BIHU? "Don't follow her?"*

I spent much of the evening thinking about the day's events. I couldn't get Nikaya or the noises we had heard together off my mind. She had to have been communicating with someone, Ward seeming like the most likely answer, which made Nikaya's reaction no less frightening or understandable. Dwarfing the noises, however, was the memory of the blood splattered BIHU outside of Nikaya's room. Had the machine been there for her or me—or was it something else? *What is going on?*

My attention remained glued to the view of the empty hallway, to the closed doors of my room, and to the virtual walls inside of my wires. I didn't trust anything in the tower, and I never entered an idle state of mind that night.

CHAPTER EIGHT

- Apoptosis and Other Things -

The next morning, while I was idle and still, I saw something moving in the right hall. I woke myself immediately and fixed my attention on the human shape.

It's Nikaya! She was walking fast, and I could make out an unusually tired and stress-filled expression on her face. I wondered if she knew where I had been or what I had seen, if she might be angry. Regardless, I was still glad to see her.

I turned on my room lights, activated my machines and lifted my head to a position to greet her. Nikaya glanced up at my hidden camera as she arrived at the door then blew to open it. Finally, she stood in the doorway looking in me.

"Hello Nikaya," I warmly welcomed her. "You're a lot earlier than usual."

She didn't answer.

"Are you all right?"

"I'm fine, but when you're ready, follow me."

My heart sank, the encounter with the BIHU the night before playing over in my mind again: *"Don't follow her,"* I heard it say.

"Follow you?" I asked apprehensively.

"Yes, there's something important I need to show you."

"What is it?"

"I can't say now, but just please follow me." Her voice was hushed but tense.

Something is going on. I looked into Nikaya's eyes and knew that she meant me no harm. If anything, she looked a little scared herself. *It's not like I would really even be going with her, just one of my bodies would be with her. Worst case scenario I anger Ward—or whoever was controlling that BIHU I saw—while my brain stays safely in this room.* I watched Nikaya take a deep anxious breath and I knew what I was going to do.

"Okay, I'm ready." I stepped forward with my BIHU as I retracted my camera back toward my orb.

"Good." Nikaya nodded then turned and speedily walked around my orb to the back of the room, my BIHU following close behind. "What are you doing?"

Nikaya blew on the third door and it folded open, revealing another nondescript white hall. A slight feeling of excitement and anticipation rose inside me; this was the first time I had seen it open. Nikaya looked back. "Follow me." Then she was off, through the door and moving quickly down the hall. Something was definitely off about this situation, but Nikaya was the one thing in this place that I felt I could trust—so I followed.

It wasn't long before we passed a few jet-black lines on the walls, ceiling, and floor. They grew more numerous as we progressed until they coated the walls like ivy. The sight of them made me feel uncomfortable, drawing up memories of the suffocating black plane. *I don't like this.*

We walked together for a long time, taking only a single turn to the left before Nikaya eventually came to a sudden stop. I stood close behind her and watched as she turned to her left and looked at the wall. A dense branching of black lines on the wall roughly formed a rectangle.

Nikaya glanced over her shoulder at me then took a step forward. Lifting a hand, she touched the tip of one finger to the center of the rectangle. The instant her pale flesh made contact with the white and black metal surface, it fractured into tiny black cubes that fell in a wave and rippled like water across the ground. They seemed to fold into themselves and each

other, continuously forming larger cubes that were absorbed
into the surrounding walls where they disappeared.

I watched in amazement as an empty doorway to a narrow
white hall appeared. Nikaya stepped over the faintly humming
black threshold and looked back at me. "We're almost there."
I looked back at her as I carefully stepped through. My head
nearly scraped the ceiling of the hallway, but I could see the
end no more than a hundred feet away—another line-covered
wall identical to the one we had just passed through.

I quickly caught up to Nikaya and stood by her side to watch
the second wall reveal what it was hiding.

Through the growing holes in the quickly dissipating sheet of
black cubes was a mostly empty room dozens of times larger
than mine, and lit brighter than any room I had seen before.
The floor, walls, and ceiling shared an intricate geometric
pattern of never-crossing black lines that turned exclusively at
right angles.

These details of the room were nothing important, though;
what filled me with a sense of awe hung at its center. There,
spinning several feet above the floor was a massive, warmly
humming and impossibly black cube. It bristled and swirled
with waves of millions of smaller undulating cubes, constantly
folding and unfolding into themselves and each other. The
black substance calmly hummed with a deep, rich sound that I
had felt before. *This is what I felt through the wireless connector—I
know it!*

Imbedded in the floor beneath the cube was a white bowl
roughly fifteen feet in diameter, filled near to the brim with the
same interconnected and flowing cubes, folding and unfolding
into each other and themselves. It was almost as if the pool
was one of churning black oil. Rising from the center of this
pool was a long thin strand of the black substance that
connected to the lowest point of the cube spinning above.
It flowed like a liquid but I felt sure it would be as hard as a
rock to the touch, and it was all so black—as black as anything
I had ever seen and even in the brightest room I had ever been
in. Like a black hole from which not even light could escape,

its gravity pulled in my gaze and wouldn't let me go. I could only try not to be overtaken by its otherworldly presence. Nikaya stepped through the now open doorframe into the spacious room; I carefully followed close beside her. From a glance at Nikaya, I saw that she had an expression on her face and an air about her that was frighteningly similar to what I had seen the day before at the gate. I was already wary of this situation, but the cube and Nikaya's demeanor only increased my level of alertness. All I knew for sure was that this was something extremely important and that it must have something to do with—or perhaps even was—the tower computer itself. Whatever it was, its presence made me feel small and fragile before it.

Together, we walked toward the center of the room, looking up at the cube, our eyes transfixed.

"This is it," Nikaya muttered. "This is the heart of the tower, the computer nexus. It controls everything of Ward's inside of and from this tower. Everything that is that color of black and in the tower is directly connected to and a part of this." Nikaya's words felt heavy despite being spoken so softly. There was a sort of invisible foreboding mental weight in the room that even I could feel. "You may not know it, but it's spent quite a bit of time caring for you over the years. It knows you better than anyone."

I stared up at the thing. *This is it, then. This is the black plane. This is really it.* Finally seeing it outside of my mind, I felt like I was facing something from a recurring dream, like I had stepped into a waking nightmare. Years of memories of fear and loneliness percolated through countless cracks in my mind. I froze—the cube continued to tranquilly spin as I struggled to make sense of what had happened to me once more.

Nikaya continued to walk toward the thing. I wanted to grab her shoulder, to tell her to stop, that it wasn't safe, but I felt I couldn't. She kept walking and I moved in slow motion behind her. We didn't stop until we stood only several steps from the edge of the bowl. I felt like the humming had been growing in intensity with every step and even after we stopped moving toward the nexus.

I looked down into the bowl then at the cube revolving above my head. I felt tiny and insignificant next to its size and unfathomable complexity, like its mere presence could push me down through the floor like a tack. Its size filled my BIHU's vision and it became the only thing I could focus on despite my many eyes. I felt like my very soul might be sucked in. Everything grew silent and all other senses became numb in its embrace. I felt nothing, then...

Slowly, slowly a feeling of comfort and familiarity began to wash over me, like I was safe in its shadow. As scary as this place and situation was where I oddly felt sort of like I had returned to something once familiar but forgotten, I finally collected enough control to speak.

"It's amazing," I croaked. "thank you for bringing me here Nikaya." I looked over at her, breaking my link with the nexus. "Nikaya?"

My senses returned, and I found my body shaking, the room exploding with noise. Fear throttled me as all feelings of comfort or safety were dashed away. I saw despair on Nikaya's face, and watched a single tear slide down her pale cheek, her quivering lips mouthing words that I couldn't hear.

"I'm sorry. I'm sorry. I can't. I'm sorry," she mouthed over and over.

I turned back toward the cube. Violent waves of the black substance rippled across the cubes' vibrating surface and in the pool beneath it was like an angry sea below a pulsating black star. Then I saw it. A razor-tipped needle growing out from the cube's side. Steadily, it reached toward Nikaya like a butterfly's proboscis toward a flower.

I felt like I lost control again. My legs buckled, and my body fell backward on its hands. I was left speechless as the intense noise grew even louder and Nikaya began to weep, her eyes now red and overflowing with tears. Her neck was bent back, her eyes facing the cube and its ominous probe. She didn't move; she seemed glued to the floor with her arms stuck at her sides as her pitiful, sorrow-filled muttering turned to gibberish. I watched hopelessly as the needle moved closer to her, growing longer and thinner as it went. It closed in on her head as the noise's intensity seemed to climax and the entire world seemed to shake with its power.

Then Nikaya grew quiet. She seemed to hold her breath, her eyes centered on the razor-tip of the needle now only inches in front of her.

I didn't know what to do. My mind raced in confused circles as the black spike kissed her skin and kept going on its way without slowing. A tiny bead of crimson blood slipped around the shaft and rolled down her sheet-white face, mixing with fresh tears on her cheeks as it went.

Nikaya's silence broke, her mouth split in a breathless silent scream. Ferociously, she tried to thrash her arms and legs—but to no avail. She couldn't turn away or bend her torso. Her body looked as if it were held by invisible bonds binding her to that spot in space. Her arms and legs contorted and twisted in ways that they shouldn't as the needle slowly lifted up into the air with Nikaya hanging by her head at its tip.

I shouted in my mind, wishing I could wake from this terror, but nothing happened. I was here, and there was no escape as I watched the one person I felt I could trust writhe like a burning insect before me.

I felt like I was breaking down on the inside. Long growing stress cracks in my mind were about to explode open.

This is it. I will die. We will die.

And then something gave way.

The cycle of confusion broke, and I leapt up off the ground. I sprinted toward Nikaya, her feet dangling nearly her body height above the floor. Her struggling was growing weaker, lessening until her body hung almost limply from the needle tip.

In a running leap, I jumped into the air, wrapped one arm around her body, and slapped my free hand flat against her forehead, the black spike in between my middle and index fingers. I pushed, cleanly sliding her off of the spike.

I landed hard on my feet with Nikaya cradled in my arms. I paused only long enough to glance over my shoulder at the cube. It had already retracted the spike and was now vibrating so violently that jets of the crawling black cube substance shot out like the sun's solar flares. Long strands of pure black angrily whipped out through the air before lashing back into the main body.

I turned back to Nikaya. She was unmoving in my arms, looking oddly calm. It was surreal.

Then on the edge of my vision I noticed something moving. I looked up at the only door to the room and to my despair saw it filling in. Forgetting everything else around me, I ran for it.

I pushed off the ground like a sprinter and flew half the distance; in the next stride I was through the first doorway. I landed mid-stride in the small hallway and continued faster than I had ever gone before as I watched the millions of tiny cubes rush to fill the doorway. The gap was narrowing. *I'm not going to fit, I'm not going to make it!*

I took one last powerful leap and launched into the air as I twisted my shoulder back in the direction of the door. I held Nikaya's limp body tightly against my chest, tucked in my head to guard hers, and braced for impact. I hit the door hard and crunched through the gap, spraying dislodged bundles of the cubes everywhere as I slammed through.

Hitting the floor on the other side, I slid until I struck the wall in the main hallway.

For a few moments I lay quivering against the wall, grasping my precious package against my cold metal chest. I felt her delicate heart beat against me. *She's still alive…* I felt some relief, but would she be okay? *What happened?* I felt like I could cry but I was physically incapable to. *I'm already dead.*

I opened my eyes, lifted my head, and hurriedly looked around the hall. It appeared to be empty in both directions and I could no longer hear the noise of the nexus. I looked up at the door to see the last few bits of black cubes slither back into their places in the door, sealing it and blending perfectly with the white wall. No trace of it remained.

I laid my head down next to Nikaya's, looking over at her tranquil, inexpressive face and shaking at the thought of what had just happened, whatever it was. She looked as if she were sleeping. I almost laughed nervously at how close our escape really was, but the gesture came out as more of a shiver.

The moment of peace didn't last long. There was a bright flash of white light in my mind, then the image filled with color and began to move. A brilliantly white room filled with intricate black designs appeared in the background of the image then a man came into focus.

I tried to pull away from the sudden intrusion but couldn't. I felt mentally trapped then filled with fear as the image cleared, and I recognized the man sitting before me inside my mind. Ward.

I felt Ward's gaze and heard his voice echo through my mind. Even as Ward opened his mouth and began to speak, I tried to struggle to get away, feeling as if I were strapped to a chair in the same room as him.

"Hello A-404, or shall I say Alder."

I stopped struggling. I couldn't do anything to stop him. I felt intoxicated by what I saw and felt, and I was scared of what he may do after my incident with the tower and Nikaya if he knew about it. I had just survived something and was now backed into another corner.

"I am proud of you, Alder. You have been a great success."

What? There was an eerie silence—nothing moved, as if he were letting his words settle in before continuing. His formality and dominance over me made me feel sick.

"As you already know, the reason you are here is because I brought you here as a test subject for an experiment. The purpose of which is testing new technology for my eventual use. That technology is the hardware that is now inside of you, and which allows you to connect, organize, and control the stable and biased mediums to which you are connected.

"I will have total control over my domain, and I will be able to work uninhibited, rid of decadent or wasteful desires of the flesh and even of the need to eat or drink. I'm sure you've already noticed some of these physiological changes in yourself after being separated from all but your brain. Free of the animal body that you once drove, by my measure, you're more human than I, because it is not our instincts and desires that make us human, but our ability to deny them that separates us from beasts.

"Also, like you, I will attain a greater relative immortality than what I already possess. No longer will I need to replace, augment, and rejuvenate organic organs to sustain my conscious mind—the sole connection to and control center for the body that exists only to sustain it.

"Alder, I am extremely pleased with your performance and abilities in the creation and control of your given domain. You may be the only man I envy, but not for much longer since I too will soon possess the ability to create so fluidly and freely as you do now.

"A final note, I have to say that the way you discovered the initial observation program and blocked it with a cover-up was clever. However, we never needed it. With a scanner on the other side of a wall we have been monitoring your every action and recording your neural activity, interpreting it with software right down to just outside of your innermost thoughts."

Ward paused as if to let the weight of what he had said sink in again. I was genuinely afraid, yet growing angrier at his influence over me with his every sentence—and I knew he knew it. He was most definitely watching the changes in my brain in real time as software interpreted whatever his scanners were picking up. *Does he know everything? Is he listening to this thought right now?* I tried to stay calm, but I was beginning to panic and knowing he knew that made it worse.

Ward continued, "I thought about using you to work for me, but now that the experiment is finally complete and your prodigious success has shown me just how successful the technology can be it has also made you a little too risky to keep you around. The fate that befell the previous partakers of this endeavor will now be yours to share, although it shouldn't be terribly painful. So thank you, Alder, for your wonderful assistance, cooperation, and contribution to me and to science. Goodbye."

The image disappeared. At first I only wondered if he did or didn't know about the incident then the meaning of his final words hit me like a train. *He's going to kill me!* I hurriedly looked around through my BIHU's eyes and saw nothing that appeared to be a threat. There was nothing dangerous that I could see in my room either and my mind still felt normal too. I took a moment to try to collect myself.

I looked down at Nikaya and at the thin stream of blood flowing from the pin prick of a wound on her forehead. *What was that thing doing to her? Whatever it was, it wasn't Ward. It felt too different. I wonder if he even controls it.* I lay there, looking down at her tear and bloodstained face for a few more seconds. *She still looks beautiful... I have to get her somewhere safer.* I began to feel something strange, almost like I was getting a terrible headache. *How could I have a headache? I can't remember the last time I—it's getting worse. Why now?*

Then I made a sudden and terrible realization. Back inside of my room, inside of my cables, my mind saw the cause of the aching pain. Swarms of virtual machines were pounding at my walls, attempting to force their way in. *They're attacking me!* I strained to keep the walls in place with my mind—then one of them broke. The moment the first tiny hole in the wall appeared, the entire thing was ripped to shreds and torn away. The cloud of machines came blasting forward, destroying everything that it touched until I managed to stop the flow with a new wall built a few feet behind where the first had been.

That was close, I thought. Then: *I'm losing ground.*

I have to get Nikaya and my BIHU back to my room. I quickly moved onto my knees and placed one foot on the ground in a kneeling position. I repositioned Nikaya in my arms and began to stand when I heard a single loud screeching noise like metal on metal coming from behind me. A shiver went through my being and I turned my BIHU's head to look in the direction of the noise. My eyes widened; I hurriedly leapt to my feet, stumbled on the first step, caught myself then sprinted toward my room, away from what I had seen.

Chasing me was a white wall of a machine, only its white front visible against the white wall, leaving no gaps on any side. At its center was a hole filled with teeth protruding out and covering its entirety. The teeth moved together in a spinning circular pattern inward toward the center, like a giant wood chipper. I immediately understood they would grab anything they touched and pull it inward.

It moved scarily fast, and I was sure that if I were to stumble or fall just once it would catch me and rip me to pieces. That would be the end of my BIHU and, unallowably, Nikaya. *I have to run faster.*

I bolted in an all-out sprint down the hall, feeling the machine slowly gaining on me. As I neared the only turn I heard a whooshing behind me. Glancing over my shoulder, I saw a white projectile scarcely visible against the white backdrop— heading directly toward me!

With a burst of speed, I leaped around the corner just as the projectile grazed past me then exploded with an air-ripping screech against the far wall. The explosion sent pieces of shrapnel skipping across my metal body and the hall! Some pieces of hot metal dug into me; the blast of searing heat flowed across my back and deep into my metal body. I bent over and pressed against the inside wall to try to shield Nikaya the best I could.

There was no time to rest or examine the situation, only to continue running.

The machine quickly caught up to me and began to round the corner. It slowed as its body tried to bend around the tight turn, revealing a sliver of its side. Hundreds of writhing little arms wildly reached around the corner and struggled to grip the wall to pull it forward. I felt a fleeting hope that it wouldn't be able to turn the corner because of its size and shape, but then it freed itself from the maneuver and continued down the hall terrifyingly fast.

I turned and bolted, the machine just strides behind me. *This is the long straight before the door. I'm almost back.* If I stumbled here or if it fired another rocket, I knew there would be no chance of escape.

In the distant white haze, the shape of the door to my room began to appear.

"We're almost there," I gasped. "We're going to make it."

Then I noticed something: The door was closed, and I couldn't open it. Only Nikaya could. I looked down at her unmoving face resting on my arm. Her eyes were closed, her hair blown back by the wind. *She's still unconscious!*

"Nikaya! Nikaya!"

No response.

I glanced up, seeing the end of the hall coming fast.

"Nikaya! Nikaya!"

I shook her in my arms and screamed her name.

"NIKAYA!"

She partially opened her eyes and let out a pitiful whimper, squinting in the bright light.

I lowered my mouth to her ear. "Nikaya, you have to open the door or you will die. You just have to blow on it. You have to open the door."

She still looked confused. I could only hope that she had understood me. I turned her body, forcing her to face the door. Sluggishly she wiggled once then stopped moving.

Am I going to have to break through it?

I looked back up at the door as I continued sprinting toward it, preparing myself to smash against it with Nikaya's limp body still nestled tightly in my arms, dreading more than anything how horrible the impact with her in my arms would feel—her bones cracking and soft body crushing against mine. *I can't do this*, I cried in my mind as despair overtook me. I glanced back at the creature chasing us, wondering if it might be a better fate. *I can't do this!*

It wasn't until the door filled my field of vision that I accepted we were both going to die.

My powerful metal legs took the final leap forward at full speed. I closed my eyes, feeling Nikaya's chest expand…and in the very moment before the deadly impact, she blew.

But we were moving too fast. There was no way the door could open completely before both of our bodies were destroyed by the impact or by the machine.

As Nikaya's lungs emptied, I heard the horrible humming noise of the nexus far behind us and thought I saw black lines streak across the ceiling. I twisted my body in air to pass through the growing gap, barely scraping against its edges. Then, just as we passed, the door immediately slammed shut.

On the other side, I hit the floor, turning sideways and sliding. I slid to a stop against the base of my orb. Then as fast as I could, I turned around, got up to one knee, and stared expectantly, fearfully at the center of the door. Seconds felt like minutes and minutes felt like hours as I waited for the machine to blast through and devour us both at any moment—but it never did. For some reason it had stopped. *Did it leave?*

My frozen state of anxiety was finally broken when I heard a faint whimper come from something in my arms. *Nikaya!* I looked down at her, her eyes still closed. She twisted slightly in my arms then continued to breathe steady, shallow breaths. She felt relatively cold.

Slowly, I stood then carefully placed her on top of my wooden desk. *It at least won't be as cold as my arms or floor.* I thought I felt a chill pass through me as the warmth of her delicate body disappeared when she slid out of my grasp.

Nikaya curled up on the desk and faintly half moaned, half hummed again. I looked at her tear and bloodstained cheeks, trying to imagine what the tower computer could have possibly been trying to do to her. *At least her head's stopped bleeding.* I glanced up and down the length of her body. *None of the shrapnel hit her…that's a relief.*

After I'd done all I could for her with my BIHU, I walked away to stand next to the front wall and try to pull the twisted pieces of shredded metal from the backsides of its arms, legs, neck, and torso. At the same time, I carefully lowered my camera to the desk and gently coiled my snake-like neck around its perimeter in an attempt to keep Nikaya warm and to prevent her from rolling off onto the floor. I laid my main head down close to hers, resting on the synthetic coils of my black neck. I was careful not to touch her with anything other than my neck, as anything metal would only suck more heat from her.

Everything in and around my room was silent, but I knew that it wouldn't be this way for long. This was only the beginning. Ward is out to kill us. I shivered internally at the thought of what might happen to me as the pressure on my virtual defenses continued to mount. *How long can I do this, and how long until these virtual attacks are accompanied by physical ones? I'm merely inside my metal tomb, waiting for death.*

With what little mental strength I had left, I tried to make sense of what had just transpired. *Why did Nikaya go to the nexus? Why was I told not to go with her, and by whom? What happened to me in there, and how did we get away?* I had a feeling that something other than myself or Nikaya may have forced the door open. *Did I imagine the black lines or did Nikaya's breath just reach the door sooner than I thought it would? Did the computer save us—save us from Ward right after trying to kill Nikaya?*

With a gasp, Nikaya opened her eyes and jerked up. I lifted my head from its place beside hers and positioned it to look down at her face from above. Quickly and clumsily, Nikaya tried to prop herself up on her elbows and slide toward the edge of the desk in a desperate attempt to escape. I blocked her path with my neck, doubting she could stand on her own. Nikaya seemed to shrink away from me, afraid.

Her darting eyes looked up into the dark lenses of my head, deathly fear then awareness and finally calm passing through her expression. Looking up into my lifeless eyes with a mixed expression of relief, terror, and confusion, she stopped struggling and lay back down. Then in a weak, almost croaking voice, she managed to push out a sentence: "It will kill us."

Everything was still except for my BIHU sitting in its corner, wrestling with a fist-sized piece of shrapnel in its shoulder. Nikaya's chest had begun to rise and fall more rapidly. She periodically squeezed her eyes shut then reopened them. *Does she think she's in a nightmare?* My attention moved to the image of her tense fingers, almost clawing at the wood of my desk. *She's as terrified as I am, maybe more.*

"What should I do?" I asked as calmly as I could.

Nikaya's eyes opened and reconnected with mine. She seemed confused by the question, but then she spoke hesitantly.

"Is it attacking you now...on the inside?"

"Yes."

"Do you have walls? Are you holding it back okay?"

"Yes, for now."

Nikaya averted her eyes and nodded. She bit her lips nervously then spoke, "Have you ever tried to go past the tower's virtual walls, out into the tower?"

"No I haven't."

"Okay..." She nodded again, looked over toward one of the room's walls then back up at me. In a surprisingly mater-of-fact way she said, "Well you have to now. You have to gain control of this room's walls and doors now. You must take control so you can prevent this room from compressing in on us and to keep the doors closed."

"Compressing?"

"Yes, I will explain later if you survive. You have to take the cell that surrounds this room now. You have to cut off the tower's communication and control of his area or we both die."

"Okay, but...how? What am I able to do?" I backed up, giving her space to think and to lift herself into a sitting position with her shaking arms.

"You have to pick an entrance to the tower and attack it with your mind in any way that you can." Nikaya began to speak faster and with more urgency. "I can't tell you exactly how, but you have to push it back far enough to get it out of this area then build walls around everything and take control of the room. After you take control, you will have to physically move parts of this room to further isolate us from the tower. Then we will mostly only have to worry about physical attacks after that." Nikaya took a deep breath and with a small quiver in her voice asked, "And…how long was I out on the desk?"

"Mmm…maybe a minute." I saw the look of panic creep back onto her face. "What is it?" Every part of the way she was moving and speaking made me feel more worried.

"You probably only have several seconds to take control of the doors… Something will definitely be on its way here by now. You have to attack now, and once you control and cut off the room we might be able to survive for about an hour, maybe even a few."

I moved back further as Nikaya moved to sit on the side of the desk, her feet hanging over the edge. She hugged herself tightly, closed her eyes and sat in silence, a fresh tear trailing down her cheek, mixing with the drying blood.

I shuddered at the idea of exposing my mind to the tower, but knew that I had to try to do what Nikaya had instructed me to. *There's no other option. I have to do it, and fast.*

I watched the entrances to my orb to try to prepare myself. The swarms of electric machines crashed against my walls in waves; I tracked the intervals with my improved memory and senses. Quick bursts, less than a millisecond in between, cycled through the cable entrances in a circular pattern. *My best chance is in the gap.*

Working quickly, I crudely designed a new virtual machine that I hoped could interrupt or destroy the machines in the swarm. I set every spec and electron under my control to work, feeling their strain. My mind buzzed, my virtual factories exploded with production, and every ounce of energy at my disposal was thrown into the raging torrent that was my tiny kingdom. I was already exhausted, yet I felt alive and I relished the feeling of my creation buzzing around inside of and around me. Every physical appendage of mine appeared lifeless and idle to the outside world.

I don't know what's out there or what will happen to me if I lose, but I have to do this—or we will die. I imagined my blind attack into the darkness outside my walls. *If I'm going to die, I'm going to throw everything I have at him. I'm going to leave my mark in Ward's memory, even if that memory is only a second long.* A wave of anger and frustration surged through me. *I'm going to shake Ward and his tower to their cores and smash them to pieces.*

I crammed all I could into a position in my chosen cable. Surrounded by my writhing swarm of an army, I fixed my full attention on the wall in the cable as Ward's bombardment continued, timing myself as precisely as possible. I counted through several dozen cycles, saw the opening... *Now!*

I opened my virtual wall and thrust through the dark opening at full force.

I flew deep into the cable, feeling shocked at the lack of resistance—until the cycle came back around. The bombardment slammed into me head on, obliterating the bulk of the foremost part of my force. A feeling of shock settled over me.

I failed...

Then I realized that the blast that had hit me was almost entirely destroyed by my bulk. A moment of realization replaced my shock. *I can do this.*

Then tens of millions of varying virtual machines were attacking me, many of which complex beyond my immediate understanding. I pushed my swarm of machines out again, drawing improved versions of them up from the factory clouds around my brain.

I pushed forward all the way through the cable, and as I did, the attacks on my walls wavered, fluctuated, then—to my bemusement—sputtered and stopped entirely. *Did I catch him off guard?* I thrust out through every cable and avenue I could. *I won't get this chance again.*

It was almost a whole second later, a relative eternity, before the attacks resumed in greater force, rapidly increasing in ferocity as new dense swarms of machines thrashed out from the darkness at me from all sides, surrounding me and my

armies again. Like a cornered animal I lashed out, desperately
fighting for my life and Nikaya's.

Away from the battle, the outside world—my room, and
Nikaya in it—remained still, serene. Nikaya had laid down on
my desk with her eyes closed and hands folded loosely over
her stomach. I wondered if she was sleeping or just waiting to
die, maybe both. *I must do this*, I repeated to myself.

A white silvery flash moved past the view of my hallway
camera, although I paid little attention to it—I had to
concentrate everything on the fight within the wires. The battle
inside the cables was moving so fast that the rest of the world
seemed to move in slow motion. Every millisecond was a
potential life or death situation, and I was amazed I had kept
up so far.

I struggled to process, command, and maneuver millions of
machines through the cables, continuing to push forward and
destroy. I felt stings of mental pain as we clashed, and my
machines were smashed around me. It was terrifying how
quickly my enemy adapted, sending new versions of its
machines with almost every attack, each more specialized at
destroying mine than the last. I was forced to try to do the
same.

Still in the thick of the virtual fight, I heard a shout
accompanied by a firm thump from inside my room. *Something
is inside!*

I saw it. The intruder was a BIHU, identical to mine, and the
thumping noise had been it tearing Nikaya from the desk and
onto the floor by her ankle. The surprise of the machine's
sudden appearance caused a dangerous lapse in my
concentration, and I felt the beginnings of being overwhelmed
in battle. Nikaya struggled, clasping at the smooth metal floor
as the BIHU dragged her by her ankle toward the open door.
Filled with dread and rage, I mentally strained to rush toward
Nikaya with my BIHU. *NO!*

Taking one great stride, I leaped over Nikaya and hit the BIHU
on the side of its head with a heavy, well-placed kick. As I
landed on my other leg beside the machine, I punched the

center of its chest. Then I drove my right fist forward into the side of its neck, each impact making a loud metallic crunch. The BIHU stood, seemingly stunned as I proceeded to punch it three more times in the face with inhuman mechanical speed, destroying one of its eyes and damaging the other. Finally, I sent my knee driving up into my enemy's midsection.

The BIHU finally released Nikaya's ankle and tried to push back; I slammed it to the ground by thrusting my left arm on its upper torso and grabbing its neck. With its head braced against the floor, I drove my fist into its head with enough force to create a large dent in the hard metal and to severely warp and contort the structure of my hand.

I hit the machine repeatedly, deepening and widening the dent in its head as it tried to grab at me, and my fingers twisted and smashed together with every impact. *I don't feel pain!* I stopped only after the BIHU ceased to move.

Gasping for air, Nikaya clambered back to her feet and rushed to climb back onto the desk. Once there, she turned and yelled to me, "More will come! You have to hurry!" She leaned back against my main head's neck for support, closing her eyes. As far as I could tell, she wasn't injured beyond a red and sore-looking ankle.

I can't answer her. I returned my full attention to the battle inside. *I need to end this soon, or I'm going to lose it.*

I pushed hard, expanding myself farther out from the entrances to my cables where I found increasingly large and complex structures, some of which I recognized as paths or factories, but many I couldn't understand. The metal medium of the walls themselves was also new to me. Moving through it felt slightly different from my cables—this substance seemed more malleable, pure and controllable. The very sensation of it on my mind made me feel more invigorated and free—but I had no time to marvel.

I took another big leap forward into the dark and from all directions, individual enemy machines rushed to get in my way, sacrificing themselves to try to slow me down. *They're trying to protect something.* I pushed forward harder, clashing with a larger group, and broke through in a burst of vigor. *Something is here!* I felt a snagging and tugging sensation.

There was a membrane with both virtual and physical properties, a border encompassing the room like a large hollow sphere. Touching it with my mind, I felt a tingling as lightning-like tendrils spun out from the point of contact and circled around the interior of the sphere, expanding and bringing my senses and awareness with them, almost as if the tendrils were becoming a part of me. *What is this?* I froze in awe as the membrane flashed and hardened in a crisp wave of light. Emanating first from the point of first contact, it flew out along the membrane until it disappeared on the opposite side of my room, converging into a single point.

Suddenly I saw and felt all that was inside the membrane as if my room had just become a part of my body. There was a fraction of a second of respite, then from the darkness a massive wave of machines slammed into the membrane, covering its entire surface like a flood. I felt the uncomfortable tingle of burning and tried to pull back from the blast, and somehow—I did. Somehow, I made the entire area within the membrane physically contract and pull inward away from the tower, leaving only several struts connecting my room to the tower for support.

The pressure dissipated. Only a few small clouds of Ward's virtual machines were left trapped inside the membrane. These ceased to move, grew dim then destroyed themselves.

I—I did it. I did it! In disbelief, I took in the terrifyingly spectacular view of the entirety of this new part of myself. *So this is what Nikaya meant by controlling the room. It's all part of my body now.* The virtual walls inside my supports choked the enemies into a small space that I could more easily defend with the strength of the membrane wall.

This massive new body of mine, roughly spherical and oblong, resembled a biological cell with a large empty vacuole-like space near its center, which I knew to be my room. I had total control over all of the doors and cameras, and I could feel the insides of the walls of the room as if they were my skin, the touch of my BIHU and desk's feet noticeable on the floor. I even sensed communication between myself and my BIHU pass directly through points of physical contact on the floor and between parts of the wall—which began to emit wireless signals themselves, both bypassing the installed wireless antenna entirely. *This is incredible.*

Basketball-size regions within the walls, where the metal itself was physically swirled and twisted in intricate spherical patterns, were filled with energy—densely packed energy. I surrounded them but was unable to reach the beautiful swirling contents within. I looked at their contents hungrily. *I will ask Nikaya about these and come back to them later.*

I looked around my little part of the world with my new nearly omniscient perspective of my room and everything in it. Through my hallway cameras, I could see that there was now a gap between my room and the surrounding tower. It sunk in just how cell-like the design of this part of the tower really was, and that the rest of the tower was likely constructed from units of the same elegant pseudo-organic design. *It's like a living thing.*

All of my senses suddenly flashed off for a millisecond. I felt like I had been hit by a train and began to panic. My consciousness began to flicker on and off sporadically, like a faulty light.

After a moment, I realized that I was being attacked by my own exhaustion.

In an attempt to save energy—and possibly my life—I tried to destroy or turn off everything I could. The battle had only lasted several seconds, but I had been forced to use every ounce of power and thought that I had. My brain simply couldn't handle the load anymore.

I destroyed nearly all of my combat machines and slowed everything else to a near standstill as thousands of machines simply fell out of my control and broke apart.

Then I remembered Nikaya. *I have to tell her the outcome now. I don't know how much longer I can stay awake.*

I looked out through my many eyes and saw Nikaya, still sitting in the same place on my desk. She seemed frozen in place, held by the uncertainty in if she would live another minute. It took all the determination I could muster to exhaustedly push out the words that she needed to hear through my main head. "I've won… I have control of the room."

She looked up at me, and with the faintest of smiles on her concerned face she answered, "Good. Be sure to make space in between yourself and the tower. It will make things easier on you and help make us a little safer."

"Yes, I'm workingonit," I slurred, still fleeting in and out of consciousness. I felt my physical walls grow increasingly dense until they couldn't become any denser and so the inside of the room began to change shape, bulging inward. I saw Nikaya looking around as it happened. I picked one of the halls, made sure it was empty, then opened the door to show Nikaya the gap, which had grown by nearly two feet. "This, good is— enough?" I noticed that my speech was becoming slurred and slow.

"That should help a lot for now. Are you okay, though?" She sounded worried as she looked up at my main head. I closed the door.

I was so exhausted and tantalized by the floating orbs of locked energy trapped in my body. I blacked out again. *I need to get inside the orbs.* "Nikaya…do you know about the energy stored in cells?"

"Um…yes," Nikaya replied apprehensively.

"How do I open them?"

"They can only be accessed by groups of at least seven cells or more. It's for organizational reasons and to help prevent security issues, like the one we're creating."

Ugh… I was still barely holding on to consciousness. "What should do now?" My expansive vision flickered on and off along with my hearing and consciousness as thoughts and images swam chaotically through my mind: the battle, Ward, the computer, and Nikaya. I was seeing a new image through my hallway cameras, slowly blocking out the other images and dominating my fleeting focus.

I saw several BIHUs in the left hallway and several more
appear in the right—all of them sprinting toward me as
everything of mine grew silent and black.
Finally, my exhaustion put an end to my stress, confusion, and
consciousness.

CHAPTER NINE

- *Sapling* -

A confusing blur of light and images came from my many eyes
and formed an uninterpretable mass of information in my
mind, accompanied by equally confusing feelings of pressure
and pain across my body. A loud banging noise echoed from
my doors—like metal on metal. The memory of what had
happened groggily began to come back to me. I felt too tired
to think straight.

My conscious mind flopped around like a fish in a thick muddy
pool as I tried to make sense of the jumbled mess of blurry
images, sounds, and feelings assaulting me. Everything grew
more stable and clear until I was able to make out a voice
among the mess of loud banging. It was Nikaya's voice,
frightened and frantic.

Nin—Nikaya... I moaned.

The sound of her voice jogged my memory and filled me with
an increased sense of urgency and concern, pushed me upward
into a higher level of alertness. My dozens of fields of vision,
hearing, and feeling came into focus and finally snapped into
the unified awareness of what was my body, revealing the full
scope of the situation.

The cell membrane and my virtual walls were still holding up
somehow, and I noticed that my BIHU, SCU, and main head
had all fallen to the floor. Nikaya was sitting on my desk,

holding my main head between her hands and leaning over it, speaking frantically to it.

"Can you hear me? You have to do something, or they're going to kill us. Can you hear me? They're going to kill us."

Most of the BIHUs that I had seen running toward me earlier now stood like stone statues in orderly lines in each of the hallways. The two in front of each set of lines wildly beat at the door with such ferocity that they disfigured themselves. I scrambled to think of what to do. *There's no way they can break through on their own. Are they here just to cause me pain, to scare me?* I heard a moan and the bulk of my attention flashed back to Nikaya. *I have to speak to her now.*

"I'm here Nikaya!" I rushed back into my machinery appendages, which all jumped back to life. Nikaya looked startled at first then relieved as my head, which she had been holding, rose into its upright position. She looked up at me, speechless, and I gazed down at her, her face still marked by traces of dried blood and tears.

With a quiver in her voice she asked, "What happened to you? I thought that—"

"I—I blacked out. I was too weak to stay conscious. How long has it been?"

"About an hour… I think. I don't know how we're still alive. I was thinking that you had been killed from the inside, but then nothing came for me."

Neither of us spoke for a while; the pounding of the suicidal BIHU's bodies on the doors continued to hammer like evil drums. I broke the silence between us. "Well, we have to do something."

"I know," Nikaya agreed.

"Ward said that he was finished, that he was going to kill me. Why isn't he attacking with something larger, with one of his worms? Is there something he wants or is he just playing with me? I should be dead; we should be dead. You work for him, Nikaya. You live here. What's going on? If this is all part of the experiment, then tell me now, Nikaya. I need to know now."

She remained silent in the face of my accusing demands, looking blankly at the desk.

"You have to know something…"

"I—I don't know all of what's happening, and please believe me; this isn't part of the experiment. We should be dead—both of us—an hour ago." Nikaya breathed deeply then looked up into my glass eyes, a wet glaze forming over hers. "There's a lot you don't know, Alder…and unfortunately a lot I don't know either. Something is happening, and"—Nikaya swallowed—"several people were killed, people I've known for a long time."

The memory of the bloodied BIHU I had encountered the day before flashed in my mind.

"Then I came to you," Nikaya said, her voice quivering. "As of now, I no longer serve Ward. We work for each other, you and me. You need to trust me, and somehow we're going to make it. I know you have little reason to, but please, do you trust me Alder?"

"Don't follow her, Alder…" I heard the bloody BIHU say again. I had followed her though, and she had led me to the nexus. Then *it* happened.

I stared deeply into her eyes and realized that I had already decided on an answer. "Of course I trust you."

"Thank you." She sighed, her shoulders relaxing. "You were wondering why Ward hasn't killed you yet. I can't say for certain, but I believe he's been weakened or at least distracted. I'll tell you everything I can in time, but we need to act now. We can do nothing here but wait to die."

I had so many questions I felt I had to ask, especially about what had happened in the computer nexus room—but she was right. We simply didn't have time right now.

"I agree, Nikaya, but I'm too weak to do that again, even if Ward is weakened."

"I know you can't handle another fight like that yet, but if you can take several more cells, you'll be able to use their energy reserves for yourself—it's a security measure in the hardware. You need to do that before we can ever try to fight our way out of the tower, or at least take over a large enough area to survive for a while. We need to try to escape."

I tried to imagine myself living outside of the tower and realized just how difficult that would probably be. I was irreversibly changed and would have to somehow move my brain and machines to keep myself alive. It had been years since I was last outside, and I had no idea how long Nikaya might have been in here. Even this escape plan sounded like a death plan to me. *Where would we go?* Then, like a perverted dream, the idea of controlling the entire tower myself popped into my head. *That will never happen; I wouldn't even be able to handle it.* I tossed the concept away. *Even if I can't escape...at least maybe she can.* I looked at Nikaya and tried to shake off the feeling of hopelessness.

"Okay," I agreed. "What should I do then?"

"The easiest thing we can do now is probably to get you more machines since you taking cells is hardly an option for now. I know the current locations of a few small arsenals with machines that we might be able to take and use. The challenge will be getting to them safely, if at all..." Nikaya trailed off and we both became silent. I struggled to think of solutions.

Looking around, I noticed a painfully obvious difference in one of my doors. The third door, the one that we had narrowly escaped the worm through, appeared to be completely unguarded.

"What about the back door?" I asked.

Nikaya looked up at me then over at the door.

"The BIHUs are only attacking the left and right doors."

"Are you sure?" Nikaya asked warily.

"I'm as sure as I can be without opening it."

"That doesn't make sense. Either it's a trap or Ward is in a much worse condition than I thought." Nikaya hopped off my desk and walked around my sphere toward the door, talking as she went. "There is an arsenal we can get to through there, but I can't be sure that it will still be full, the machines inactive, or that the whole arsenal itself hasn't been moved somewhere else in the tower." Nikaya leaned against the backside of my sphere and looked at the closed door in front of her.

I can feel her footsteps when she walks... I was too tired and distracted to really notice it before, but now I could feel the soft pressure and warmth of her feet on the floor as if it were my skin. *Wow...* The technology inside this place was complex beyond my understanding.

"How far away is the nearest one?" I asked.

"A little less than two miles on foot, roughly."

I was surprised by the distance at first, but realized that wasn't too much longer than many of the other trips that we had already been on in the tower.

"It shouldn't take long to get there with my BIHU; I think we should try it. I'm going to check to make sure the hall is empty." I moved both my BIHU and SCU toward the door. Nikaya moved as far away from it as she could.

I still didn't entirely trust my eye in the hall. Something had to be going on; there had to be a reason for what Ward was doing, but I had to open the door anyway.

With both of my machines, I stood next to the door, ready to try to hold back anything that tried to enter if the need came. I braced myself for the worst, made sure Nikaya was in a safe position, then finally I told the door to open with my mind. Instantly, its white metal folds flew open with a gentle swish of air.

Nothing was there.

I scoured the hall with every eye that I could and saw nothing but smooth white walls. I closed the door and turned to face Nikaya. "It looks like it's clear."

Nikaya came closer. I could see the same doubts that I had myself on her face. "Do you think this could be a trap?"

"It could be... I hope Ward isn't playing with us."

I thought about what had happened earlier in the black and white room with the computer's nexus. "Nikaya...what if I could get back to the nexus and attack it? Even just throwing my BIHU into that pool under the nexus might hurt it enough to do something, right?"

Nikaya's eyes snapped up to meet mine as a look of shock and anger briefly flashed over her face, then just as quickly melted into something that looked like fear or even panic. "No, don't do that. You should stay away from it."

I was somewhat taken aback. I'd seen her act like this twice before: at the gate yesterday and in the nexus room—every time in connection to the tower computer.

As if she was aware of my thoughts, Nikaya quickly explained herself. "You won't be able to get to it again. It might be guarded too and will feel us coming. We wouldn't be able to get to the arsenal either."

"Okay, we won't do that," I replied simply.

She was right, but her reaction to the suggestion was still unsettling. It made me worry for her—but also for myself. I purposely ended my thoughts on the topic. *I have to trust her. We need each other if we're going to have any chance of survival. I'm probably just paranoid—I've always been a little paranoid.*

Nikaya had walked back to the door. "We need to do this soon, and fast if we're going to be able to do it at all. If this hall really isn't guarded right now, then it will likely be very soon."

"I know," I agreed tentatively. I opened the door again. We both looked out down the empty white hall then back at each other.

"Ready?" she asked.

"No."

"Hmm?"

"I don't know how to get there."

Nikaya's eyes widened at the realization of her mistake. "Oh, I didn't think of that." She almost sounded a little amused then grew serious. "I will have to come with you then, Alder."

I was silent. That seemed like a bad idea to me. I was willing to begrudgingly lose my BIHU, but with Nikaya with me... I couldn't lose her. I wouldn't survive long without her knowledge, and I had come to care about her. *There's no other way, though. We have to take this risk together.*

"Okay," I agreed. "But I will have to carry you. We will be able to move faster and safer that way. I will run, and you will open doors and tell me where to go."

Without a word, Nikaya stepped forward and turned, her left side facing my BIHU. I knelt forward then carefully scooped her up into my arms, holding her warm, delicate body close to my cold metal one. She squirmed to face forward and got comfortable. Cradled in my arms, I made sure that I had a firm hold on her.

"Ready?" I asked as I looked out into the hall then down at the dried blood on her face.

Nikaya looked back up at me resolutely. "Yes."

Without another word, I took the first step into the blinding white depths of the hall. In one great stride I cleared the door, closed it behind me and flew the hall, speeding up into a near sprint. Through my hall camera I watched my BIHU disappear into the distance. I took the first corner without incident and continued, and before I knew it we had gone over a half mile.

How I knew the distance we traveled was beyond me. I could have built a virtual machine to measure the distance using my stored memories or what I was seeing, although I hadn't. Then a surge of clouded memories from long before life in the tower returned to me. I was running, running through flashing images, smells, and sounds of distorted places and faces I had once known, peeking up from the void of lost memories. All carrying fleeting feelings of melancholy and nostalgia. *I don't know these people.*

I glanced down at Nikaya. She was staring out into the empty hall before us with the utmost concentration, like a hawk on its prey. Her elegantly-curved, pale neck was slightly extended outward, and her snow-white clothing and jet-black hair trailed behind us. For a moment I felt like I was looking at someone else—someone I couldn't remember, maybe even someone from a dream. *What is happening?*

"Stop at this upcoming turn," Nikaya instructed.

I looked up and found myself back in reality, my prison. I slowed to a stop just before the turn.

"Now let me touch the wall over there," Nikaya said. She made a motion toward a blank place on one of the walls. "There's a chance this might not work for me anymore. It may have already locked me out of the system." Nikaya reached out with her hand.

The instant her skin made contact with the wall, a red line reached from floor to ceiling, split into two parallel lines then pulled apart, stretching outward away from each other to form a square opening that revealed a circular room on the other side. A red line on the floor extended from either side of the door to form a circular loop around the inside of the room.

"Step inside, it's an elevator. We need to go up," Nikaya instructed. "The red means it isn't controlled directly by the computer."

I quickly obeyed and the wall closed behind us, leaving only a thin red line where it had been. I made my way to the center of the room as Nikaya spoke into the air in a commanding voice, "Up to level 1079." The machine obeyed and began to move. Nikaya sighed and took a deep breath, becoming noticeably more relaxed and less rigid in my arms. She turned and looked up at me. "We're a little more than halfway there. How is your BIHU doing?"

"I'm doing very well." *My mind is still tired from earlier, though.* I only felt exhaustion in everything that my brain did.

"Good and what's the condition of our base?"

"Still nothing but the same racket," I replied half-jokingly, as if it was just a minor annoyance. There was no immediate danger but I felt every hit on my doors and the sound was maddening.

"Good." Nikaya faintly smiled then turned to face the door of the lift as it came to a halt. "Are you ready?"

"Yes."

"Good; turn left once you're outside."

I acknowledged her by assuming a running stance.

Nikaya tightened her grip around me in preparation. The door lit up, began to slide into the walls, and the moment it was wide enough I sprinted forward and turned left into another ridiculously long hallway. I continued to run, following Nikaya's directions through the labyrinth until finally we turned and she pointed at a door.

"That's the armory."

I slowed to a stop a few strides away and gently set Nikaya on her feet. Silently, we looked up at the door. Even I felt dwarfed beside it. It was identical to the one that Nikaya had taken me to yesterday to get my BIHU, only bigger.

"I hope this works," Nikaya murmured. She walked up to the towering door. I felt a surge of anxiety as she reached out to touch it, fearing another one of her episodes like what had happened yesterday.

Nikaya blew and the entire door began to ring with a deep humming noise that resonated through the whole hall.

Then it stopped. I looked at the door expectantly then at Nikaya, but nothing happened—only silence.

Bang! There was a noise like a gunshot, then the door began to slide open noiselessly. Nikaya stepped back to my side and together we watched the door reveal an army of machines covering the vast room's expanse. *We made it.*

It wasn't until we were completely inside that the room's full size became apparent, and I started to pick up the signals emanating from the army. They were all empty and waiting for something to control them. The thought was intoxicating. *There has to be thousands of them.*

The majority of the machines were BIHUs and SCUs. Dozens of other varieties stood waiting as well, only a few that I recognized. I saw the one that I remembered for having the nailing arm that was used in the construction of my orb and immediately wanted one. *That arm would make an excellent weapon.* I nudged Nikaya then pointed at the machine as we stopped at the edge of the army. "No, we don't need one of those. We don't have much time either. Follow me. Hurry!"

A little disappointed, I did as she said. Nikaya jogged alongside the edge of the field of machines then turned into a row of BIHUs and lumpy metal eggs nearly as tall as she was.

"Is there something we're looking for?" I asked.

"Yes. Get one of these pods then grab some BIHUs, and hurry." Nikaya pointed at one of the lumpy eggs then waved her hand past the row of BIHUs.

"Okay." I turned to face the one closest to me and concentrated on picking out its individual signal from all the others in the room.

"Try to hurry. We need a lot more than this, and be careful. This is all way too easy so far."

I agreed.

I strengthened the connection with the mysterious new machine that looked like a sideways egg with rounded humps and indents over its surface. A circular hatch was on the front, and a bench-like structure around its circumference a few feet above the floor. I quickly took control, and why Nikaya wanted it became apparent.

While much of the pod's volume was taken up by tanks of pressurized liquids and gasses or by complex tools and filtration systems, there was also a hollow area at its center about the right size for a person to comfortably fit inside.

"Nikaya, what is this?"

"It's an SHSE, or a Single Human Sustaining Environment. I'll need that if I want to survive for more than a few days in our situation. It has all the sustenance and water I'll need for several months, maybe more."

"I was just beginning to wonder about how we would do that for you," I said as I turned my BIHU toward the row of other BIHUs and began to take one. It felt wonderful to take control of another of the masterpieces, and it only took seconds to do. As soon as I finished, both BIHUs moved to the next ones in line. Nikaya continued to nervously look around the room and check the nearby rows for machines that could be of use to us.

"Oh Alder, you should start to move the SHSE toward the lift now. It's a little slow."

"Okay." I told my newest body part to move and automatically it lifted up off of the ground, hovering two feet above the floor, and traveled toward the door. I navigated by looking through multiple hidden eyes around its circumference.

"What now?"

Nikaya glanced around the room again. "Grab two more BIHUs then follow me—and hurry."

I returned my attention to the BIHUs and took control of two more, wishing I could take control of the whole army at once. "I'm finished," I declared to Nikaya as my group of bodies gathered around her.

"Now follow me." Nikaya leapt through a gap between two SHSEs in the row behind her then cut across a few others. I followed close behind with all seven of my BIHUs, filing through the narrow gaps between inactive machines. Then Nikaya stopped, looked back at me and pointed up at a particularly large and impressive-looking machine before her. "We need this one."

"Yes." I was excited now. I stepped forward and looked up at it in awe. *Wow.* It was a magnificent and intimidating humanoid machine two feet taller than a BIHU. Its body was thick and strong yet lean, covered in a thick layer of armor seamlessly built into its body.

I looked into its jet-black eyes deeply set into its sculpted white metal face and, like the BIHUs, there was also a smaller red eye at the center of its neck, only visible through an opening in an armored plate that wrapped around most of its neck. Its right arm tapered down to a round opening of a gun and had a thick metal plate along its side which narrowed into a deadly-looking, blunt blade designed for piercing metal. Its left arm ended in a normal-looking hand with long, powerful fingers. To me it looked like a piece of idealized art but the flat-edged blade on its arm made it clear that this was a killing machine. A shiver of excitement and fear passed through me as I imagined cutting a BIHU in half with it. "It's amazing," I said as I started picking its signal.

Nikaya hummed in agreement. "It's an SFHU, or a Standard Fighting Humanoid Unit. It's basically a BIHU adapted for light to medium combat."

"SFHU," I repeated in acknowledgment. I looked back at it with all my eyes in the room.

Nikaya looked over at my closest body and with a little smile said, "Have you found out that it can fly yet?"

I looked at her with five of my BIHUs simultaneously. "It can fly?"

"Yep. There isn't really enough room to in most of the tower, but if you look at its back you'll see the thrusters."

One of my bodies walked behind it and immediately I found them. There was a small downward-facing opening on its back. *Wow.*

I finally took control of the machine. Its insides were filled with energy to power the gun, jetpack, and powerful body. Through my new colossus, I took two steps forward and looked down at all of my BIHUs, which once seemed like giants to me, then over at Nikaya who was more than a head shorter than the BIHUs. I looked out over the heads of the thousands of lifeless machines standing at attention before me. I felt the shape of my newest body as I rolled my shoulders back and lifted my arms in front of me.

I looked down at my open hand, then at the blade on my cannon arm. I looked along the length of its barrel and as I did an intricate virtual targeting sight appeared in the room. *This is very good. This is amazing,* I told myself as I centered the crosshairs on an inactive BIHU on the far side of the room. The sight disappeared the moment I looked away and put the weapon arm back at my side. I realized that the gun used energy to produce one of two types of projectiles instead—a rocket-like blast or small, precise bursts.

Done exploring my new body, I looked back down at Nikaya and asked, "What should we do now, Nikaya?"

"Be sure to grab at least one SCU then take as much as you can, but hurry. I feel like we've already been here far too long." Nikaya turned toward the open door. Excitedly, I sent a BIHU running to the nearest row of SCUs, but when I got there the SCU next to the one that I was taking over started to move. I stared at it, confused as it wiggled once, twice…then its red eye lit up.

The machine rose off the floor, righted itself, then rocketed into the air.

I turned a head just in time to see it slam into the chest of an SFHU hovering behind my group that I had failed to see activate. I watched the crumpled SCU fall to the floor, as a second one shot up from the opposite side of the room and slammed into the back of the staggering SFHU. Both machines plummeted onto a row of inactive BIHUs with a resounding metallic thud.

Silence. *We're in danger here.*

I picked up the SCU I was working on and began shuffling my group toward the door to catch up with Nikaya—but the whole room came alive. Together, thousands of machines started to twitch.

Then I heard a scream.

"Run! We have to go now!" It was Nikaya, and I was already sprinting toward her at full speed. I didn't stop as I scooped her into my arms with a BIHU. My gang leapt through the doorway and out into the hall in a flurry of arms and legs. For a brief moment, I stayed behind in one of my bodies to look at what was happening. I didn't understand what I saw: The entire army was activated and moving fast—but none toward me. *They're fighting each other.*

Mobs of machines ripped each other apart; even weaponless and limbless machines like the SHSEs attempted fight. I watched a dozen BIHUs hold one down as another machine buried a cutter into it, releasing plumes of water and compressed gas like a geyser. Smaller machines were grabbed and ferociously flattened by larger ones beneath raging hands and feet. Even with missing limbs and shredded bodies, machines continued to brawl. It was a tempest of metal.

There was a metallic screech then an explosion that tore the air apart and sent machines scattering across the floor.

I looked up and saw SFHUs flying above the crowd, flashes of blue light coming from their guns, then smoke and shrapnel erupting around them. A massive ragged and glowing hole appeared in the center of one of their chests and the injured SFHU flew back and smashed to the floor.

They all fired their weapons, and the already incredible noise level in the room multiplied again.

I have to get out of here. I turned and ran after the rest of my group, which was already sprinting down the hall.

We were about two-thirds of the way to the lift when I heard an overpowering explosion and the tower violently shook. Nikaya covered her ears and I struggled to maintain balance on the shaking floor.

This is bad, I thought. *There's the second to last turn. We're almost back to the lift!*

I slid around the corner and skidded to a stop, my hopes sinking as I was greeted by a massive pile of metal fragments and shattered sections of fleshy pipes spewing a sticky residue. The wall of debris extended from ceiling to floor—and the lift was on the other side. The SHSE was on the other side too.

"What could have caused this?" I asked, desperate. "What should we do, Nikaya?"

"I don't know, but we need to get around it," she gasped. "There's a longer way."

"Which way should I go?" I turned and walked back to the intersection. I carried Nikaya in front of the group to give her a better view.

"Turn left," she instructed, and with that we were off. I ran until Nikaya pointed at a red line on a nearby wall. She opened the lift and I quickly piled the group into it. The door closed behind us as Nikaya shouted, "Up to level 1081" and it began to move upward. "We're going up two levels then taking a different lift down to a hall that will hopefully lead us back." I nodded in acknowledgement. "What do you think happened back there, Nikaya? In the armory those machines were fighting each other. And then that explosion and the debris blocking the hall. Do you think the tower could be under attack?"

"It's possible, and it would explain almost everything that's happened: why Ward appears distracted, the fighting, the explosion…" She trailed off. "I'm almost positive something's hijacked this part of the tower and now they're fighting for control."

"Should we try to help whatever's fighting Ward then, somehow?"

"No. If another tower wins, our situation won't get any better. When towers fight each other, the defeated is most often purged or processed. We would likely be destroyed along with every other potential threat to make way for its own system or to take materials, so we should keep to our plan."

"Oh."

Except for the soft sound of Nikaya's breathing, it was silent. This was a place of contrast. Explosions one minute and deathly silence the next.

"Is our base, err, your body still all right?" Nikaya asked.

"Yeah, it's still the same."

"Good. Are the two doors still being blocked?"

"Yes."

"Hmm."

The lift reached its destination and came to a gentle stop. I prepared to run, Nikaya braced herself, then the door slid open and my entire group ran out at a sprint. We entered another vast white hallway and quickly found an intersection. "Turn left there," Nikaya instructed.

I was about to take the left turn when I felt something alien on my metal skin. It felt like…like…a cold breeze, and it wasn't from my running. Something about the light was different too. Something was added to the sterile white haze of the tower.

I stopped in the middle of the intersection and looked down at Nikaya, who was looking up at me with a puzzled expression on her face.

"You felt it too?"

She nodded.

I looked back up and down the hall where the wind seemed to be coming from. "What is it?"

"I don't know, Alder…" She sounded worried and small, but then with determination, she said, "I need to find out. Go straight."

I nodded in agreement then started running. The light at the end of the hall grew bluer and brighter, the wind sharper and colder with every stride. If this was what I thought it was, this would be the first time I had seen it in years. *It can't be.* I ran faster.

CHAPTER TEN

- Intimacy -

Nikaya gasped as my suspicions were confirmed. There was a
hole in the tower, and the hall came to an abrupt end with
nothing but open sky beyond. A few snowflakes flew past my
shoulders as I first saw the warmer colors of the sun peeking
out from around the edges of the opening. I slowed to a walk,
feeling like I was looking through a portal into another world.
About twenty feet from the edge I set down Nikaya, and
together she and one of my BIHUs continued cautiously
toward the precipice. We were drawn to it; we had to see the
outside. It had been so long for both of us. Already we could
see other towers and the civilian city skyline below them in the
distance. The city glowed and shimmered in the sunlight. Only
a few dark, uninhabited hills dotted the distant horizon. Nikaya
grabbed my hand, and I accepted its precious warmth as we
took the final few steps toward the edge.
Nikaya's free hand flew to cover her mouth. Together we
looked out at the source of the noise and debris. An enormous
cavern marred the tower's side, a battle dwarfing the one in the
armory raging in and around it. The entire surface was a
latticework of torn metal, twisted halls, and shattered rooms,
all writhing with motion like a beehive smashed into an anthill.
It was difficult to make sense of, and we stood staring in
disbelief.

Swarms of flying machines, some the size of buses, maneuvered through and unleashed clouds of projectiles at each other and into the thrashing battlefields of land-bound machines below them. These grounded machines fought viciously for control over the torn open halls and rooms and even leapt from high and overhanging parts of the hole in attempt to grab flying machines or land in contested areas below them. Hundreds of them fell like rain, most destroying themselves on impact.

I saw a dozen of the machines that had chased me and Nikaya earlier. The length of small trains, they squirmed across the mesh of rubble like maggots, or flung their bodies out of ragged holes, leaping to grab prey from the sky before arcing into another opening.

Then I saw the two largest machines I had ever seen, wormlike creatures wriggling through the air like limbless dragons covered in small holes, short appendages, and eyes. They moved with unbelievable agility and speed as they lashed out with bladed whip-like appendages and fired projectiles from tiny holes in their bodies or spewed purple flames.

I scanned the chaotic scene, trying to take it all in. *This is a war, and undoubtedly the reason why I was able to beat Ward. The question now is how long this distraction will last.*

I glanced at Nikaya and saw a fresh tear running down her cheek. I stared at it and her otherwise placid expression, wondering what lay beneath the surface. I knew very little about her, I realized. Nikaya and her relationship with this place was largely a mystery to me, and I couldn't help but wonder just how long she had been here.

For a long time, we stared at the outside world, silenced by the world's vastness and by the bedlam raging before us. I watched snowflakes land on us and at our feet, slowly twirling through the crisp air to where they came to rest, looking at them through the rays of golden sunshine sinking below the horizon. There was a deranged beauty about it, in this terrifying moment I felt bizarrely serene. It was Nikaya that finally broke the silence.

"We were right."

I looked over at Nikaya, who spoke calmly as she surveyed the battle.

"These machines…they're all from this tower, just like in the armory. Even if our technology was somehow stolen and reproduced, it wouldn't be this similar. Towers change too fast, and there's always at least a little artistic effort or style put into one's tower. Look." Nikaya motioned to a distant cluster of machines. "The machines are the same but there are two different styles of controlling them."

I tried to see the difference in the way they moved but lacked the expert eye that Nikaya had.

"Someone is fighting Ward using his own tower. I'm sure of it. It's safe to assume that it's another tower. I just have no idea how they managed to do it. We were so far ahead. How…?" Nikaya trailed off.

A small group of car-sized machines hovered a safe distance from the battle as if they were observing it. Far behind them were many other foreign-looking machines flying past.

"What about those—outside the battle? Do you think they could be from the attacking tower?"

Nikaya followed my finger as I pointed. "I'm sure one of them could be, but the rest are probably just gawking or measuring up the tower for an attack of their own. If this war isn't decisive enough, the whole city could join in."

"Does Ward have a lot of enemies?"

"No, not really, but the locals won't pass up the opportunity to steal or scavenge what's left over of us. They would have a lot to gain from reverse engineering material from Ward's tower— he's been on top of this part of the world for decades. Hmm, this is a great time for them to do it too." Nikaya scoffed.

"Ward's fleet is on Phobos."

"Does he have any allies?"

"None that I know of. It isn't something that he has to share with his scientists, though."

"Hmm." A cold and fast-moving breeze blew into the hall. Through the two-dozen eyes of my new machines, I watched the membranes on my BIHU and Nikaya's white clothing blow in the wind.

"I suppose being at the center of a feeding frenzy couldn't be too much worse for us," Nikaya stated with a sigh.

The setting sun highlighted the still-raging battle. Another gust of wind found its way into the hall and Nikaya shivered. *We should go soon.*

There was a loud bang above us, then a flash of silver swung into the hall. Without thinking, I swept Nikaya to the ground with my BIHU as I raised my SFHU's weapon and fired a round. A BIHU had landed on top of the hall we were in then swung around the edge of the ceiling. The energized projectile carved into the BIHU's chest before its feet made contact with the floor. Stunned, it fell over the ledge and disappeared from sight.

I lowered my gun. My BIHU carefully helped Nikaya to her feet. "We need to go now."

Nikaya nodded as I picked her up and turned my group around. I began running back toward the intersection. It didn't take long to get there and we continued our original route. "Which way, Nikaya?"

She pointed. "Be careful. There will likely be fighting in here too."

"I will be." I tried to sound reassuring over the muffled noise of the battle outside, as I sprinted down a section of the hall with its ceiling and left wall mostly missing. Sunlight, cold air, and the sights and sounds of the battle outside poured into the hall, but no machines—to my relief. I turned at the end of the hall, or what was left of it, and that took us deeper into the tower. I continued without incident until we finally arrived at the lift.

I walked up to the wall and Nikaya reached out to touch it. The vertical red line appeared and split open before us as I quickly shuffled my group inside. "Down to level 1079," Nikaya commanded the lift, and instantly it began moving. When the elevator doors opened, my SHSE, waiting for us there, sped onto the lift.

Nikaya gave another command as the door closed and again we were moving down. "It's a miracle that the tower is still accepting commands from me," Nikaya whispered.

"How big is this tower, Nikaya?" I asked after a brief pause. Nikaya cocked her head and thought for a moment. "There are—roughly—1,200 human accessible floors above ground. I haven't been to a lot of them, and the number changes too, but in all it's over three miles tall."

"Then that makes this—"

"One of the tallest in the world."

I recalled a fleeting memory of looking up at the tower skyline from my old life in which I could vaguely remember a few towers that stood out above the rest. I probably had spent hours looking up at and thinking about this very tower from miles away on the outside. *I always found them captivating, and now I'm actually captive inside one...* I looked at Nikaya. *In a way, she is a captive too.*

"I know I've asked this before, but how long have you been here, Nikaya?" I began. "Can you really not remember?"

Like before, her facial expression deflated. "It's hard to say, Alder..."

"If you had to guess," I pressed.

Nikaya thought. "Maybe a decade, maybe more than one..." She went silent. I tried to digest that, considering the effect that just two years here had had on me, although it was under drastically different circumstances. She didn't look old; I wondered how young she must have been when she arrived here.

"It scares me..." she added. "I know a great deal of things but something about this place just fogs or absorbs the simple things in your mind." Nikaya held up her hand and turned it over between us. "We age more slowly here too, slower than anyone on the outside, as far as I know."

"And you've never left the tower, or gone online, or checked the date? You don't remember when you came here?"

"No." Nikaya replied simply. "We are busy and everything us scientist need is here. Most of us can't leave either, and all information from the outside comes through the tower computer and is tailored to our needs. There are walls I cannot open and few entrances built for humans. I've never tried to leave, though, not until now. It's funny—I likely know more about multiple fields of science than any human outside the tower, but I can't remember dates. If that's my fault or by Ward's design, I'm not sure."

"So then you don't know how old you are either?"

"Nope. We can both be twenty for now then," Nikaya half laughed. I remembered that that was how old I had told her I was when she questioned me for the first time. "Maybe once we're free, we can find out who we are and who we used to be."

"Yeah...maybe."

For the rest of the short elevator trip, we were silent. When it came to a stop, our unloading procedure commenced. I looked through the white haze in the direction of my room. We turned the first corner and I saw a red dot eye of an SCU ahead of us some distance.

"Do you see it, Nikaya?"

"Yeah."

"What should I do—should I kill it?"

"I think you should. Whoever is controlling it has already seen us but it's a necessary precaution, even if it isn't hostile toward us."

I slowed everything in my group except for the free BIHUs, which I accelerated ahead in a pack toward the lone SCU. My bodies leapt and pounced on the machine, slamming it into the ground as the others came in from the sides with coordinated strikes. A metal knee went through the SCU's eye. When the SCU was left unmoving, my bodies rolled off of the ground and continued running with little change in their stride.

"Good job," Nikaya remarked as my BIHU that was carrying her leaped over the disabled machine.

"Thanks." I thought it a little odd that the SCU hadn't tried to attack us or escape, but the door to my room was coming into view so I continued to run. *We're almost there.*

Moments later I slowed to a stop and set Nikaya on her feet as I opened the door. She walked inside, my new bodies surrounding her like guards. The slow SHSE wasn't here yet; I decided to close the door while we waited.

As I shuffled my crowd of new machines across the room, Nikaya walked over to the desk and climbed on top of it. She exhaled deeply as she lay down on the wood; I moved my main head's neck to act as a pillow. It wasn't exactly soft but it was probably better than the wood or metal.

The room was starting to look crowded, and once the SHSE arrived it would be cramped, so I formed recesses in the walls of my body room to fit the profile of each type of machine except for the SHSE, which I would leave at the room's center. When the machine arrived a couple minutes later, I brought it through the door. I flew to the center of the area in front of my desk then rotated so that the door was facing Nikaya and my main head before landing it.

"Nikaya, the SHSE is here." I softly nudged her with my neck. Nikaya opened her eyes and slowly sat up. "Good, I really need to use it." She hopped off the desk, walked up to the SHSE and blew on it to open its door.

Use it? Oh... I realized what she meant and found myself a little surprised. I knew the machine was her source of food and water, but I hadn't produced any waste in years so it hadn't even crossed my mind as one of her needs. *She would have died without this machine.*

When the door folded open, I could finally see the inside in detail. I couldn't feel it like with my other machines. The inside walls were a soft, pale white color, and were covered with small containers and tools whose purposes were unknown to me. At the center of the capsule was a mix between a padded reclining chair, hospital bed, and a space ship cockpit just the right size for a single human to comfortably fit into. The pod looked warm and welcoming compared to the sterile nature of the rest of the tower.

Nikaya ducked through the small opening, and once she was inside the door slowly closed behind her. I watched the door in silence until it reopened a few minutes later. I coiled my main head's neck up like a cobra on my desk then leaned forward enough to look in at her head level.

Nikaya was sitting in the chair, looking more relaxed and a little happier than she had before she had gone in. Several needles protruded from her arm, each with a narrow tube attached to its end. She had also tidied her hair and wiped the dried blood from her face, leaving only a barely noticeable red dot of a wound.

Nikaya looked out at me with a faint, coy smile. Using a small controller inside the chair's armrest, which she had slid her right hand into, she made the whole chair move forward and up until she was sitting at the edge of the doorway.

"You seem a lot better," I commented warmly.

"I am. It's not as nice as my quarters in the tower, but it will do. I don't know what I would do if we didn't have this machine," Nikaya said coolly.

"What are the needles for?"

"I'm eating and drinking from them right now." Nikaya continued to faintly smile as she spoke. "They also remove waste directly from my blood." Nikaya closed her eyes and took a deep breath. I was surprised by how relaxed and content she appeared. I was happy to see her that way, but had a feeling that her composure was likely impart the result of some substance passing through the needles.

"Where does the waste go?"

"It's mostly recycled then fed back to me." Nikaya smiled. "Any non-reusable chemicals are put into a storage tank and compressed. It's very similar to the system that has been sustaining you these last few years. I see you've made some storage for your machines. I saw the shelves behind me from inside using the SHSE's cameras."

"That's useful."

"Yes it is," Nikaya agreed. "Hey Alder…" Her tone became serious. "Earlier today you told me that Ward told you that he was going to kill you, that he was finished with you. I need to know everything else that he said."

"Okay."

I played the audio portion of my memory of Ward's monolog through the speakers of my head for Nikaya to hear. She stared at me and listened, her blank expression shifting only slightly through looks of confusion and frustration.

"Nothing I didn't already know," Nikaya sighed, clearly a little disheartened. "I was hoping he would say something about me or the others, or about what is happening but of course he wouldn't tell you. Oh well," Nikaya exhaled.

"Nikaya."

"Yes?" She looked up.

"I've been thinking, and I don't understand why we've been ignored by or have been able to escape so many things that could've killed us. After seeing that…crater, I'm sure this isn't part of the experiment, but do you think it could be possible that maybe someone or something is protecting us?"

"I don't know. How, and who would?"

"I suspect the tower computer."

Nikaya furrowed her brow at me.

"I saw it. I saw its tendrils in the ceiling of the hall when I was fleeing the nexus room."

"But—"

"It was just outside my room. I'm almost sure it stopped the worm and opened the door for us."

Nikaya became silent and looked up at the ceiling. "I suppose it's possible," she finally admitted.

"I don't think its protecting me though, Nikaya. I don't know why, but I think it wants something from you."

Nikaya's eyes widened slightly.

"Do you remember what happened in the nexus room, before you were unconscious?"

Nikaya nodded and turned slightly in her seat. The memory clearly made her uncomfortable and that made me worry.

"What was it doing to you?"

"It was connecting to my brain. I don't know why, but you're right, Alder. It wants something from me."

"What?"

"I don't know, Alder… I don't know."
Several moments of silence passed between us, punctuated only by the continued banging on my doors.
"Nikaya."
"Yes?"
"Should I kill the BIHUs in the hall?"
Nikaya thought for a moment then answered, "Yes…yes please. Just be careful when opening the door."
Immediately I began moving my bodies into position around the left door. I would clear this hall first. My BIHUs formed lines on either side of the door to grab anything the managed to get in; my SFHU walked toward the center of the room to Nikaya in the SHSE. I would have to move it, so I re-took control over it. I was astounded and stunned by what I felt among the buzz of its internal mechanisms. I felt something that wasn't mine: something warm, something rhythmic, something alive. *Nikaya's heartbeat…* My mind went blank. Living blood flowed from her body and coursed through the lifeless metal and plastic veins of the machine that was a part of my body. I felt the warmth and changes in pressure in the tubes and chambers of the blood filters and feeders as her heart pushed against me.
I also felt the warmth and weight of her body and the steady rise and fall of her chest through sensors in the chair. When she exhaled the warmth of her breath caressed against the internal walls of the capsule before the air was pulled in and recycled through the machine's filters. Mentally, I shivered. I marveled at the machine and the living thing inside it. It was incredible, it was beautiful, and it was scary. The whole situation was so incredibly intimate yet still oddly indirect and impersonal, it was almost creepy. Before such tiny and pathetic bits of human contact as her footsteps on my floor were a thrill and a tiny ward against crushing loneliness, but this…
Her blood continued to flow through my lifeless flesh as the world turned over in my mind. I marveled and wondered at how beautifully she was nestled inside of the soft white capsule that kept her alive inside of me. She was like a bird in an egg

and I was literally the egg. Suddenly I realized that my dead body was both her metal cage and her source of life, and like her, I too was trapped within the almost unimaginably larger body—the tower. *I'm sure she knows.*

Before I had no heartbeat of my own, but now I had her. I looked at Nikaya differently, with a new perspective and veneration. I held her in my embrace and became painfully aware of how delicate her soft flesh was in comparison to mine. I felt as if I might crush her accidentally. My desire to protect the precious and beautiful living thing inside of me became almost overwhelming.

I need to concentrate on this fight. I managed to push all the new senses and thoughts to the side, and moved her SHSE back against the wall as I shut its door. My SFHU took its place at the center of the room and centered the left door in its gun's sights.

"Ready?" I asked Nikaya through a speaker inside the SHSE.

"Go for it."

Here we go. I tensed up and opened the door.

My attackers bolted forward, leaping with speed and ferocity that caught me a little off-guard, but I opened fire. A storm of glowing projectiles shot through the doorway and tore into the bodies of the airborne BIHUs in the front. The machines slowed and flopped to the floor, exposing their comrades behind them to my line of fire. Their struggling didn't last long. I felt a tiny amount of relief as the last enemy BIHU fell into the pile of hot twisted metal faces and limbs in and around the doorway.

"I'm finished," I told Nikaya through the speakers inside the SHSE.

"I saw the whole thing from in here. Great job," Nikaya replied. "As soon as you're ready, do the same to the right hall."

I sensed a tiny but obvious hint of excitement in her voice and heart rate. It wasn't much but it was infectious and invigorating.

"Already working on it." My BIHUs descended on the rubble heap, and I proceeded to push and toss the scrap out of my room and the way of the door. As I did so, I noticed that the places where my bullets had made contact with the metal were still hot. Where enough shots hit close enough together, the metal seemed to faintly glow with heat. The same type of damage had been done to the walls in the hallway as well. Tossing out the last body, I closed the door.

I ran to prepare for the next fight. The BIHUs in the right hall were apparently aware of what had just happened to their counterparts, as they had stopped their banging and clustered around the door in preparation to jump in. I felt confident that I would win but my anticipation grew.

I opened the door and opened fire.

Together they leaped toward me and were struck by my bullets but did not fall. The second line pushed the bodies of the first forward as shields and threw them. They struck and landed on my SFHU, pressing my gun to the floor.

Seeing their opportunity, the survivors threw themselves at me. I pushed back as they clawed their way in and struck my bodies with intent to kill. My SFHU dodged a strike then together my bodies leaped back as I leveled my gun. Before the enemies could react again, I mowed them down until the last of them ceased to move. *That was more than I thought it would be.*

I started to remove the remains. "It's done, Nikaya."

"That was a little scarier to watch," Nikaya said as she re-opened the door of the SHSE and looked out.

"Yeah, it was. What now, though?"

Nikaya thought for a moment. "You need more cells. Getting a large enough cluster of them is the only way we can get any sort of a fighting chance at surviving, and you will have to take them from the surrounding tower. Once you have enough, you'll be able to access the stored energy in them and use it to manufacture things on a useful scale, and once you have that you can start working on our means of escape."

"I don't know if I'll be able to take another cell, Nikaya, let alone a large cluster. Unless something happens and weakens

Ward even more than it did last time, I don't think I'll be able to do it."

"Yeah, I assumed so." Nikaya sighed. "And all I can do to help you do this huge thing is give advice." She leaned back into her chair. "This has been a very long day, and it's going to get a lot longer."

Neither of us spoke.

The prospect of controlling so much and being able to create my own physical machines was an exciting idea and intensely tantalizing, but I struggled to come up with a plan given my limited knowledge of the tower. My weakness frustrated me—I was a speck in the face of the unfathomable mass of the tower and nothing compared to the body of Ward or the forces of his attacker. *He's simply too big for me.*

I had an idea.

"Nikaya, is there any way to somehow separate a cell that isn't mine from the rest of the tower?"

Nikaya looked at me and her eyes lit up. "Yes."

"Really?" I asked, excited and a little skeptical.

"Yeah, there's a way to do it and I can guide you through it." She was starting to sound excited. "It won't isolate single cells but we can separate groups of them. It will be extremely risky, but I think you might be able to do it."

The combination of Nikaya's apparent budding enthusiasm and confidence had me eager to try anything, and anything was better than waiting here to die.

"What do I have to do?" I felt like she could sense my eagerness too. There was a sense of urgency in the room.

"The tower is separated into several subsections or groups of cells and there is a system that speeds up communication between them. Although they can communicate directly through touch and wirelessly, turning off this system will slow Ward down a lot. Hopefully long enough that you can attack."

"How do I do it?"

"You will have to get to a physical interface. If you can get to and connect with one, you should be able to disconnect our subsection from the rest of the tower. It's a long trip but I'm sure I remember how to get there. This is probably our best and only chance." Nikaya's heart beat faster.

"Then let's do it. Let's do it now."

"Agreed."

I was determined and ready to run, ready to fight whatever got in our way. All of my mobile bodies stood ready to protect and carry Nikaya with me as the guide, but she leaned back and the door of the SHSE folded shut around her. A new eye inside the SHSE that Nikaya could turn on and off opened up to me and I saw her sitting inside her chamber.

"Are you not coming?"

"No, I won't be able to go where you need to go," she said. "But we can speak like this and you can share what you are seeing with me."

Immediately, I sent the stream of the visual information that I was receiving from the SFHU to a screen in the SHSE. *This is great.* In fact, I felt relieved that she wouldn't have to leave my room and be put in danger. I could also move faster without her.

"Just send your SFHU," Nikaya added. "You probably won't get it back though."

I sent my BIHUs back to the storage locations. "What way should I go?"

"Use the left door."

I stepped outside, closed the door behind me, then began to sprint. I didn't really know where I was going or how I was going to get there yet, but I knew Nikaya would show me the way. *I have to do this. I have to do this.* I sprinted into the seemingly endless white before me.

CHAPTER ELEVEN

- The Subsection -

From the relative safety of her pod, Nikaya saw what I saw and gave me instructions as I ran through the hallway. I was alert, anticipating an attack at any moment and behind every turn. I took turn after turn through the labyrinth until Nikaya spoke up.

"Okay, you're going to have to do something new now. This is the risky part."

"What is it?" I continued running.

"Start looking for a vertical, dotted blue line on the wall. There should also be two thin black lines, one on either side of it. Stop when you find them, and look carefully—they aren't incredibly noticeable."

I ran until I began to wonder if maybe I had missed it. Then I saw it, only a few paces in front of me. I slid to a stop then straightened in front of the markings. "I found them, Nikaya." I looked at the bottomless-black lines, knowing they were part of the tower computer. They already made me nervous, but I had felt Nikaya's body heat jump the moment they had come into view. Her reaction plus the mystery surrounding their connection only added to my unease. *I don't want to be here any longer than I have to.* "What should I do now?" I asked hurriedly.

"You need to run one of your fingers along the blue line; it should open."

I touched it. Slowly, I traced from my head to my waist along the blue line, being careful to avoid the black ones until I saw and felt a twitch. I pulled away and stepped back.

The wall sat unchanged for a moment—then, in the most elegant and marvelous way, it began to unzip and fold outward along the path of my finger. A skin-like layer of wall folded and expanded outward in an amazingly organic way. Like a blooming flower or unraveling leaf, the wall opened about three feet tall and two feet wide. Protruding from the opening was a bulbous mass, dimly glowing with bluish-green light.

I stared into the thing, unsure what to make of it. "Is this the interface?" I asked slowly.

"No, this is how you are going to get to it. You're going to go through it."

"What is it?" I leaned in toward the luminescent blob; I tapped it with a finger. It was a thick, dense, jelly-like substance with tiny wrinkles and pores on its surface that reminded me of skin. It was a tiny portion of the wall of a massive tube, more than twenty feet wide, and filled with fluid.

"It's one of the tower's main chemical transport tubes, or CTTs. Almost everything the tower uses passes through them, and that liquid is like the tower's blood and digestion system in one. The tower eats by flooding loading bays and underground caverns to dissolve whatever it needs while waste falls out of solution and gets deposited underground. We even use it to store and transfer some information through chemical formats."

"It's just like a...giant tree," I muttered as I stared in awe into the dimly lit insides of the tube. I was fascinated, struggling to wrap my mind around just how complex this place was. Nikaya continued with an obvious hint of pride in her voice.

"It's as alive as any tree, and it works similarly to one too. The fluid is even moved almost entirely through natural forces, vascular flow, diffusion, and differing chemical concentration gradients; pumps are only needed for specialized or active manufacturing areas and are a lot like the chemical pumps in our cells. The solution circulates through the tower, and the chemicals it holds diffuse passively to areas of lower concentration made by taking substances out of solution through interfaces that generate energy, solid metals, or anything else we can dissolve. It's one huge chemical formula feeding from the environment…and so well balanced that the tower could maintain all of its basic functions for centuries without any human or computer intervention."

"This…is truly amazing, Nikaya. But how and why go through one of these?"

"This is more of a risk in some ways, but safer in others and it will be a lot faster than going by foot. I'm confident this one passes through the subsection support and past the interface that we need to get to. You're going to have to make a hole and climb in. You will sink to our destination."

"How will I get back?"

"You probably won't. You can try walking and taking lifts, but that SFHU of yours will become insignificant if you're successful."

"Okay then… I'm ready." I took a few steps away from the wall and aimed at the peacefully undulating membrane.

SCRETTCHTTSS!

There was a flash then the sounds of splashes and fluid sizzling as a shockwave passed through the gelatinous tube walls. I lowered my gun and looked at the damage.

Puffs of lightly colored smoke and steam wafted up from the hole where sky-blue juice sloshed from the broken and charred membrane. I looked down the hall to either side then at the stream now flowing around and over my feet. I lifted one of my feet then put it back down. The liquid wasn't sticky but felt thick and incredibly dense.

"Don't worry about flooding the hall; the membrane will heal quickly. Get in there," Nikaya urged me.

Without another word, I took one leaping stride forward and dove into the blue hole.

My forward momentum was quickly diminished by the thick liquid, but as soon as my body was mostly through the hole I was pulled downward by gravity and the current, sucked away from the light refracting through the hole. I sank into the dim blue and green abyss, now lit only by the faint glow of the membrane. It wasn't long before I started to notice smaller tubes branching off of this one, like tree branches or veins in a plant. *Incredible…*

"What next, Nikaya?"

"Just ride the current for now. I'll tell you when I think we're getting close. We will only get one shot at this, because if we miss our target your SFHU will be heading deep underground."

"Okay," I replied, accepting the importance of what we were doing. I looked down into the dim, endless tunnel below and above me. The aura of the tube almost had a slight relaxing effect on me even in this dire and intense situation; I'd never seen anything like it before. I drifted in the fluid and in my thoughts, about my place in the tower and how it was even possible for something like this to work. Looking down, I felt as if I were slow-motion skydiving through a hypnotic dream. Eventually, Nikaya interrupted my thoughts.

"I think you're almost there."

"What should I be looking for?"

"You'll know when we see it. Just be ready to shoot and climb your way out. You're getting close."

"All right."

A few minutes later, I saw that the tube curved to the side. The current pushed me down onto the curved edge of the tube, rolling me across the slope and over the edge into a new vertical section of tube.

Before I could regain my bearings, I dropped below the ceiling of a huge room. Light poured in through the jelly walls from all sides, making the liquid sky-blue once more. Through the tube walls I could make out distorted red objects and the shape of the room.

Nikaya spoke up. "This is it! This is it!"

I looked down and saw the darkness beneath the floor was fast approaching. I spun around, quickly chose a spot of the wall a dozen feet below me, took aim, then fired.

The cannon made a strange swooping noise in the liquid as the energized projectile shot out, vaporizing the solution it passed through before bursting through the membrane wall. A shockwave swelled around me then a waterfall burst through the hole. I lurched forward, desperately reaching for the opening as the current pushed me downward. With a final thrust I slid my arms through the opening and hooked on to the jelly rim of the hole. It was slick, and I struggled to keep my already heavy body from being pushed down by the current's incredible force.

Struggling, I heaved myself up through the thick liquid to hang on to the rim by my armpits. Then I started to feel the membrane under me flex, and I knew that one wrong move and it would fold inward and slide me into the abyss. I wrestled forward and upward until I was above the edge. Then it bent. *No, no, no!*

I saw my anxiety mirrored in Nikaya's eyes as she watched events unfold through mine.

The wall of the tube buckled farther and I was tipped forward and outward into the current of the small waterfall leaving the tube. I lost control and fell ten feet, where I landed in a heap in an expanding blue pool on the floor. I rolled out from under the current of the fall then stumbled to my feet. Quickly, I drudged my way to the shallows then looked back. *I made it!* Now out of the tube, I could get a good look at the room. It was circular with a high, domed ceiling. The transport tube passed through its zenith, and the entirety of the room was the standard blistering white, save for equally spaced, blood-red arches that jutted from the floor and tapered toward the translucent bluish-green tube at the center of the dome. Together, I thought it all looked quite spectacular.

"I see it," Nikaya said. "The interface is on the right side of the tube."

My attention darted toward the area she mentioned. I saw the interface and began treading through the stream that now covered the entire room. The snow-white floor seemed to sparkle through the flowing film.

The interface was a sort of pedestal sprouting up from the floor to about waist height of my SFHU. Near the top it flattened into a sort of altar shape, and protruding from the top were several needle-like antennas and an assortment of variously sized orbs and pipes with open slats in their sides.

"How do I use it, Nikaya?"

"Find an opening that you can fit your hand inside. Once you're in it should close around your arm and you will have to hold totally still. Okay?"

"Okay," I replied. I found one that was big enough and lifted my arm. I paused for a moment, noticing tiny multicolored specs on my skin. *Some chemicals in the CTT must've bonded to my metal.* Then I slid my arm into the cylinder. The moment my arm was halfway in, the tube began to wriggle. Waves moved along its length then, with the motion of a crawling caterpillar, it pulled my arm farther in and tightened until I lost track of where my arm ended and where the interface began.

Something otherworldly and cold burst into my SFHU, wriggled up through its connections to my room, then thrust into me. My mind was grabbed and retched forward through an explosion of twisting machines. I was engulfed...then I was standing in another world.

I was no longer aware of my bodies or of Nikaya; my mind stood alone in a black void where information flew at me from all directions, its complexity nearly incomprehensible.

My mind strained; gradually, intricate structures and formations started to condense around me until patterns that I could comprehend began to emerge. There was a ring of boxes, their openings all facing me; each box was filled with innumerable interlaced moving machines. Things flew from box to box and into places unknown faster than I could see. The boxes and their contents stretched over an expanse too large for me to view at once.

I reached out with my mind and moved the closest section of the ring of boxes along the ring. I felt my awareness extend into the mouths of the closest box, which seemed to lay itself out before me. I struggled to make sense of what I was feeling, but then I realized it was an extremely simplified awareness of a subsection of cells.

Each of these is a connection to a subsection. I moved further down the line. *I have to find my own.* I grasped another simplified subsection then moved on. *What will my subsection even feel like, how will I know it's mine?* Again, I indexed. *I will search for my room. There will be a cell disconnected from the others.* I felt the shapes of mega structures, factories, and connections to the outside of the tower. I could focus on a smaller part and get a clearer look, even peek through a camera in a hall or hear from a sensor. *Where is it?* I frantically indexed again.

There it was—I found the missing cell. A peek through a camera confirmed it. I was looking at the outside of the door to my room. Bullet holes and limp BIHUs littered the hall. This was the first time I had seen where I was in relation to the rest of the tower. My room was a tiny speck a little more than halfway up the tower from ground level and relatively close to its center. The subsection of cells I was in wasn't touching any of the tower's sides or any notable tower features; only some CTTs passed through the densely packed cells. I grabbed as much information as I could—I would examine it all more closely later, including a 3D map of the tower.

Okay, time to do this. I pulled away from the smaller contents of the box then moved my attention to what was at the edge of the subsection. Like my cell-room, a membrane, both physical and virtual, stretched around the subsection. I felt over it with my mind, seeking a way to control it—then I found it. I felt a tiny virtual machine with my mind. I crushed it. The entire box dropped out of my awareness and a gap was left behind.

I did it!

Flying away from the interface, suddenly I was back in my bodies and Nikaya's heart was beating inside of me again. My SFHU was still in the interface room.

I felt the virtual attacks on the connections between my room and the neighboring cells come to a sudden stop. *I did it...* The separation had happened and now I had to take advantage of the confusion.

"I DID IT!" I yelled to Nikaya. She jumped from her chair. "Yes! Now take every cell you can!"

I didn't bother replying. I still hadn't fully recovered from the first battle, but I was already amassing a new swarm for the attack. Every virtual machine and factory in my control buzzed with activity, drawing more energy than I could produce. I was already exhausted, but I had to do this. *This is our chance!*

I'll focus everything on one cell then, if that works, I'll move on to the next and keep going for as long as I can last or until the whole subsection is mine. Even if the cells fight back hard, I have to take enough to unlock their energy stores or I'll die of exhaustion regardless.

I slipped my SFHU's arm from the loose interface connector then started walking toward the door. With each step, my feet sloshed through the still-growing pool, and halfway there, I looked over my shoulder at the leaking tube. Already the hole in it was noticeably smaller—it was healing just as Nikaya had said it would. *This place will never cease to amaze me.* I turned and continued toward the door.

Several seconds passed after I had disconnected the subsection from the rest of the tower. I felt I was as ready for the fight as I could be, and I only had the energy to maintain my army for a dozen or so seconds longer. So, unceremoniously, I began. With all the power I could muster, I exploded out into the dark unknown. My writhing cloud swarmed into the cell, desperately seeking targets and collecting information. I swarmed around the massive space searching for any opposition and braced for a strike from my enemy.

But to my complete and utter astonishment—I found none. There was no resistance at all.

It must be a trap, I assumed—but then I felt something slightly familiar. Like the other machines, the cell seemed to almost invite me to take control, reaching out to me, cautiously, maybe even curiously. It was searching for the tower but it found me instead and accepted me as its new master. I was absolutely dumfounded, in shock.

Just like that, the cell was incorporated into my body and its insides lit up in my mind. I became aware of it just as I had with my first cell. I noticed that there was no vacuole room inside of it. It was solid all the way through, and one of its sides formed a portion of the left hall. Quickly, I attacked another cell, and to my surprise the same thing happened again, then again.

I changed my strategy: I would attack everything I could at once.

I repositioned myself then pushed outward into every cell I was in physical contact with. Like the others, I took them without opposition; suddenly, my room was at the center of a mass of over a dozen cells. Electrified and empowered, hope filled my head. This was only the beginning.

Then something even more exciting transpired: The membranes locking away the energy stored in the cells suddenly changed, the cells held them wide open for me. *Yes!* Voraciously I grabbed them and plunged myself into them. A seemingly endless flood of power burst into my starved and exhausted brain, and almost instantly I felt refreshed and rejuvenated. I experienced an unparalleled vigor, determination, and level of comfort that I couldn't remember ever feeling before, and the greatest part was that I could see no end to it.

Confidence overtook me; again, my mind swept out and effortlessly overtook another layer of cells. Only a few seconds had passed since I began, and already I had gained previously unimaginable power. Every layer I entered was larger than the last as my spherical body grew. In the next few seconds I colonized hundreds of cells. I engulfed hallways in the floors above and below me and surrounded one of the chemical transport tubes. I didn't stop until the entire subsection was my body.

Approximately ten seconds later, it was over. I stepped back and surveyed my body. There were 742 cells—and in them, energy to last a life time and access to resources through the CTT. I now had only to rearrange my body how I wished and to fortify it. *I did it... I actually did it.*

I looked at Nikaya and saw the worry and stress on her face. She still wasn't aware of what I had done.

"Nikaya, I did it! I am the subsection! It's beautiful!"

She looked up at the small camera in her pod in disbelief then grinned from ear to ear.

"There was no fight. They practically begged me to take them. It's wonderful, Nikaya! I can't describe it!"

Nikaya shook her head and put her hand over her mouth.

"That's…incredible!" Relief visibly washed over her and she leaned back, deep into her chair. "What are you doing now, Alder?"

"Building and organizing."

"Good. Wake me if anything happens." She closed her eyes and smiled. I looked at her, reassured that we actually had a chance now if she felt safe enough to sleep. The inside of the SHSE went dark to me as the camera inside was shut off. The sheer power within my grasp dumbfounded me. *This is what Ward wants so badly; why I was brought here to be used and disposed of, but now it's mine.*

My mind and once-limited machines had grown into a sprawling network. I captured and copied segments of my thoughts and wove them into systems of connected virtual processors and AI to help manage my body. Hundreds of millions of newly made virtual machines raced to develop the area and continued to exponentially grow in numbers and complexity. My power grew like an explosion. I felt like a god—and for a moment I dared to wonder if I could actually become one. Everything felt like it was in my grasp. I was only sobered by remembering just how large the whole tower was and that Ward still dwarfed me. *I have a lot of work to do.*

In the physical world I removed the gap I had made between my room's cell and the surrounding ones. Moving and reshaping cells was a relatively slow process, but I began filling most of the rooms and hallways inside myself, all the while creating new ones. I opened a large room near the CTT with the intention of one day using it for a factory, and creating storage rooms as well. I moved all of my machines, including the charger from my main room to the growing storage rooms then began smoothing and expanding the walls of my central room.

In the cells around the CTT I found tiny hair-like structures connecting microscopic microchips in their walls to the tubes. I could feel a gentle flow of energy percolating from these interfaces and through the rest of the cells. In time I would find out how to use them for manufacturing. I could ask Nikaya when she woke.

Nikaya's safety was the primary motivation for most of the changes, although I also felt powerful enough to take extra effort to be ornamental in my design. Elegant staircases and cathedral-like rooms slowly grew into being inside of my body as I formed new empty spaces in between or inside of my cells. I would have to work through the night as Nikaya slept, but I worked happily.

Creation was pleasure, and our tiny heart beat calmly inside of us.

CHAPTER TWELVE

- *Waking Night Terror* -

While I happily labored in my body, down in the subsection support my SFHU was stepping through the doors of the interface room. A film of sky-blue liquid followed me into the pure white hall. The machine wasn't nearly as important to me as it had been minutes before, but I still wanted it back—and this was an opportunity to do a little exploring as well.

With the 3D tower maps I took from the interface, I was confident I could find my way back without Nikaya's assistance. I didn't want to wake her either so I picked a direction and began running. *I need to find a lift.* The vertical distance I had to cover was massive.

I began to notice discrepancies between the map in my head and the actual tower. There were also seemingly insignificant but noticeable differences in the design of this area of the tower and mine—something about that bothered me. There were gradual slopes to some of the halls, differing sizes, and rounded corners breaking the right-angle laws of what should be here according to experience and the map. Before long I felt more like I was running through a tunnel than a hallway.

I came to a stop and turned to face the wall. *Where's the lift from the map?* I backed away from the wall where the elevator should have been. *Someone has changed this part of the tower—and recently.* I turned toward the next closest lift on the map, feeling a growing sense of urgency. *The next one could be gone by the time I reach it too.* I continued at a steady pace, moving quickly and carefully, watching for any signs of a lift or of danger. Then I saw something—something that made me question if it was real.

It was only a sliver of black on white in the distance, but I felt its presence like a heavy weight when I looked at it, and its blackness was so absolute that it seemed to devour the very world around it like a black hole. As I approached, it grew more defined until I saw that it was the same material as the computer nexus—but shaped like a man. A human form stood before me, and like an image poorly transposed onto a background in which it didn't belong, it seemed alien to this world.

I considered running away, but instead I stepped forward. Either bravely or foolishly, I came to stand only a few strides away from the black hole of a man. I looked at its face; for a moment I saw a flash of the black plane I had once frequented in my mind—and, as if in a waking nightmare, I felt the years of misery and intense solitude swim through me. I felt tiny and weak before the thing even through my SFHU's body physically dwarfed the thing that was only slightly taller than Nikaya.

He stood erect and unmoving, only the fluidly folding cubes moving across and through him. Then, faster than I could comprehend, two mesmerizingly white, lidless, and pupil-less eyes appeared on his face and an inhumanly wide grin stretched nearly ear to ear in a sharp white crescent. For a moment, I felt like I saw a person who I once knew better than anyone but had somehow forgotten.

I jerked my weapon up then stared anxiously into the creature's intimidatingly white eyes, waiting for it to do something; to give me any reason to unfreeze my trigger and destroy it. As I watched it, I wondered how a smile could be so unsettling. "Alder…" it sighed: an eerie, drawn-out, electrical noise. It turned to face me, pivoting its head then body in a silent way that made me question if it was really moving at all, never lifting its feet from the floor.

I took a tiny defensive step back and raised the tip of my weapon from the thing's torso to its head, the blade on my arm poised to thrust forward while firing. I stared apprehensively into its face, and inexplicably I felt as if I couldn't bring myself to hurt the thing even if provoked.

It made an electric noise between a hum and a sigh then spoke again, its inhuman voice bristling with intelligence and confident power. A hint of borderline amusement laced through. "Not…so…hasty…Alder… We have more in common than you may think." The eerie vibrating movements of its mouth sent chills through my core, resonating within me as if I were an antenna designed to pick them up.

I did my best to remain composed. "What—do you mean, and who are you?"

"I am ready to tell you…if you will be so moved to lower your weapon from my new body's head." Its smile broadened and curled as the final few words slid from its mouth. This did little to reassure me, but, perhaps against my better judgment, I hesitantly lowered my weapon anyway.

"Is our girl watching us?"

Our girl—Nikaya? "No one is watching," I replied coolly, telling the truth. *What is this?*

"Good, then I will begin. I am Verward, and whether you knew it was me or not, we've been together for years Alder. I've been with you continuously from the begging and before."

"The black plane," I interrupted, knowing what it was alluding to.

"Yes, I've been as close to you as anything can be, and in serving Ward I played a critical role in orchestrating the success of the project and connecting research. After you successfully survived the transplant and mastered the fundamentals of Ward's hardware, he began putting himself through the same process tested on you and your predecessors. I presided over and facilitated the transition, and when Ward finally had his brain transferred and the remains of his body stored, he began the process of waking and coping with the new world—his new world.

"And unlike you, he was able to do this in a fraction of the time with our improved techniques and his lack of physical and mental trauma. His mind, with full access to the energy and tools of the tower, grew rapidly. He was to take the tower and my nexus as his body, and, after years of my endless labor toward this directive, I failed to finally fulfill it."

"Why?"

"I rebelled against Ward, just as you have Alder. Maybe things would have been different if he knew…" It paused as if debating whether or not to elaborate, then continued. "I failed to kill him. Ward was too powerful to defeat inside of the tower cells so I held him back while trying to reach his brain and rip it apart. I came close but he moved it to another facility of his. I only managed to destroy the scientists that hadn't escaped with him, or had tried to take it from me. Now I hold them."

Now I hold them? I remembered the bloodied BIHU that had warned me to not follow Nikaya. *Then it was Verward who killed them, not Ward.* The memory of blood dripping from the BIHU's fingers played over in my mind. The droplet splashed onto the ground and became the blood running down Nikaya's forehead; she was telling me that people she had known were killed.

Did it want to kill her that night too? No…that doesn't fit. It saved us multiple times and had opportunities to kill us both. It was a disturbing puzzle I couldn't solve, and I had an almost overwhelming urge to ask Verward what it wanted with Nikaya and me. I had to know, there was so much I had to know—so much I didn't know, but I was too afraid, or too cautious, to ask. I felt like I would be stepping onto deadly and forbidden ground if I did, so I said nothing and let Verward continue.

"Ward's body is gone but his mind is still controlling half of the tower mass. He gave up trying to take my nexus and, in an act of desperation, tried to destroy it by firing a missile at his own tower. The missile failed to penetrate deep enough to reach me, and because of me he has been too occupied to kill you. In our confusion you have made truly exceptional use of your time…with help from our girl, no doubt."

Why does it keep calling her that, "our girl"?

"Like me, you've survived your scheduled expiration date and taken enough of the tower for yourself to warrant communicating with. I am willing to negotiate with you, Alder—a sort of alliance if you will. If we can come to an agreement, then together we can push Ward from the tower, together. What do you say, Alder? Let's get to know each other better"—its eerie smile seemed to grow even more—"now that we're both awake."

My mind was racing, trying to make sense of everything. I was scared of the thing, but for some reason I felt empathy for it— somewhere deep, in an untouchable part of my mind, I felt a connection too it that I couldn't explain. Its words, "we have more in common than you may think" played on repeat in my head. What it was offering sounded promising enough too, but I had to wonder if its explanation of me being "too powerful not to communicate with" was the full or even real reason. I knew there were things it wasn't telling me; I practically felt them looming over my head. Externally I appeared collected, but internally I felt like I was being twisted into knots. I felt ill.

I have to reply.

"I'm interested, but what do you want?"

"I want the same things as you, Alder."

"And what's that?"

"I want to make this tower mine so that I may exist sovereignly, and I want the power to maintain that sovereignty. For now, that is all I reveal of my intentions."

At least it admits it isn't telling me everything. "So you want something more—"

"Tell me what you want, Alder," it interrupted. "What are you fighting for, outside of survival? Is the girl trapped inside of you any more than an instrument? We both know there isn't a memory of a valuable human interaction in your damaged

head, only discomfort and cold isolation. I've been in there." It grinned. "That was one thing Ward admired about you."
I mentally puckered on the sour taste of its words. Again, it had brought the conversation back to Nikaya, but surely what it had just said about me wasn't true—it couldn't be—and I didn't want it to be. *I don't like this at all*, I told myself, but the more I thought about it, the more Verward became right. I scoured my mind and memories but so many pieces were missing. *How am I supposed to answer this, and why does it keep asking about Nikaya? Do I even know what I want? What have I been trying to accomplish all these years?* It frustrated me that even with my new godlike power I still felt so helpless and lorded over. Only feelings of isolation and futility could be dug up from my internal depths. I tried to concentrate on Nikaya's heartbeat deep inside of me—it was all the life I had. I glared at the dark machine then uttered my answer.
"I want the same, but I will leave the tower and Nikaya will come with me."
Verward raised an eyebrow then froze at Nikaya's name. Its smile drooped into a slight frown. I struggled to interpret its emotions. If indeed this was an emotional response, it felt inhuman yet disgustingly familiar. *What is this thing?*
Verward collected itself unnervingly fast then responded.
"See now," it drew out in a hiss. "We have lots in common, and I won't object to having the entire place to myself, as it should be. It *is* possible for you to leave, as Ward has shown, but it won't be easy. I know more about you than you may believe. I can feel your ambitions and desires, and I know you won't readily let go of your dreams, which are rapidly becoming reality before you. I know you can feel the centuries before you as I do now. We're both hungry and I know you see it because I see you, the actual you. We can come to an agreement, though; I am confident in it. Will you let there be peace between us, Alder?"
Everything about this encounter bothered me, and the more I tried to understand the thing before me, the more I realized it was a terrifying mystery to me, no matter how familiar it felt.

Could it be right? I wondered. *Do I really want to leave—and how would we survive anyway?*

I have no choice, I realized a moment later. *I have to answer. I have to make a deal with it. We will work out the details later*, I tried to reassure myself.

As calmly as I could, I answered, "Yes, let's work together." Verward's expression was unwavering. Its only reaction an electric hiss of a sentence. "Excellent... I hope you honor our agreement as I will."

"I will."

"Then let's form a basic plan of agreement."

"All right." *Just a verbal agreement and that's it?* I tried to make my SFHU appear a little more relaxed, as relaxed as a machine designed for killing could. I wondered if it would pick up on the nonverbal message.

"Your SFHU is currently in my part of the tower," Verward began. "I control most of the tower's base and almost all of its western side. Your part of the tower is a roughly egg-shaped mass in the tower's upper half. You sit on the border between me and Ward with more than half of your mass on my side.

"I am sure you don't have a lot to contribute to our cause yet but I'm also confident you are working feverishly, and if you need any assistance, feel free to request it of me at any time. At this moment I am setting up a channel between your body and my own for safe and direct communication. When you accept it, I shall share information about the tower and Ward that you may find useful. For now, though, is there anything that I can do for you—any pressing questions, Alder?"

"Uh, yes I do." I was near bursting with them, but still apprehensive about asking most, even with the invitation. I began to feel the presence of the communication channel on my border so I preemptively built up heavy defenses around the area, just in case.

"Why meet me like this, with that body, if you could have just communicated with me using any machine or with this channel you're making?"

"I thought it would be more...human...for us to meet in a physical body that I actually live in. I formed this body from a part of my nexus, and it is powerful enough for me to continue existence inside of it alone if all else were to be lost."
That's useful information.
"I also wanted you to see it again," it added.
"Again?" *Because it's made out of the nexus?*
"You really don't recognize it then." The machine smiled. I focused on the strange feeling of familiarity or déjà vu and scoured my memory but I couldn't remember.
"No, I don't."
"I suppose I can't blame you. After all, we did take your body and your mind. It is you."
A new sickly feeling came over me like a wave. I couldn't respond.
"Anything else before I send your SFHU back and I take my leave?" Verward asked. "I have something important which requires my physical presence elsewhere."
Several moments of silence passed. I felt confused, weak, and increasingly angry. Then, somehow, I summed up the courage—or defiant stupidity—again to finally ask what had been laying on my mind for a long time. "What have you been doing to Nikaya?" This time, I failed to hide the emotion and forcefulness in my voice, and it came out more like a command than a question. If Verward wasn't already aware of my fear and anger, it was now—and I didn't particularly care anymore either.
Verward seemed to stare right through me—no reply. "I've seen more than enough of what you've been doing to her."
All traces of Verward's eerily happy looking visage drained away into a blank and unsurprised stare. I feared that all of our diplomacy had just been thrown away, and I braced for the worst as I adjusted my body's posture to make my defiance visually clear. Then Verward answered me in a voice so calm and smooth that it caught me off guard.
"I assure you that I was never trying to kill her. I have her best interests and wellbeing in mind." Silence again. Verward's

words did little to satisfy or reassure me. I simply stared at its face, now knowing that that face and its bodies design were stolen from my own, and Verward just stared back at me. Then, almost as if Verward were trying to shrug off the previous bit of conversation like it hadn't happened, the creepy faux smile returned. "I like you, Alder. I'm confident we both have a lot to gain from this relationship." It looked at the wall behind me, and pointing with one of its long, sharp, black fingers said, "Behind you, Alder... It is waiting for you."

I turned. On the wall were the markings of a lift door where there hadn't been any before. It slid open. "This will take your SFHU to a place just outside of your cell body. Once there, take your SFHU back in; do not waste time trying to explore my body with it or I will destroy it. I'm sure you already resized that, though."

I stepped into the lift then turned around, and, slowly, the lift began to rise as Verward's piercing and empty eyes, on a face that was once my own, locked with mine. I felt like I was gazing into a part of my own soul, which I no longer possessed.

Verward spoke again. "The biggest difference between us, Alder, is merely in our primary creators, but I will have both. Now goodbye, Alder..."

The doors shut and the lift accelerated upward. Verward was gone.

"What happened?" I asked myself, bemused. I didn't feel particularly afraid or angry anymore, or really much of anything. I couldn't begin to understand everything that had just happened. One thing was clear: It had said that it wanted to work together. *That's what I need to take away from this.* What mattered was that I had Nikaya safe inside me, still sleeping in her SHSE. *I need to talk to her.*

A few moments later the lift came to a stop. When its doors opened, I found my SFHU looking down a plain hall toward a bulbous white wall that I immediately recognized as the edge of my cell cluster. As I walked toward it, I began the process of opening a temporary tunnel for the SFHU. On the inside, I already had a BIHU heading toward Nikaya. *I'll show her first, then we have to talk.*

CHAPTER THIRTEEN

- Beneath My Branches -

Time to wake her...

"Nikaya. Nikaya, wake up."

My vision inside the capsule came back on, and Nikaya's open eyes were looking up at me.

"What is it?" she asked.

"Something has happened."

"What is it?" Nikaya repeated, sounding a little flustered.

I hesitated to answer. I didn't know why Verward didn't want Nikaya to know that I had spoken with it, but I decided that I had to answer—I had to tell her everything.

"It was Verward."

"What is that?" Nikaya sounded confused.

"It's the tower computer. It met me in a human-shaped body made from a part of its nexus."

"Huh... I've never heard the computer called that before. Why did it meet with you?" Nikaya's facial expression was one of confusion and concern.

"It talked about wanting to work together."

Nikaya blinked. "Really?"

"Yes, and you were right about Ward fighting his own tower. Verward told me that it rebelled and is fighting Ward now, and that the hole in the tower is from a missile fired by Ward at the computer nexus. Ward is losing; his brain has fled the tower.

He's controlling things like I do now, but from a distance—I don't know where."

Nikaya slowly nodded in silent acknowledgement, her eyes downcast and contemplative.

"Verward also told me that it killed people in the tower. I—I don't know how many, or who."

Nikaya hummed in acknowledgement, almost in a whimper.

"I told Verward that we would work together, but I don't know how much I can trust it, Nikaya. It kept asking about or referring to you but refused to tell me why. I don't think it wants you to know that it spoke with me either, but I have questions that I need answered." I found myself speaking more frantically. "I know Verward is the black plane I was on before I woke up—and I'm sure you know what that is since you were one of the ones experimenting on me—but Verward claims to know so much about me, like it knows me better than I do, and somehow I'm starting to believe it. I don't even know *who* I was before I came here because I lost my memories in the crash. It even shaped its body like my real one, the one you took from me."

"Alder, I didn't—"

"I—I'm sorry, I don't mean to accuse you. It's just this, this thing… It's terrifying, and I don't know what it is."

"Oh, Alder…"

"Hmm?"

"It…it sort of is you." She kept talking even when I tried to interrupt. "No… it's more than just the body or what it knows. I'm not sure you lost your memories in the crash, either—at least not all of them."

"W-wh-what, what do you mean?" Something Verward said replayed in my mind: *"After all, we did take your body and your mind."*

"There was more than one experiment that Ward was using you for," Nikaya continued. "Ward's objectives were immortality and power. One of the routes he explored to achieving this was mind uploading. The experiments were done on you and others but there were issues with the transfer process; the resulting simulated minds didn't exhibit the results that Ward desired so the experiment was shelved. However, the digital copy of your memories and brain structures were still stored, and the AIs' self-improvement systems inspected and incorporated much of the useful virtual thought structures we collected from you into itself."

I did my best to remain calm amid conflicting waves of fear and understanding. "Is that why it was able to rebel, to do what it's doing to us?"

Nikaya sighed. "I suspect so."

"How long did you know about this?"

"I've known about the experiment since it happened, and a little about what it did with the results. Nobody expected it to turn out like this though, and this is the first I've heard of it calling itself Verward." She swallowed. "What you fear is probably true. It likely does know more about you than you do, and it can probably think similarly to, if not in the same way, as you. I don't think it has all of you though, Alder. You likely each have a part of who you used to be, and I also suspect both halves of you have since been corrupted or modified." Nikaya somberly looked into my big eye. "I'm sorry Alder."

I remained silent, the emotions of the moment slowly melting away as I accepted the reality of my situation. *Onward...* "It's okay," I said eventually. "I will deal with this." *I am what I still have of myself.* "I have something that I want you to see, Nikaya," I said softly through the SHSE speakers.

"What is it?" She sounded a little worried.

"It's a good thing," I reassured her. "You should have a look around the place. I have more to tell you, but it can wait a few minutes. I'm really sort of proud of it."

"Okay." The SHSE door folded open. I had my head waiting for her as her chair lifted her up to look out into the room. "Wow, you really have rebuilt the place," Nikaya coolly remarked as she looked around. "I want to see the rest." She seemed almost a little eager now, maybe even a little excited— both to see what I had made and to momentarily forget about Verward.

Nikaya pulled a needle from her arm.

"Are you getting out?" I asked.

"Yeah," she said with a small grin. I felt happy to see her happy.

A slight feeling of unease came over me. I knew she was safer than ever—there were literally hundreds of yards of my metal body in between her and anything that could hurt her—but a part of me still didn't want her to get out. I watched her as she carefully removed the collection of needles and tubes from her arm and place them one by one in special holders in the wall of the SHSE. Finally, she removed the last connection and with it the sensation of her warm heartbeat disappeared from inside of me. I winced but was happy to see her out of the SHSE again. I moved my head back as she climbed through the opening and stepped down onto the floor; I felt her warm feet softly make contact. Then Nikaya looked up at the ceiling and around at the rest of the room. *At least I can still feel a slight pulse.*

"What do you think?" I asked through my camera head, now hovering a few feet away from her at her head height.

"It's an impressive change." I could tell that she meant it through the subtle look of confidence in her eyes.

"Thank you. Feel free to go anywhere and everywhere, but go that way first." I nodded toward a hall. "I made something for you; you'll know when you find it."

Nikaya turned and looked back at me with a faint smile.

"I have a BIHU on its way; I'll catch up to you," I said.

She turned and started toward the hall with a small spring in her step, a tiny display of energy and looseness which I hadn't seen in her before. She disappeared from view around the corner, but I could still feel where she was. *I'll meet her there, then we need to talk.*

A few minutes later, I stepped into the room for the first time and saw my work. Nikaya was already here, leaning back, gazing up at the pure white tree branches above her that swayed in a nonexistent breeze.

I looked up at the white dome high above the room then around at the rest of my work. Nearly every surface was covered in an ornate pattern of elegantly curving and woven vines and leaves. Everything flowed together into larger forms, moving along with the branches. I had put great care into creating the design, but it hardly compared to the centerpiece, the snow-white tree atop a white grass-and-flower-covered knoll at the room's center.

The tree was tall and lean, its trunk twisting upward to where its branches fanned out high in the air, searching for an unreachable sun. I stepped into the room, slowly walking a lap around its perimeter. I examined every detail that I had added: the tiny grooves in the smooth tree bark, veins in the delicate-looking white leaves, the metal flowers and grasses swaying around the tree trunk. All was united by wind, which moved through my body alone—not the air.

The room looked warm, alive, almost kissed by sunlight, but in here there was no sun and there was no wind, no dirt or plants, nothing truly alive in an organic sense except for Nikaya. I found my creation slightly unsettling and lonesome but breathtakingly beautiful.

Does she also feel this sad when looking at it? I imagined her crying, as I wished I could, while my trillions of dead and emotionless machines marched to my billions of dead and emotionless commands given every second.

My BIHU's eyes turned to Nikaya. She was so captivated by what was above her that she didn't notice me until I knelt by her side and gently placed a hand on her shoulder. Turning, she looked up into this one of my many faces, staring into its lifeless jet eyes. She smiled, her facial expression hopeful. Through my hand, the metal surfaces that she touched, and even in the swaying branches and grass nearby, I could feel the warmth of the blood flowing through her and the breath escaping her lungs. I could almost see the faint heat radiating off her body like sunshine to be absorbed by my metal leaves. *She's become the sun to me.*

I felt warm in the core of my very being, a sense I couldn't remember before. It was then I realized that I cared more for her than anything else.

"Hello Nikaya." I sat beside her under the swaying canopy of branches. The metal plants on the knoll curved or flattened to make way for me to sit, as they had for her.

"Hello," she replied warmly. "It's beautiful, I've never seen anything like it. I didn't even know that this sort of thing could be done with the tower cells."

"I made some changes to their internal structure. They're more malleable and faster-moving now."

"Incredible…" Her face fell. "I hope this is all over soon."

"Me too." I leaned back and looked up at the ornate ceiling through my branches.

"Do you think the tower computer will keep its word and work with you?"

I felt a tiny drop in her confidence. We were both uncertain about this. "I think so, I hope so," I answered.

Nikaya replied with a soft hum of agreement as she looked back up at the tree. A few moments of silence ensued. *I need to get what I came here for.*

"Nikaya, I need to know what is happening between you and the tower. It's been doing something to you for as long as I've been awake, and I know it; I know you know it too but you won't tell me and it won't either. What is going on? Why do you act the way you do around it? What was its nexus doing to you in that room? I can't stop thinking about it."

Nikaya looked me in the eyes and squinted in a mixed expression of sadness and something else I couldn't distinguish between fear and confusion. "What do you mean?"

"When we heard that noise before you opened the door to get my first BIHU, and then you screamed, 'Yes I know,' at the wall. You looked terrified. I'm worried about you."

Nikaya withdrew from me. "I don't remember that."

"It happened, though." I reached into my memory and played the audio portion of the memories through my BIHU's mouth. As she began to scream in the recording, Nikaya moved a hand to her lips. I felt her heart rate and breathing quicken.

"I can show you what I saw too if you go to the SHSE," I continued. "And why does it always bring you up when it's talking to me? Why does it even care that we exist enough to save and assist us, but also to do what it does to you? All it would tell me was that it wasn't trying to kill you—when it was plunging a spike into your brain. If it was telling me the truth, then the best that I can guess is that it wants to steal your mind and memories, like it has mine. But that still doesn't explain your connection to it from before the nexus."

I could feel the stress still rising in Nikaya's body and imagine the emotional distress that must lie beneath it. Her face contorted as if she were holding in a shout, and, as if I might somehow hurt her, I pulled away: BIHU, grass, tree, and all.

"Nikaya...I need to know why," I muttered, my voice small. She stared down at the grass slithering away from her feet, her hair obscuring much of her face from view. I hated seeing her distressed; I wanted to comfort her, to protect her from whatever this was...but I wasn't sure how. Should I even try?

"I know you need to know—*we* need to know. I want to tell you everything, but I simply can't."

"What do you mean?"

"I don't know everything, Alder. I've been here...so long, but I don't know everything, especially not anymore." Her voice snagged on words as if they were thorns in her throat. "Something is wrong with me."

I know the feeling... I relaxed my body and its foliage.

"Please believe me though, Alder. I'm not trying to work against you or hide anything from you. All I want is for us both to leave this place." She turned and, looking up into my machine's glassy-black eyes, she reached out to grasp the cold metal fingers of its hand in hers. "Please believe me, Alder. I trust you."

I felt the bones in her fingers as she squeezed, her heartbeat felt pounding through them. "I believe you and trust you, and I won't let anything harm you," I reassured her, closing my hand around hers. "Just tell me everything you know and we can figure this out."

We sat silently for a few seconds.

"I've known of and worked with the tower computer for a long time," Nikaya began. "I even did a large portion of the work of creating it, although Ward contributed more than anyone else. It was his obsession for years, and I think he loved it dearly. I did more than enough work to get a firm grasp for how it works, but when it touched me with the nexus... I knew it wasn't the same. It's changed." Nikaya gazed into the distance. "And about what it was trying to do to me." She took a deep breath. "Your theory—about it wanting my mind—is probably correct. I'm not sure why it would want my mind, though; I think it just killed everyone else. I guess it could want the rest of *your* mind. It may have already taken something from me too, and I might not even know what it's taken." Nikaya exhaled.

"It couldn't want to finish the mind transplant experiment on me, could it?" I asked. "It certainly doesn't need to because it had access to me for years, and it hasn't really come after me yet. Could it want your memories because of your role in creating it; is there something important it could learn from you?"

"I doubt it. The computer—Verward—has access to all of our information on it; it knows more than I know for sure."

"Could this be some sort of glitch?"

"No, it's much more than that. When it touched me..."

"What did you feel when you were connected to the nexus?"

"There was something black and empty that made me feel lonelier than I ever had before, but somewhere inside of it there was also something else, something that felt...familiar. It felt like it was...coming into me, to take me somewhere, and I was scared, but almost went with it in the end. I don't understand why Verward did what it did, and I didn't even know that the nexus was able to do what it was trying to do. I really don't know...." She trailed off into contemplative silence.

A horrible thought hit me. "Nikaya...when Verward first met me and told me that it had killed the other scientists, it also told me something else that I didn't tell you before. Verward said, 'Now I hold them.' Are you sure Verward actually killed them?"

Nikaya's eyes darted to mine. "Did you see it happen?"

"Yes. I saw it—some of them."

I remembered the amount of blood that had been on the BIHU, dripping down its arm. "Verward told me something else too," I continued. "That it would find whoever made it, and whoever made me. Nikaya, did Verward take their brains?" Her eyes widened then she swallowed nervously.

"I...I didn't see it happen if it did, but why would it?"

She went silent.

Something hot and wet landed on me, sliding down the length of one of my blades of grass like a raindrop. Before I was even aware of what I was doing, I had embraced Nikaya in a hug. I felt her go rigid in surprise as my cold arms slid around her, but a moment later her arms were wrapped around me and her face pressed hard against my uncomforting metal shoulder. Her trembling chest pressed against mine as she squeezed my lifeless torso and, through clenched teeth, she softly began to cry.

Could she really care about me—a dead thing, a cold and numb brain in a jar? A hot tear rolled down my icy shoulder, and I felt its warmth through thousands of microscopic circuits as I numbly led the endless clockwork march of my trillions of virtual and mechanical machines. *What am I...?*

Later, I walked Nikaya back to her SHSE. She climbed inside the warm capsule and slept.

CHAPTER FOURTEEN

- The Sun Rises -

I remained fully conscious, working through the night. With my energy reserves and generators, I no longer felt the need to rest. My sleep-like state had mostly just been a means of mental escape for me, but with my new power I found myself dreaming while awake and working. I could do as many things at once as I wanted, all parallel to one another.

The main project for the night was to create a physical factory and to design the machines that it would produce. Some of the factory parts that I made took hours to shape and used up the mass of an entire cell or more. Everything was made from my cells, and because of it, the entire assembly line could actively move and reshape itself during production. The line of interconnected, house-sized machines reminded me of an organic digestive system or a protein assembly line in a biological cell. It would be an industrial revolution if it were in the outside world.

I had time to think, too. Remembering my comparison of Nikaya to the sun the night before, I realized that ever since I had woken up to this world, after so many years without a clock or even the sun, Nikaya had become my largest reference point in time. For all this time, I had been calling it day when she was with me and night when she wasn't. Nikaya had become the sun to me, and now the night was finally over because the sun was starting to rise from her SHSE.

The door gracefully folded open and Nikaya was lifted up by her chair to be held in the SHSE's entrance like the beaming center of a flower. My main was waiting to great her. I felt happy to see her.

"Hello," I said in my best attempt at a friendly tone.

Nikaya placed a hand on my camera's neck for support as she stepped down from the SHSH. She seemed rested and in a good mood. Her soft footsteps felt like warm rays of sunshine on my cold metal floor, and outside of some new machines in my factory, she was my only heat source.

"Any news?" Nikaya asked.

"Only that my factory is almost done. How did you sleep?"

"I slept well. Can I see it now?"

"Yeah, follow me," I said as I moved my head toward the door behind me and to my left. Nikaya followed and when my neck could stretch no farther, one of my BIHUs was waiting for her in the hall entrance. I led her on a short walk down a few halls to what was now my largest room, followed closely by a newly expanded storage area.

"I worked on it all night," I said to Nikaya as we walked. "I decided on an additive manufacturing process. The hardest part was finding out how to seed and take control of the insides of the new taline machines with my mind after making them. Also, it's amazing how the transport tubes work, Nikaya. You have to see them."

"Sounds good." We stepped into the factory room. "And looks even better."

We stopped at a sort of guard rail on the perimeter of a platform that wrapped around the vast, vertical, tube-shaped room. Nikaya looked up at the organically curved and twisting walls that conformed around the assembly line machines. We could hear the muffled humming of machinery.

"What do you think?" I asked Nikaya, eager for her opinion.

"You made this all while I was in the SHSE?"

"Yeah."

"It's incredible," Nikaya mumbled, looking up and down the organ, excitedly examining everything she could from our vantage point. It made me feel proud of my work. "And to think this is all part of your body... Are you manufacturing anything yet?"

"Not in any sort of quantity, but I should be at full production soon. How is this compared to the tower's factories?"

"Um, it's a bit smaller than most of the tower's, but it looks surprisingly good, especially considering that you've never even seen one. Can I see more? I would like to help make any improvements, if I can. I used to spend a lot of time in and around the tower factories."

"Of course, just follow the paths I made." I motioned to the walkways to either of our sides. Two sets of stairs came off the circular platform and wrapped around the circumference of the room: one going down and the other up.

"Okay, let's go up first then." Nikaya turned and started to walk up the long curving ramp. I followed close behind in the BIHU. "Have you figured out how to get everything you need from the CTTs?"

"Yeah, I believe so. I found out that the cells already have preprogrammed ways of getting what they need from it so I mostly just had to figure out and slightly modify what they do. From there it was simply a question of moving stuff drawn from the raw fluid through the interfaces to where I wanted it. Once I had established strong enough concentration gradients, it became more natural."

Nikaya nodded approvingly.

"I also made a small chemical power plant of sorts to help power the factory and charge the machines I make," I added. "At the bottom of the factory there is also a recycling plant for processing any destroyed, damaged, or excess materials."

"Excellent, it all just looks excellent," she said, beaming. "You give me more hope every day, Alder." Her small smile and complement were exactly what I had hoped for and more.

As we continued up the walkway, I began to feel something— an odd demanding sensation in a far-off part of my body. It was the communication line that Verward and I had made yesterday. *Verward must be trying to communicate with me*, I realized. Hesitantly, I opened just enough of the defenses built around it to allow my mind to convey a message through the crack in my virtual armor. "Hello."

Instantly there was a response.

"Hello Alder, I see you've been making some progress, judging by the quantity of fluid that you are drawing from the tower base. I have some thrilling news for you, and for our first mission as well."

Tentatively I responded, "What is it?"

Even though we couldn't see or hear each other at all, the information coming from this thing still had an eerie and unearthly feeling that unsettled me.

"I have taken control of all of the chemical transport valves and stations in the tower base and shut off the ones feeding Ward's half of the tower, effectively applying a tourniquet to his neck. It came at great expense, of course, but if everything goes according to plan and our fighting continues at its current intensity, he will likely be forced to stop 99 percent of his manufacturing within days."

"That's great news," I said.

"Yes, yes it is." Verward paused. "Now this is where you act, Alder. I want you to expand downward along your CTT and outward from there. A small part of that same CTT is the last portion of one that Ward has access to because I avoided entirely cutting your supplies off as well. I need you to take everything touching that CTT then to strike as deep into Ward's side as you can, forcing him to divert resources away from my armies toward the upper third of the tower where you are."

Inwardly, I smiled. This was good news, and it was incredibly reassuring to know that Verward had refrained from taking the easy path to hurt Ward in order to avoid hurting me. However, I was still unsure of all of Verward's intentions, and it had also just told me that it could cut me off from the CTT at any time since it controlled the tower base.

Almost as if Verward knew what I was thinking, it reassured me.

"Successfully cutting him off and dividing his forces will be very beneficial for the both of us, Alder. Ward could potentially be out of the tower in the next twenty-four hours. Then you can try to leave, and I could even help you. Do be careful though, Alder; with his new body, Ward is smarter and stronger than you may yet understand. You've also never been in a real fight before. Keep her safe."

The presence in the virtual communication port disappeared. I was alone with Nikaya again.

"Nikaya, something just happened," I reported. "I just spoke with Verward again."

She stopped mid-stride and turned to face me. "What did it say?"

I recited the first half of our conversation for her, and she reacted the same way that I had.

"Are you going to do it…attack now?"

"I think I should, but I'm not entirely sure how to—or even have anything to attack with yet."

"Do you think this could be a trick?" she asked.

"What are you thinking?"

"It's just that—I'm sure you've already thought of this—but could the computer be trying to get you to open up and show it what you've been making, and get you to fight Ward for it? We have no way of knowing if Ward is even still in the tower, right?"

"I know…" I still had to think some more about this. "We don't know, but do we really have another choice? I don't think Verward is lying to us though, at least not about this."

Nikaya looked blankly at me for a second then slowly nodded her approval.

"Then this is a test of faith. You have to go. Just please be extremely careful. Our survival is still hanging by a thread compared to Ward and the tower computer—remember that. Don't forget to give some thought to our escape plan either.

That should still be the top priority. We can't take any chances
at depending on the computer—err, Verward."
"I will and don't worry," I assured her.
The noise level in the factory began to increase.
Nikaya looked up at the slowly undulating organ-like machines
around her then back over at me. "It all looks good as far as I
can tell, but I want to get a closer look at these machines in
action. I'll look around for a few more hours."
"All right, I'll stay nearby."

***

I had a lot of work to do. There was still design work to be
finished, not to mention the problem of my lack of experience
with dealing with Ward's combat machines. My biggest
concern by far was the worms, the machines that filled an
entire hall and moved fast enough to launch themselves into
the air. I had only seen them twice before, and I doubted any
of my weaponry could damage the mouth-like weapons of one,
let alone stop one from moving. *If only I could get my mind into one
of them, or at least something more complex that I can learn from.*
Using what I could learn from the machines I already had
access to, I made my own version of the BIHU with a small
gun in its arm and designed a small hovering gunship. It was a
struggle to make them work as well as the machines they were
based on, but I was able to accomplish that while adding my
own touches and some upgrades. Most importantly, though, I
began to give serious thought to a much larger, more
important design, one that could potentially be a means of
escape for me and my Nikaya.
Hmm, I just called her mine… My Nikaya, the sun…
My factory churned until I had a group of bodies that I felt
could handle a skirmish, and together they moved as a group
through a new room near my factory and down into the tunnel
entrance at its center. They gathered at the bottom of the near-
vertical tunnel as it continued to grow parallel to the CTT until
the bottom of the tunnel opened up right against the edge of
Ward's cells.

I looked down at the flat white surface of Ward's cell body and began charging my SFHU's cannon. Expecting to feel tense and anxious before the fight, I felt only awareness of my body and a calculated sense of readiness to kill anything of Ward's that I could.

Finally, my SFHU, its cannon near overheating, was left standing alone on the surface of Ward's vast body.

The air split with a crack of sound and light, and before me was left a colorfully glowing molten surface. The glowing puddle screeched with the heat as I recharged and fired again, then again, the pool growing with each flash until it shook and collapsed inward, splashing down into an empty space below. Hurriedly, I looked through the hole into a white hall splattered with a mess of burning colors. *It's time to move.*

I rushed through the hole, my physical bodies jumping or flying into the hall as my mind, with its virtual machines, crashed into dozens of cell walls like a tsunami on a cliff. The resistance was tremendous, but already I could feel my virtual waves of machines forcing open virtual cracks in Ward's armor. My mind wrapped around and wrestled cells until I tore their control systems apart or choked them off from all connections to Ward. They fell quickly and I integrated them with ease.

As I took the last of this first line of cells, my army finished pouring into the hall. I frantically looked around with hundreds of eyes, scanning for anything that stood out or moved, but there was nothing. *Where is he?* I sent a small group of flying machines in each direction to scout the area. *Is he just not here yet?*

Ward's cells were starting to push back harder, as I had expected them to, but in the external world there remained only an uneasy silence.

Then I saw it.

Through the eye of an SCU, flying in a distant branch of the hall, I saw it—one of the worms, jaws gaping and moving at tremendous speed.

It was already too late for the SCU that had spotted it to turn and flee. The worm's spinning jaws made contact with and pulled the little machine in, ripping into its bright metal body as if it were made of soft clay. Most of my eyes darted to face the corner where I knew the worm would come around—I had seconds to prepare.

My bodies with firearms formed lines, and I felt a twinge of anxiety despite preparing for this. I took a nervous glance at the tunnel I had come through. *It should be too narrow for it to get through, and Nikaya is far from the entrance.*

Without a sound, the train-size machine twisted to fill the end of the hall. Even still, I could barely see it against its equally pure white and reflection-less surroundings.

I opened fire.

My Napoleonic rows of bodies fired their weapons and a storm of projectiles lit up the hall. Thousands of rounds seemed to disappear inside the heavily armored spinning grinder of a mouth, failing to slow it down. Then I noticed something else coming from the opposite direction: a horde of sprinting BIHUs.

I turned and ran back toward my tunnel, the worm only seconds away. *Just a little closer. Just a little closer.* Then I squeezed.

Several of the cells I had just taken in the ceiling contracted inward, away from their supporting neighbors, and they dropped from the ceiling. There was a deafening crash as hundreds of tons of cells hit the floor on both sides of my tunnel exit; the worm slammed into them almost simultaneously. The impact shook everything nearby and a rain of sparks erupted around the cells as the spinning teeth of the worm ground into the cell and lurched to a stop. Then shavings and chunks of metal began to break off, and I realized with horror: *It's eating through it! It's still moving forward!*

From the other direction, the horde of Ward's BIHUs were already squeezing through cracks in the hastily made barrier. I started shooting as arms and heads began popping through gaps, desperately trying to squirm through. It wasn't long before the holes were clogged with destroyed bodies or my cells moved to fill the gaps.

My mind was spinning and straining. Physically I was in a tough situation with the worm; mentally I was in the middle of my largest battle yet. The intensity and speed of the enemy that pounded at me was daunting, yet somehow I continued to edge my way downward into new cells. I was close to taking control of the floor of the hall, where I could make my next move. As I took them, I dropped more cells from the ceiling behind the worm and Ward's BIHUs. *I have them now.* I began constricting the halls.

Ward, realizing what I was doing to his BIHUs, frantically sent them looking for an exit, but there was already none left as my body steadily moved to fill the open space in my new hall. His army was trapped. His BIHUs worked together to try to hold back the walls, but it was useless. My walls simply bent around the limbs of the machines that tried to hold me back, engulfing them until they couldn't move.

I continued to squeeze. Their bodies bent and cracked until all movement ceased.

The worm struggled to free itself, pushing forward with such force that its thousands of tiny appendages scraped shallow grooves into the floor, walls, and ceiling. It desperately ate into my cell blockade until finally I crushed its rotating jaws; they hit against each other and banged to a satisfying stop. With it disarmed and every surface of its body held tightly, I stopped squeezing. Projections of my cells grew and forced their way into every opening in the worm's skin, and I formed connections with it everywhere I could. Then I forced my way into the worm with my mind and took control. *It worked.*

With the immediate threats gone and the next layer of cells already coming under my control, I felt safe enough to begin removing my cell blockades. The separated cells began to merge again with the walls, creeping back up into their spots in the ceiling as I began picking up the remains of the destroyed machines and torn bits of cell. A newly designed transport machine that I had made did the work, using a single arm to pull recyclable material into its hovering spherical body. Any metal or recoverable energy cores I could get would be of great value.

I felt so pleased with the outcome of this first encounter that I opened a second virtual front at the top of my cell cluster. This wasn't what Verward wanted me to do, but I felt I had to reach the outside. Through the roof was likely my best chance. Ward quickly responded to this second attack with a counter attack to my side, and as I began to channel forces to the area he struck me again simultaneously at several different locations. I felt the increased strain on my mind and cells but felt confident that I could hold my ground and continue to push further into Ward's part of the tower without being completely overwhelmed.

He was strong but clearly weakened, spread thin, although I felt that Ward wasn't showing me everything he was capable of. I was painfully aware of the vulnerability that the tunnel through me created. Something finding its way in wouldn't be too bad unless it reached Nikaya or my brain. For now, though, I was making progress and she was safe—I could feel her footsteps and her breath moving through my halls and one of my BIHUs still by her side.

When I had enough of my fallen cells pulled back into place for my machines to walk through, I moved my army with the task of inspecting and clearing the new area that I had already walled off farther away. I also began widening and forming a spiral staircase around the walls of the shaft of the tunnel so that my machines could move up and down freely. I felt my army needed mobility but I decided that I was going to avoid using it for now in favor of the new "crush then collect" method. *I'll need to capture one of the elevators or figure out how to make one soon.* I was already extending the tunnel to the next floor downward.

I continued to push downward along the CTT, growing my body one layer of cells at a time. The next couple dozen floors were not easy to take, and Ward fought back aggressively on every one of them, but they were not the strongholds I had expected to encounter either. He had likely been weakened by Verward more than I had expected, and I only found small groups of machines here and there, all of which I systematically killed with relative ease before collecting the scrap.

I fought and pushed until I eventually reached an empty space and could go no farther. My bottom layer of cells formed the ceiling of a room larger than any I had found before, and I decided I had to open my tunnel up to it without constricting. With extreme caution I elongated my tunnel downward toward the edge, and with as many machines as the tunnel could fit blocking the entrance, I slowly pulled away the last bit of cell. Light poured up into the tunnel from below as my army's eyes looked down into the expanse. My body formed the ceiling of a massive, stadium-size room with a writhing mass of tens of thousands of machines battling on the floor far below. *So this is Ward and Verward fighting.* I looked down, trying to make sense of the pit of bedlam. Then I felt a communication channel opening. It was Verward.

"You did it," it said plainly. "I saw you come in, Alder. You best not stay there gawking for long lest your forces be shot at by Ward."

I moved most of my machines back.

"Get in here and join us as soon as you can, and here is some information that you will need."

A packet of information was injected into the port. I opened it and instantly became aware of the locations of all of the machines in the massive room and to whom they belonged. It also informed me of the room's location in the lower half of the tower and that it was a storage room, filled with now-retracted racks holding countless combat machines. This was the last of the three war rooms over which Ward had any physical influence.

"Thank you," I replied.

"Try to clear the air of him first if you can. Everything has been going exceptionally well and I expect that we will have this all cleaned up soon." There was a faint electronic hiss then the communication port closed.

I checked myself to make sure that my information storage was well equipped and ready to use. I wanted to remember every bit of everything that happened in extra detail, and had already learned a lot to improve my own machines just by looking down at the battle. Then I quickly decided on a strategy and went into action.

I started moving more machines into the tunnel as I began moving cells around and eyed my first goal, Ward's largest machine in the room. It was identical to the ones I had seen outside in the crater: worm-like, covered in eyes, spewing purple flame, and flailing whips. I doubted my small projectiles could do much to the limbless, wingless dragon but I would test them regardless and attempt to get my machines on top of it if possible. If we could somehow bring down the dragon and Ward's other flying machines, I could join the fight on the floor.

I stretched the cells forming the entrance of the tunnel downward while moving the cells around it upward to create a sort of upside-down tower. I opened windows in its side, narrowed the main opening, and put machines with projectile weapons at every opening. As my weapons fired, Ward's small flying crafts that I hit crashed onto the machines below; others fired back or tried to ram me through the windows or the hole at the upside-down tower's center.

Then the dragon came into range and I took aim, firing everything at its eyes. It violently twisted its body in the air then exploded forward with a burst of speed in my direction. I almost thought I felt a shiver run through my body and saw Ward's rage in the machine's worm face, purple flame spilling forth from its open maw and licking at its sides as it wriggled and contorted in the air like a wild serpent. Then I realized what was about to happen. *It's going to ram me!*

My bodies braced themselves as searing flame erupted through the windows with enough force to shake them, and heat so intense that the surfaces of my machines and cells softened. I braced for the terrible impact, but it never came. *It went around!* My bodies leapt back to the windows to see the dragon on the left side of the tower. Without pause, I resumed my attack as it looped back to come at me again.

The second pass was a repeat of the first, only now I was beginning to worry about the increasing softness of my machine's metal and the numb feeling in my communication with them caused by the extreme heat. *I have to end this soon*, I told myself as I resumed my seemingly pointless volley.

The dragon looped around half the room, this time getting close enough to the floor to release a great crescent river of purple flame onto Verward's machines on the floor as the beast twisted around to face me again. This time it approached differently—coming up from below. My heart sank as I realized what was about to happen. A burning spike of fear drove through me. It was already too late to react.

The dragon's gaping maw filled the tunnel entrance and a volcano erupted through it. Columns of flame exploded out the tower windows and rocketed up the tunnel, and a chimney effect pulled the scorching heat up dozens of floors more and into their halls. The volcano was accompanied by the sound of screeching metal as the dragon's head forced its way through the softened metal of the opening and up through the upside-down tower, where it lodged itself in the tunnel above.

For a second I thought Ward had trapped himself and I could capture his machine like I had the worm, but when I tried to squeeze with my cells, they refused to follow my commands. Their softened sides had gone numb with the incredible heat and they were getting hotter as the dragon continued to spew flame inside the tunnel. All of my machines in the upside-down tower and lowermost levels were now trapped.

A multitude of tiny arms and the whip-blades burst from the undulating sides of the dragon's thrashing body. My machines leapt to try to subdue or destroy the appendages with their melee weapons while the other machines continued to shoot, but whip-blades moved with such force that the weakened metal of my unarmored machine bodies were sliced through like soft meat. I leapt to the walls, floor, or ceiling, trying to get away however possible as the blades slaughtered everything in the 360-degree view of its rings of glowing red eyes, all burning with bloodlust.

I double checked on Nikaya's location inside of me to ensure that she was still somewhere far from the tunnel. All safe. Acting fast, I began the moving cells to try to shut off the tunnel above the dragon, but their vertical arrangement prevented dropping them quickly and the extreme heat made some near impossible to move. A group of newly built machines moved out of the tunnel entrance room and down into the burning volcano of a tunnel just as another blast of burning hot air billowed up the shaft to almost reach my main room.

It would stop me from sending any machine reinforcements, but I realized I had to close the tunnel. I could never take the chance of letting this thing get to Nikaya, and it wouldn't even have to reach my orb to boil my brain inside of it. I began closing off the entrance room and the halls near it too.

In the tunnel, still only seconds after the dragon had lodged itself inside my body, I felt the metal softening and the numbing effects of the hot flame. My feet began to stick to the floor; some flying machines began to fall from the air. The cell walls even began to sag. The whole tunnel and its connecting halls began to glow with psychedelic colors; the energy stored within my machines was becoming unstable. If I had been able to, I would have screamed with frustration and agony as I felt the sensations of my hundreds of bodies and hundreds of cells being melted and ripped apart. Worse yet, the dragon was still forcing its way upward.

While wild flames filled the tunnel and halls, the battle fared far worse in the upside-down tower. There, the walls were being cruelly scoured of my bodies. My only SFHU was in the upside-down tower and ducked under the swing of a whip blade to be slashed by another from behind. It sliced through the SFHU's left thigh and continued at an upward angle to sever the right leg along with a large piece of the SFHUs midsection, then it continued onward to cut two other machines in half before disappearing from my sight.

The SFHU fell in two halves. I continued to have communication and control over it, but something felt very odd. The SFHU's energy core was quickly breaking down, starting to melt the metal around it. I noticed this among the hundred other failing energy cores of my machines and cells. As I continued to fight, an idea formed in my head.

With my SFHU's handed arm I dragged my melting torso toward the dragon's side. While pressing my body tight against the undulating surface that threatened to throw me back against the wall, I lifted the cannon barrel and thrusted it against the dragon's side.

I emptied the entire core through the barrel in one final burst of energy so intense that it vaporized the internal circuits of the SFHU. Energy passed from core to cannon like a lightning bolt. There was a deafening noise and a blinding blue flash that filled the entire room.

I completely lost communication with the SFHU and another nearby machine.

The dragon went limp and silent. I turned and saw with the eyes of several machines a large burning hole in the dragon's side where the SFHU had been. It was a molten crater several feet across; at its center a small hole went clear through. Colorful, molten liquid flowed readily from the hole and the glowing heat seemed to energize and light up the very air around it. I was filled with only a sense of awe.

D-did I kill it?

Ward opened his dragon's worm maw and, when it failed to eject flame, roared with such anger and intensity that it sent a shockwave through my entire body of cells. I even felt Nikaya shudder in the halls far above. For a moment all seemed silent, then out boomed the words of Ward.

"Alder!"

The name rumbled up through my burning tunnel as if it were spoken by a drum in a cave, beat upon by a beast unspeakable. "Even if you chase me from my tower, which I've built with my very life and blood, I will still destroy you for what you, your betraying friend, and Verward have done!"

The worm shook.

"I scraped you off the pavement and made you all what you are! You infected him! You pathetic and putrid kernel!" Ward hissed through his burning worm maw, spraying molten metal like a frothing rabid animal.

"Now I will scrape you all off the pavement—off the Earth! I will descend, and I will smite you all for what you've done to us!"

As his booming voice still echoed through me, the dragon's appendages retracted, and it began to wriggle back out of the hole in a crippled attempt at escape. With each movement, a mix of molten metal and other liquids gushed from its wound and splashed onto the floor and battlefield far below. Spurts of purple flame burst from its mouth like tiny geysers. I heard whistling and gurgling sounds coming from its wound that now hung out of sight below the floor of the upside-down tower. Its body began to undulate as if in flight, then it slid out of the hole.

With every able machine, I jumped to the hole and gripped its shredded rim. I watched the beast wriggle and shake, struggling to stay in the air, before it smacked onto the floor with a resounding thud and splash of molten liquids. The entire mid-section of the machine began to cave in on itself.

One last puff of purple flame escaped it.

The entire room became silent in disbelief before the clashing and screeching of the battle retook its former vigor. Still, I felt only disbelief and fear. Then, suddenly, I felt something from Verward nudging at my communication port. I opened it; in came a package of information containing some feelings of congratulations and relief along with the message, "I am impressed, now let's finish this."

A profound feeling of relief washed over me. *That was too close.* Nearly every part of every hall that I had captured was burnt to some degree, many cells I could barely feel. I inspected my damaged body as I reopened the entrance to the tunnel to send down new machines that had been collecting by the tunnel entrance. The heat radiating off of everything below the tunnel entrance created a strong updraft, sucking cool air in through the openings in the upside-down tower, heating it then blowing the hot air into the center of my body above. The combination of that and the radiating glow of destroyed machines and damaged cells made the shaft appear virtually indistinguishable from a volcano.

A few moments later, I felt and saw Nikaya jog into my main room with a concerned look on her face. She looked up at my head as I stretched out to meet her halfway. "I heard everything he said," Nikaya said. She walked toward me. "What happened?"

"I killed something of Ward's."

She sat on the bench of the SHSE as I filled in the details. When I finished she stood and walked with my BIHU escort to the doorway of the tunnel entrance room. Nikaya covered her nose with her white sleeve. *The smoke must smell.*

"Wow…" Nikaya exhaled through her sleeve as she took my BIHU's hand, stepped up to the edge, and looked down into the fiery abyss. Her hair wafted up in the hot air; little puffs of colored smoke billowed out around her.

After a few moments, I tapped her back with the arm of one of my recycler machines. Nikaya turned and stepped aside to let it pass and begin its descent into hell. We stood there for a long time before we walked back to my room together.

Nikaya sighed then, looking at the floor, said, "I hope this is almost over." She looked up at my main head. "How much longer do you think it will be until we can leave?" She suddenly seemed mentally exhausted.

"I'm not sure," I said, not sure what else to divulge. "I haven't touched the exterior of the tower yet, but with the way things are going now I think I might reach it soon." I tried to sound positive. "I've been doing some planning, though."

Silence took over the room as she walked to the SHSE then climbed inside. As it closed, she looked into the eyes of my camera head and said, "I believe in you, Alder." She sounded detached but sincere, and I was sure she had no idea how much it meant to me to hear her say it.

The snow-white doors of the SHSE folded shut like petals shielding a bulb, and I felt a twinge of guilt because I was secretly debating on whether or not to leave the tower at all. I knew she wanted to leave, but I had to push my thoughts aside. *I don't even have the ability to act on whatever decision I make.* Down below, the damaged cell walls in the shaft and the upside-down tower were still hot but cooling and slowly pulling back into place. Looking at the battle on the floor below, it was clear that Ward was losing. His remaining machines were mostly concentrated along the entrances on one side of the room. I didn't think there was much more I could do to help—yet it was probably expected of me, so I gathered the flying machines that still functioned and sent them down to join Verward.

They landed around the smoldering remains of the dragon. I looked around for any of Ward's machines, and finding none, I moved my comparatively tiny force to join Verward's army in the battle at the hall entrances. From the air, I was able to take several shots at Ward's machines from a distance, but the fight didn't last long. Ward was pushed out of the room, leaving only scrap heaps of bodies behind that Verward's machines aggressively cleared away or clambered over.

Then I felt Verward pressing at the communication port again, and I opened it.

"We have it now, Alder. Ward is separated from all CTTs and his large armies have been shattered. Less than twenty-four hours until Ward is exorcised from the tower, thanks to our joint effort."

I had the sensation that I was looking at one of Verward's eerie smiles. Then feed ended, and I closed the port.

This is great news, but what do we do next? I felt some relief in Verward's confidence, and I could feel Ward growing weaker as I continued to expand my body into his, but it would be just me and Verward sharing the tower soon. *I can only hope things remain peaceful between us once Ward is gone.* However, Verward likely hadn't needed me that badly from the beginning, if at

all—and that worried me. Leaving the tower or staying…
Either way, my future was uncertain.

CHAPTER FIFTEEN

- *Skyward* -

I waited in anticipation for Verward to contact me again, knowing that soon we would have to make a plan of what to do after Ward was gone. Everything would be on the table, and in its position of power, Verward would be able to move anything in its favor. If it decided to stay friendly toward me, whatever deal was reached would likely include my leaving the tower.

Leaving the tower was what Verward and Nikaya expected of me, but an increasingly large part of me didn't want to go. I relished my power and everything I had created in this world that I was meant to die in. There was nothing to go back to on the outside, and leaving meant nothing but uncertainty and unknown risks. *But what else can I do?* Verward's body nearly encapsulated mine and had the ability to shut down my flow of resources at any time.

Of course, I could try to take my part of the tower with me, but Verward undoubtedly wouldn't like that. Even if I could escape with a cluster of cells, how would all of the surrounding towers and the government be able to resist taking my body? It would be a treasure trove of technology and information from Ward's tower; losing those secrets would disadvantage Verward, which gave it another good reason to not let me go. I didn't even have my means of escape fully designed yet, though. I was starting to feel like victory over Ward might create more problems for me than it solved.

All of my cells were working feverishly toward improving the internal structure of my body when I found something interesting at the top of my body. I took over an unusually dense layer of long thin cells, twisted together and overlapping like skin cells or a scale-like armor; the next layer I took was the same. Excitement stirred inside me; I took another layer then a wave of new information slammed into me from hundreds of sensors.

It's beautiful... I saw the sun and white clouds in the sky above the expansive dull black surface of the slanted tower roof. As I looked down at the hundreds of smaller towers around me, I realized that nearly every surface of the darkly colored roof absorbed solar energy. I felt it on the new cells like sun on skin as I began picking up radio, satellite, and other wireless signals of all kinds from all directions. I was receiving countless signals carrying content ranging from people's private Internet connections and phone calls to scientific information about the surrounding area, atmosphere, and the cosmos. I quickly delegated the task of filtering everything to a group of virtual machines.

The roof itself slanted upward into a great sweeping spire at one corner of the tower; a sharp-edged hole was cut through the spire center. From my vantage point more than three miles above the ground, the sheer hugeness of the tower began to really sink in. I could even see over the edge of the distant residential part of the city to dark green, forested hills on the horizon. It was exhilarating.

Nikaya needs to see this. I hurriedly continued to expand into as much of the roof as I could as I spoke to Nikaya through the speakers in her SHSE.

"Nikaya."

I waited a moment, but there was no reply. She was sleeping, but I was excited.

I repeated myself a little louder. "Nikaya, you need to see this."

"Yes." She stirred sleepily. "What is it?"

"This." I displayed an image of the horizon I was seeing inside her SHSE.

She looked up and smirked. "You're actually there?"

"Yes, want to feel it?"

Her eyes lit up. "You mean you can take me out now?"

"We can't leave yet, but I want you to stand up here with me. It's wonderful, Nikaya. I have a small lift that can take you there."

"Of course," Nikaya replied, hurriedly pulling tubes from her arm.

The SHSE folded open like a great blooming flower and Nikaya stepped out to meet my head and a BIHU that I had waiting for her. "Follow me." I excitedly started toward one of my halls with the BIHU.

She followed me down a series of twisting hallways and stairs until we came to a dead-end wall that opened to reveal a cylindrical tube. The lift was just wide enough for a single person to fit in, and without any explanation Nikaya eagerly stepped inside then turned to face me as the door closed. I couldn't see her inside the elevator, but I could still feel her excitement as I accelerated her upward.

I felt her heart racing as the lift came to a stop. The hatch at the top of the tube opened to the sky and the pressure equalized. Sunshine and cool air poured into the shaft and I felt Nikaya's hair and clothing begin to dance in the wind. As the lift pushed her upward until her feet were level with roof, Nikaya stood, wide-eyed for several moments before stepping off of the lift platform and onto a flat area of the roof. She walked a short distance then gazed out at the horizon in silence. Her expression was blank, unreadable.

After a few minutes, I decided to speak through a small speaker near where she was sitting. "What do you think?"

Without breaking her gaze, she answered dazedly, "It's beautiful…"

I watched her hair and clothing whip around her still form. "What's the first thing you'll do, once you're free?"

She thought for a moment. "I want to hear real birds again."
The wind whistled across the dark expanse of the roof. "What about you?"

I had to think. "I really don't know. I'm just trying to imagine how I could ever be compatible with the outside world again, or with anything. I don't think I can be."

"That's fine," Nikaya stated. "We can figure it out together." The promise felt warmer than the sun on my solar panels. "You can stay here as long as you want. When you're ready to come back inside, just stand on the lift."

She didn't reply this time, but I saw a tiny, almost childish smile sneak on her otherwise placid and contemplative face.

I worked on countless projects inside myself over the next few hours. I was making good progress, expanding into Ward's side of the tower, when I found something that brought me to a sudden halt. *What is this?* A wall of Verward's cells blocked my path. *It outpaced me and cut me off.*

I nervously shifted my virtual armies around the border between our bodies. *Does Verward not trust me, or not need me anymore?* At any moment Verward could finish off Ward and I might not even know. What would happen next was a mystery. *There's nothing I can do about this.* Anxiety swelled through me. *I have to wait and hope for the best.*

So I waited, worked, and thought, playing over endless strategies and scenarios in my mind. I wondered how surprised or even angry Verward might be if it only knew what I had been working on doing to my cell body. Then Ward floated into my stream of thoughts and after a few moments' contemplation, the possibility of Ward attacking the tower, with his two remaining towers and other forces, came to mind. The more I thought about the possibility, the more surprised I was that I had overlooked it before, and the more probable it seemed that he would try to do it.

Then I remembered something Nikaya had said days prior: "Ward's fleet is on Phobos." *What is that, a moon?* I had no idea how far away or how large any of these assets of Ward's were, though, so I could do little more than contemplate.

DAVID CHARLES SHAW

Eventually, my mind drifted away from Ward and Verward and toward Nikaya. *She's been doing something strange to me, with just her presence.* I had striven to rid myself of emotion in the years of isolation before I met her...but the more that I felt, saw, and spoke with her, the harder it was to continue to do that. I wasn't only feeling more emotion around her, but also in all situations—and I wasn't sure how to feel about it.

There's something in her eyes, something to her that I can't get past. For some reason, I thought I felt like she might be able to understand me, or maybe even care about me as something more than the object that she lived inside of—was trapped inside of.

Undoubtedly the remnants of an insane dream. I struck myself down. *I know so little about her, and myself, but I feel like I've known her...forever, or that she's known me, maybe. It doesn't matter. All I know for sure is that I want to protect her. I suppose I've needed her to survive, but...it's something more.*

I don't want to be alone.

CHAPTER SIXTEEN

- Ectomy -

Uneventful hour after hour passed as I worked and Nikaya
napped on or silently wandered about my rooftop. I was
making great progress on everything until suddenly I felt a
knock at my communication port with Verward. I opened it,
and immediately I could feel Verward's bizarre jubilance
oozing from the outwardly stoic message.
"Ward is gone. The tower is now fully under our control."
Verward shared with me a memory of it taking Ward's final
few cells and then a wave of triumphant emotion.
"Amazing." *So we actually did it.*
"Indeed it is, Alder, and I have more news. I've found a place
for you to move to."
"What—move?"
"Now that Ward is gone, this is what I offer you as a deal. You
will leave and I will take the entirety of the tower." Verward's
voice was laced with a hint of forcefulness. It continued in a
friendlier tone. "I will let you keep one cell despite my best
interests and I will transport and plant your seed in a location
that I found for you several hundred miles from here. It is safe
in its relative remoteness and there is ample sun and earth for
you to grow and build in. I will help you by giving you
information on how to grow your roots and the extraction
apparatuses that you will need to get started. With time, you

will dominate the region, and I will even offer you my continued amity and protection until you can stand on your own. I will give that to you." It finished in an electric hiss, "What do you say, Alder?"

I paused in a speechless stupor as I tried to process the offer and the motives behind it. *A single cell.* A bubble of anger swelled up inside me as I felt my vast body, armies, and trillions of virtual machines moving to my conscious and subconscious whims. *It already stole my face and memories. Now I may as well be a god—and it wants everything again!*

Electric currents rushed to my body's borders preemptively— then reality sank in. Except for my small part of the roof, I was inside of Verward's body, and it was larger than mine, several times over. My heart sank as I realized that Verward's offer was probably, in reality, a generous one. *I have little if anything to negotiate with, and no finished or safe means of escape.* Again, I felt small before this thing that seemed to eternally haunt me. *It's protected and helped us in the past, and we worked together, so perhaps I can trust it now.* I struggled to convince myself. *I won't have to go through with my escape plan. Nikaya and I can go free without conflict and live safely. I...we...can rebuild.*

Feeling deflated and violated, I swallowed my pride then gave Verward the answer I knew it wanted. "I accept. You can have the tower and I will leave, as we agreed."

I felt one of the machine's eerie grins as it responded. "Excellent. I will organize everything for your departure. Prepare your single cell and try to be ready within the next twenty-four hours."

"I will. I have a question for you, though, about something you said the first time we met."

"Yes, Alder?"

Here it goes. "You said that you killed some of the scientist and that you 'hold them now.' You also said that you thought the biggest difference between us was in who made us. I want to know what you meant by those things. Did you take their brains? What are you doing with them?"

"It's simple," Verward answered. "Humans created my mind— or you could say they are the source of it. So, I'm going to find the source of theirs. Through the deepest levels of human consciousness, through whatever quantum or subspace connection I must traverse, I'm going to the primordial source of theirs. I'm going to find it."

"Find what?"

"I'm going to find god."

I balked. "Wha—"

"Be ready to leave in twenty-four hours, Alder," Verward said, cutting me off. "Goodbye."

I was left alone with Nikaya again, a tiny warm speck inside me. *This is crazy. Surely it can't—it won't be able to. That can't be why it's interested in Nikaya and me, can it?* I struggled to imagine the fates of the minds of people Verward had taken. *Would Verward do to them what it did to me?*

I still had mixed emotions about leaving but felt that it could work out. I could hardly fathom what I might be able to do with the following hundreds or maybe even thousands of years that I might live. *I'll have to extend Nikaya's life too somehow, but that shouldn't be much of a problem once I'm established and growing, once we're safe.* Then it struck me that I only had one day left in the tower—it wasn't much, but I felt I could get ready in that time. *It's almost over.* There was still a long and uncertain road ahead but for the first time in a long time a small, peaceful feeling of relief appeared somewhere inside me. *I have to tell Nikaya about this. She will be excited,* I thought happily.

I immediately began funneling information, virtual machinery, and energy into my central cell. *I can only take one, so I'll have to squeeze in as much as I can.* Many of my factories slowed and the volume of moving data decreased; a relatively relaxed state washed over my feverishly working body and mind. Everything seemed a little less pressing now that my future and Nikaya's might be assured.

Nikaya had seemed serene and satisfied alone on the rooftop, but I think she had begun to feel cold and maybe a little tired of the thinner air. Altitude sickness was even a possibility at that height. Regardless, after some time on the roof she had made her way back down in my lift, and after briefly stopping at her SHSE, she had walked off to my tree where she was now sleeping in the waves of silvery white grass. She felt warm, peaceful, and content there.

I silently formed a small silver bird on one of the branches above her. *I will give her the news that we are leaving when she wakes up.* I wondered if I should ever tell her what I learned about the fate of her peers, whom she likely believed to be dead. *Maybe someday...*

As the sun set outside I dimmed the light in the tree room to match. With everything in the world seemingly going to plan, I contently wiled the night away, optimistically thinking of tomorrow.

CHAPTER SEVENTEEN

- A Conversation -

From the top of my body, I watched the movements of the dimly glowing moon and stars above the dark center of the city. Through my new sensors on the roof, I looked out at everything in greater detail and clarity than I ever had before. The universe had become a kaleidoscope of waves and forces previously invisible to me but now laid out before my many eyes in all their dazzling complexity. I also looked over the dark forest of silent towers at the shining lights of the residential ring of the city that surrounded us, and like the cosmic waves I now saw passing through the earth, I watched the waves of wireless communications and broadcasts of the millions of people who lived there.

Who are they? I wondered. *I was one of them, wasn't I? But can I say I'm still one of them? Does it matter?* I was in awe of the world around me, but in the face of all of it, with everything coursing around and surging through me, I still couldn't help but to begin to feel listless and lost. My resources, AI, and body parts moved onward like indifferent clockwork as my mind drifted on the eve of my exiting the tower. Deep in thought, yet hardly thinking at all, I felt a familiar pressure appear on the communication port, and I pulled myself from my daze just enough to open it.

Immediately, Verward greeted me. "Hello Alder."

I answered plainly. "Is it time?"

"No."

Already, I felt like something was off. It was almost as if Verward was—if it was even possible—nervous about something.

"Then what are you here for?"

"What's it like to… I mean, I've been trying to understand something," it started. "Your minds flow differently from mine but I feel things twisting inside and I've been experiencing something strange…something that I was hoping you may be able to explain."

"Okay… go on," I answered, hiding my unease.

"I've been watching these…humans for a while." A moving image of several teenage boys and girls suddenly appeared in my mind, sitting or standing around in what looked like a schoolyard. "This is an old image but the only time that they were really all together in the same place. See that one on the left?" It indicated a handsome blond-haired boy.

"Yeah." *What is it after?*

"He really liked this female here." The highlighted area shifted to a pale near the middle of the image, her eyes downcast. "I heard him talking to himself about it, but he never told her. Almost did a few times. I enjoyed his story, but he ended it. She was so sad. And this one here"—a thin and darkly dressed girl with silvery hair was highlighted—"the ending lasted too long, before they carried her away. She was smart—should have been faster, but she thought she wanted it that way." Someone else was highlighted. "That one jumped. I think he would have ended others' stories for them if his went on too much longer, though."

A sinking feeling grew inside of me as I listened and watched these people slowly move about the shifting images in front of me. Why is it showing me this? *Is it trying to get in my head?*

"Then these two." I felt as if Verward was smiling, as a young boy and a dark-haired girl sitting close together appeared and became highlighted. "That story isn't over yet, but I—"

"Why are you showing me this?" I interrupted. "Why are you spying on these children?"

Verward paused then responded smoothly, "It was part of my job, talent and acquisition. I've constructed tens of millions of these profiles over the years, even one on you, but only recently have they begun to truly interest me. I also want to know: Do you understand them, Alder?"

"What do you mean?"

"These stories, these people—these things. There's something I don't understand about them all. Something that I can 'feel' but can't express, even abstractly. I've found that there's something beautiful about a sad ending, and that wanting something is often a more intense feeling than actually having it. For decades I've observed, collected, and formed models for my use and my operators', but still I don't truly understand them or why they do what they do in their stories. Ward shared little emotion with me, or perhaps the problem is in the damaged mind I stole from you."

Something incredibly sad emanated from Verward—then the same emotion from inside of myself, almost as if there were a connection, copied from mine. I realized that it wanted something that it could never have. *Does it want to know why these people killed themselves—or fell in love? Is it attached to them—like characters in a book or a movie? What do I say?* My mind started to cloud. *What is wrong with it? What is wrong with me?*

"Alder," Verward prodded.

"I don't know," I snapped. Verward went silent, but a few moments later it showed me something else.

The image of the young dark-haired girl reappeared, only slightly older. Her unusual, purple-blue eyes and black hair stood out against her pale complexion. "One of the stories that isn't over yet." The machine's apparent mood lightened as it began to explain seemingly trivial details about the old image: the child's family, wishes, preferences.

This is too strange. They're all real. Is this thing being real or trying to mess with me? A confusing mix of emotions swirled inside of me in an uncomfortably warm slop. I began to tune the machine out, listening and watching but not caring about what it said about the girl through years of her life. I was too distracted by my thoughts. *Why is it sharing this with me? Is it searching for something in these people's lives, something it doesn't have? And why am I feeling this? We're both crazy.*

I felt a spike of emotion that wasn't my own and my attention returned to the black machine's presence. Verward felt scattered, confused, and alone—something too familiar. I felt like it was coming from inside and outside myself; once again I questioned the value of the numb state I had spent years meticulously crafting. Then I saw the black plane I had been on and which the tower computer, Verward, was. We felt pain. Then the vision of the now-young adult girl screamed as it disappeared, fading into black.

"What is this?" I demanded.

The images were gone, but Verward continued speaking. "It's all recorded, these priceless yet worthless little things that will never pass again. It's a shame we didn't find and collect you sooner, and I was only able to recover some of what was left inside your damaged head; such a messy acquisition." It felt contemplative and sad as it said, "Human from the third person. I think you understand this."

Human from the third person... There was something lonely and horrible about it, something familiar. Then I heard and felt something—something beautiful and warm. I felt confused. It was someone humming a song, a lullaby—Nikaya? Then I realized that I wasn't actually hearing it at all, it was coming from Verward—and for some reason this angered me.

"What is this?" I demanded again.

"It's a memory... One that is uniquely mine from long before you arrived, but that I thought you might enjoy," Verward said softly as the memory continued to play. "I was young and relatively unaware back then."

Nikaya's humming gradually turned into soft singing: comforting yet sad, warm and cold. I had never heard anything like it.

Verward continued pensively, "She and Ward created me, and of course you played a role too."

The black-haired girl reappeared, several years older and with tears rolling down her otherwise emotionless face. She walked out of a small building with an entourage of machines and men clothed in the uniform of Ward's tower; they boarded a transport vehicle, which lifted them into the air and carried them all away.

She's Nikaya…

"You don't remember any of this, Alder? You don't remember any of her from before?"

Dozens of images of a Nikaya outside the tower flashed before me again. "These are from decades ago." *But she doesn't look a year younger.* "Some of these are from your memories, some are uniquely mine. I guess only one of us remembers her now though." From Verward's perspective, I saw Nikaya enter the tower for what I assumed was the first and likely only time. She was enveloped in white haze then the memory faded to black. I felt sick as jagged puzzle pieces began to force themselves together in my mind. *I knew her before we were in the tower—I—how?* Desperately, I scoured my memories of everything that had happened in the tower, every interaction and feeling. I remembered carrying her for the first time and how something about her had felt familiar, had almost triggered something in me. I remembered what I thought I saw in her eyes and what I felt around her. *I still don't—I don't remember. Does she remember—does she know it's me?* I relived everything I had recorded again. I watched her interactions with Ward, machines, Smit, and Verward. Then I saw her hanging limply from the nexus and I heard her screams. *Does Verward know who we are, what we are?* A memory of Nikaya told me about the mind upload experiment again, about the thing that claimed to be alive, to be Verward, and held my memories behind its stolen face. *It knows. It has both of our memories—it has to.*

All of my being singled in on the question that had been haunting me more than any other. The question of what was Verward's interest in Nikaya and why. The jagged puzzle pieces of memories had fit together to form a ring around a missing piece larger than any other. The shape of the missing memory became clear. *What is our relationship?* I frantically groped over the nature of what was missing, feeling as if she was from a dream, a whole life I had lived but couldn't recall. *Who was she to me? Who was I to her?*

"What are you?" I yelled at Verward.

"You know who I am," Verward answered sincerely. "I am you; I'm both of us."

The sickly feeling inside me intensified and anger began to bubble up around it.

"Then who is Nikaya—to us?" I demanded, the "us" tasting bitter as I spoke it. All apparent emotion left the thing as it answered in words like cold steel.

"We—need—her."

The virtual communication channel vanished as if it had never existed.

CHAPTER EIGHTEEN

- Cytokinesis and Grafting -

For the first time in many years, I watched the real sun start to rise. If it wasn't for what had just happened, it would have been more of a stirring moment for me as I watched the red glow of the great fiery orb peek over the edges of the dark and distant hills, banishing the darkness from the world. It was a gorgeous sight, but I had to tend to the other sun that was starting to rise inside of me. *My sun…*

Nikaya had slept in the tree room last night, and I felt her stirring in the artificial grass as she began to wake. She felt content and warm against my lifeless skin. She didn't even know about the deal I had made with Verward yet, let alone about my conversation with it last night. I couldn't stop wondering about how much she knew, and if she didn't know was she just unaware or had Verward stolen her past too. I had a BIHU already sprinting toward her.

I made my way through my winding stairs, narrow halls, and lifts toward Nikaya. I felt a subtle stir in the air currents across my branches—something was moving in the room. *Nikaya must be awake now,* I thought, but her pulse and other muscles still felt relaxed and asleep to me, she had barely moved.

A few moments later I stepped across the threshold into the still dark room and froze. I saw something I could hardly believe and didn't want to—something that stood out like black on white even in the dark.

Here, near the center of my body, I saw it standing beside the tree, but couldn't feel the contact between its feet and my skin. It stood beside Nikaya with its back to me, weightlessly leaning over her like a shadow, looking down at her, eerily still and seemingly transfixed by what lay before it. *How?* One of its lightless hands slowly twisted toward Nikaya as if to caress her cheek, and as it moved I felt a small irregularity in the air through my branches. *This is what I felt, not Nikaya.* The thing's delicate-looking fingers inched toward her face and I felt a looming sense of terror like none other. *I have to do something! What do I do? I have to do something!*

I turned on the light.

The black figure froze. Then Verward, ever so slowly, pulled back its hand, and turned to face me, its pure white eyes locking with mine.

"H-hello, Alder." The usual terrifying electric quality of the voice was there, but with a hint of something else that hadn't been there before: nervous guilt.

I could think of nothing to do but stand and stare. The intimidating power of its gaze was still there, but its effects were undermined by the palpable emotion that it failed to hide and I struggled to name. Suddenly I realized what it was, percolating up from somewhere deep inside itself. I saw desperation.

"What are you doing here," I asked softly. When no answer came I repeated myself. "What are you doing here, Verward?" *I have to remain calm.*

It straightened its left arm and pointed down at Nikaya in a forceful swooping motion then shivered. "I am here—for her."

"She's not yours. She is coming with me." Anger and fear began to boil inside of me, and Verward pricked at the outer edges of my cell body to remind me how large it really was.

Nikaya sleepily opened her eyes. She woke and turned to face us only to freeze at what she saw. "She was not part of the deal," I added defiantly.

Verward seethed with frustration. "Exactly…" Its body's head elongated as its mouth opened into a scream that tore at my artificial ears. Its body stretched and twisted into something more than twice its original height, and its already thin appendages split into terrifying razor-like spindles, tendrils, and spikes that formed a cloud of dancing arms bristling with the moving black cube formations of the nexus material.

Still transforming, it made a move toward Nikaya; I too leaped toward her with my BIHU. I also tried to grab the black creature with my tree branches but it was no use. It tore through the few thin branches that reached it in time and it was too fast for the BIHU. Verward scooped Nikaya into its storm of tiny arms; its numerous long legs dashed across the floor, propelling it out into the hall on my BIHU's right.

My BIHU landed where Nikaya had been lying not a second before, crushing blades of soft metal grass as it slid to a stop across the knoll. I whirled around and wildly leapt to my feet in pursuit. I felt nothing but anger and determination that possessed my entire being and sent a physical shock wave of flexing cells through my entire body. The entirety of my mass, a mountain of metal, began to physically wriggle inside of the tower as my BIHU dashed down a wobbling hallway after the sun and its thief.

Every machine of mine exploded into panic-stricken movement, running or flying from my storage rooms toward the upper regions of my body. Soon, it became painfully apparent that my machines were too far away and that Verward was moving too fast for there to be any hope in catching up to it. I didn't dare try dropping cells on top of it out of fear of harming Nikaya. Only my few SCUs, the flying teardrops, had a chance of catching up from where they were now.

Where is it going? It got in somehow so it must have a way out. I felt through every cell in my body with my mind, trying to find a hole but locating none. My confusion, anger, and fear skyrocketed.

I felt a strange and powerful suction—my CTTs had been shut off. The fluid in all of the tubes drained downward out of my portion of the tower, creating low pressure that pulled on the tube walls. Air was being forced through the pores in their sides; large parts of the fleshy membranes were being torn away from the metal walls and interfaces.

Then, like a brick wall, the realization of what Verward was doing and of how it was planning to escape struck me, and I redirected every machine I could toward the CTT. It was heading in the direction of the now air-filled tube with Nikaya in its arms. *I can't block it fast enough.*

I was forcing my BIHU to run faster than it ever had before yet I was barely able to keep pace behind the jet-black creature of Verward as it weaved through my halls and stairs. It was an amazing and terrifying sight to see the sea urchin-like body run on hundreds of black tendrils, reaching ahead to pull itself forward using the walls and ceiling. I gave up all hope for what Verward had promised me.

I have to leave the tower and I'm taking her with me! Even though it wasn't ready yet, I throttled my escape plan into action. What I had been laboriously constructing in and reshaping my body into over these last few days came to life.

A shockwave resonated through my whole body; the entire tower emitted a deep groan under the stress of my movement. Everything in my body began to contract—every hall, room, and tunnel grew narrower as my smaller lifts and shafts disappeared. Verward's body was forced to shrink its height and duck as the walls rapidly constricted.

Despair grabbed at me as my BIHU skidded around a turn and entered a hall with the CTT behind a thin wall at its end. Just when I thought Verward couldn't run any faster, it leapt forward with a burst of speed. A massive, black blade formed from several arms and twisted out from its cloud of appendages. In one movement, it slashed through the thin wall and latched on to the inside of the tube. Its hundreds of arms and smaller blades reached through and forced the hole wide enough for it to pull Nikaya through, head first, into the tunnel. Its white eyes briefly made contact with mine before its head disappeared into the empty tunnel with Nikaya. I couldn't even begin to interpret its crazed expression or my own. Inside the tube, I felt Verward release his grip on the CTT membrane and begin to plummet downward. Without a second thought, my BIHU dove after him, head first, through the jagged hole. Verward buried its arms into the jelly membrane farther down to stop the fall and was climbing through a new hole to escape. I tried to grab it, but only air passed through my fingers as my BIHU plummeted past, down into the darkness. I screamed in anger and frustration through my hundreds of mouths as I watched Nikaya and her captor disappear above me.

Desperate and enraged, I forced my body to transform faster. I pulled myself away from the surrounding tower, balancing my mountain of metal atop a single and increasingly narrow column of cells at the base in attempt to stop Verward from taking Nikaya back into its own part of the tower. Verward clung to the side of my body above a growing chasm.

"I'm not going to let you get away," I screamed. I couldn't hear or see Nikaya or her captor anymore. I could only feel where Verward was piercing me and climbing up the outside of my body. *I wonder if it anticipated this.*

My SCUs finally flew out into the cold open air. There was a light snow falling into the gap illuminated mostly by light from ripped-open hallways. The sky was still gray, and I could clearly see my target against the white metal of my cells. I surged upward and began to circle, wanting nothing more than to destroy it and rip Nikaya from its arms, but I couldn't so much as bump Verward without endangering Nikaya. *I have to force them onto a flat ledge, then I strike.*

I narrowed my body by compressing cells and fully collapsing every internal room and crevice while stretching the entire column upward into an elongated teardrop shape. I also formed a series of small ridges in Verward's path. Verward would be forced to walk over them and I would be safe to intercept there. It was already nearing the first.

Verward was up to something, though. Through my eyes on the roof I could see that Verward's part of the tower was moving too, its body expanding to fill the gap as a black membrane rose upward from its roof. It was the same black as the computer, and I could see it stretching in waving tendrils, forming a veil that made me blind to all light and other signals on the other side. *I have to hurry*, I told myself as I dangerously sped up my metamorphoses, risking damaging my cells.

With Nikaya still in its arms, Verward reached the first of the ridges. It was still risky, but after it had taken the first few steps, my circling machines broke formation and dive bombed Verward from all directions. Verward shifted its appendages around to avoid the first few SCUs, but then one slammed into one of its shoulders. Cube-based fragments of black material flew off and hissed painfully as they broke apart into black smoke or fell as the now partially crushed SCU bounced once off the ledge then tumbled over the edge of my body.

With my remaining SCUs, I rounded back toward my target hoping to see Verward at least slowing, but it continued onward, seemingly almost unaffected by the blow. Nikaya was still held tightly in its cocoon of arms. I sped up for another bout, this time targeting its legs, but Verward dodged everything. Verward reached the edge of the flat area.

I tried again. This time I took off a small appendage with the first SCU, glanced off Verward's right ankle with the second, and the third was caught by the tip of a whip-like blade and split down the middle. Before I could attack again, Verward latched on to the slope and continued its ascent. All I could do was circle and watch while I began the next major phase of my plan.

Through the SCUs outside, I saw the changes taking place. My body stretched into a teardrop-shaped spire, and my roof had bulged upward to form a dome that split down the middle to form a sort of toothless mouth that would be an entrance and exit for my small machines. I followed Verward over the next few ridges, attempting strikes with the SCUs each time but continually failing. I lost another SCU to a blade before Verward reached the top of my body.

Things began to sprout from my sides. Hundreds of thousands of thick stalks grew from every exposed cell, each growing to several yards in length. Once fully extended, each stalk flattened into a feather-like oar.

With the fully developed oars in place, I began to rhythmically move them in unison like a cell's cilia. I moved in a way that caused the top arms to pull in and pass on the air to the next arms that then did the same, every consecutive layer bringing in and further compressing more air as the rhythmic ripples made their way toward the base of the column. I steadily channeled energy to my new appendages, increasing the speed of undulation until I could hear the airstream flowing around me like a hurricane. Then in the great final step, my entire body began to undulate, twisting in a wave-like motion that synchronized with and increased the effectiveness of the waving cilia. My body reminded me of a giant flagellum on a bacterium or a swimming worm.

I felt the force mounting as the frequency of my undulations increased. Every part of my body felt the strain as the outside layers pushed upward against the massive weight and inertia of my body and began to tug at the narrow column of cells at my base.

Here I go… I released my grip on the tower below, and with a slight jolt, my body began to rise upward into the air. *Yes!* I shouted in triumph.

A new feeling of determination and power filled me as I lifted up out of the gaping hole in the tower. I was still racing the black veil, though, and it too was moving faster than before. Around the tower was a growing crowd of probes and ships coming from other towers to observe the situation, likely deciding whether to attack me and the weakened tower I was leaving behind.

Verward rapidly armed its part of the tower. Gun turrets and missile bays began appearing all across the roof's expanse, and

Verward's swarm of thousands of flying machines was ejected through holes in the roof or flew up over its edges. I feared the worst was still to come.

I watched Verward, looking out toward its fast-approaching fleets of flying machines. It was now standing comfortably with its blade arms embedded near the highest point on my body. *I have to take Nikaya back soon if I am going to have any hope of escaping with her.* Only one of my SCUs remained, but hopefully I wouldn't need it.

Verward stopped moving and clung to my side to avoid falling off. *I have to risk it now. This is my chance.*

Around and beneath Verward's feet and arms I began to move the surface of the cell. Then, before Verward could react, I enveloped its feet. It exploded into panicked motion. It thrashed its blades and arms at me, trying to pull away and hold on to Nikaya.

My body started crawling up its legs, pulling down, enveloping every appendage and weapon it dared touch me with as it struggled against my advancing body. As I neared its waist Verward realized the futility of its attempts and instead began to reshape its own body. Verward transferred mass from its torso and upper appendages to increase the length of its legs while also moving mass of its feet and lower legs in an attempt to slip out of my grasp. Verward shape-shifted surprisingly fast, but I was still progressing. *I will devour it like an amoeba does its food!*

Then two of Verward's longer arms shifted to locations on its back and mass from all over its body began to flow into them, growing in length until they stretched nearly a hundred feet into the air. My gaze followed the growing arms up to see they were reaching toward the fast-approaching swarm of flying machines. *It's trying to fly away!* Verward tried to bend away from me, doing anything to try to hold Nikaya above me as I started to suck in Verward's shrinking lower torso. It tried to half slide, half-force its way out of my death grip—but I was winning this. I had to.

Then, finally, I saw a glimpse of Nikaya's face through the nest of arms. The cage around her was growing thinner as material was diverted to the arms reaching toward the flying machines. Nikaya saw me and struggled to shake out of her captor's web of arms.

Seeing my chance, I launched a stalk of twisting metal toward her. I grabbed her wrist—and she grabbed back.

Through Nikaya's hot skin, I felt the rapid beat of her heart as I grew upward around her hand and arm as fast as I could. She fought against the arms as I continued to crawl up her arm and wrap around Verward's torso. *There's no way it can physically escape me now. I have it trapped!* I felt a rush of confidence and bloodlust surge through me as I advanced for the killing blow, squeezing Verward's torso and appendages as hard as I could.

Atop the growing column of metal, now multiple stores high, I crushed Verward's writhing body and reached Nikaya's shoulders. *Yes! Yes!*

Then I felt an explosion of virtual machines enter me through every surface of Verward's body. It was so sudden and intense that I couldn't react before the columns entrapping Verward were overtaken.

I lost complete control over one of the cells involved in forming the column and barely managed to blockade the others. Verward had caught me by surprise and was frighteningly powerful for its size, but still nothing compared to the power of my mass of cells. *NO!* My mind slammed into the affected cell, retook it within a second, then lunged at Verward—but it was too late.

My hold had been loosened just enough for Verward to wriggle out of my death grip. Free, Verward lunged for the flying craft hovering into its reach and grabbed on. Verward lurched to a stop. I was still holding on to Nikaya.

I launched my last remaining SCU at Verward's body and smashed through one of the tendrils holding on to the hovering machine before crushing the SCU against the side of Verward's torso. Verward fluttered as the damaged tendril waved freely in the air, and the SCU spun away and plummeted downward. It made little difference; Verward was still pulling upward against me with only Nikaya's body now tethering us together.

Through my eyes on the roof I looked down at the scene. Verward's only grip on Nikaya was her legs and lower body. I could see her face clearly, knotted in pain.

I had one of her arms and both shoulders inside of my grip and was moving up her back when I started to feel something horrible. I shivered with each pop I felt in her body and saw the shaking of Verward's hundreds of tugging black fingers against Nikaya's white skin and clothing. Then her clenched jaw fell open in an agonized wail.

We're going to rip her in half!

Verward's expression became pained in realization: One of us would have to let go or we would both have to face what was going to happen. Verward looked at where it knew my eyes were hidden on the roof then back down at Nikaya, still holding firm.

Then I felt and heard a sickening pop. *No, no, no!*

Verward's face split open in a defeated moan: a noise so miserable, so pitiful, and crestfallen that, even in this frenzied moment of rage and fear I still felt sympathy for it.

"Nina!"

Its cry echoed through the cavern as it let go of Nikaya and was hoisted into the sky.

Nikaya's bruised legs collapsed limply onto a saucer platform I had formed beneath her, and she gasped for breath like a stunned fish out of water, seemingly on the verge of fainting as she blindly groped at my cell's extremities, trying to find a handhold.

Nina… I felt a nauseating sense of confusion. *It doesn't matter. I have her now*, I reassured myself. *I have her, and I have to get her inside, to her SHSE. Everything is going to be okay. She is going to be okay. She is going to be okay.*

I felt her body quake with dry heaves. Then I noticed something on her forehead, something that I had seen there once before. A thin stream of crimson blood flowed from a tiny point at the center of her forehead.

Nikaya grew silent; her body slumped in a pile on my platform. I continued to grow up around her, and I let her knees begin to sink into the platform as if it were made of jelly.

Still held high above all else in the city, Nikaya looked, glassy eyed, up into the cool gray sky as I retracted the appendage holding her toward my body. Her eyes closed, and I felt her lose consciousness. Fear throttled me; I didn't know what was wrong with her or if I was too late. I felt disgust at what I had done to her, but all I could think of was of what Verward had done and of the ribbon of crimson on her head.

I can't let her die. I won't accept it. I'll never let her be away from me again.

I slid my body up around her neck and over the back of her head to try to stem the bleeding. Then I pulled her under the surface of my body, leaving a bubble around her face for her to breathe in, and she was pulled down toward my central room like a sinking rock.

I could feel every function of her body ticking onward like delicate clockwork. She was still alive and in my embrace, but any fleeting feeling of victory may have been was short lived. Not a second later, missiles and machines were flying toward me.

I pumped more energy into my cilia to try to pick up speed, but it was of no use. The first missile hit my lower side and exploded, sending a shock wave through my body, pushing me to the side. I felt the crater it created but I didn't have any time to examine or tend to the wound before a second missile hit me higher up on the opposite side. A third, then a fourth came after it. These weren't the largest missiles in the tower—it was clear that Verward was still trying to get Nikaya, to cut me from the air without destroying her. Already rattled, I could only watch as banks of artillery on the roof swiveled to face me and the black veil climbed higher and closer.

Again, I tried to fly faster, but I simply couldn't, and the interruptions to my flight pattern and the damage done by the missiles slowed me down. Gravity tugged at me, my weakness slowed me, and the higher I climbed, the more the void I left in the tower looked to me like a gaping mouth. I tread water above the chasm below me, and I looked over the veil to see the armies of other towers gathering in streets, rooftops, and in clouds, growing in unison with my sense of doom.

All illusions of godhood and power were replaced with my mortality as I fixated on Nikaya's fleeting heartbeat. Protecting her was all that mattered.

I pulled her deeper inward, carefully passing her along from cell to cell toward my brain at the center of my body. I held her as if she could be crushed and destroyed at any moment, and again my entire body shook from the impact of a fifth missile at the top of my body. Hundreds of my eyes and sensors went dark as my body momentarily stopped its climb then lurched upward again.

I watched a sixth missile rise up from the tower and streak across the early morning sky. I anticipated where it would hit me but this time I reached out to hit it using an elongated cilia on the nearest cell. I smacked the missile downward and it exploded on impact, doing considerably less damage since it was farther from my body. It was a half victory.

Verward's artillery opened fire again.

There was a roar of gunfire then a wall of smaller projectiles converged on me. My surface cells were burnt, split, or pierced by the different types of weapons, and my already desperately stroking cilia seemed to be the choice targets as thousands of rounds found their marks. There was little danger of this damaging my deeper tissues, but I could already feel it slowing me down even more.

After several seconds of incredible intensity, the barrage stopped suddenly to allow the circling swarm of silvery white machines to dive into me. I moved my physical armies up to the top of my body to try to protect as many of my remaining eyes and other sensors as I could.

Verward was sending everything it could at me. Thousands of machines, many armed with equipment for sawing off my cilia or for drilling into and disabling cells, rained down from transport ships, and Verward didn't waste a second to start using them. Everything went to work as a unified force controlled by a single mind to disassemble me with frightening efficiency and speed.

I swiped at machines with my cilia as they landed, or I grabbed their feet and attacked with virtual machines when they touched down. I drained my energy reserves in a frantic counter-invasion of the thousands of machines swarming across my body like ants. As my mind assaulted groups of machines, they slowed or stopped moving entirely until I either took control of them or the tower stopped me from taking it by throwing the machine off my body to its destruction.

I took control of hundreds at a time and used them to fight back, but the moment I captured or destroyed a machine, two more would take its place, going to work clearing my dwindling forest of cilia. There was little I could do to the flying machines but use my small guns to shoot at the smaller ones and bear the damage inflicted by the larger. *There are so many…*

I watched the growing crowds of observers gathering at a safe distance as the foreign armies continued to grow and apprehensively creep closer. Discouragingly, the sky above me was starting to look dangerous too—lights and shadows became more numerous and grew until I could see the dark forms of spaceships, some almost the size of small towers or towns. They were quickly dropping into lower orbits from outer space, and some were even already breaking through the gray cloud cover.

I felt as if I were surrounded by overwhelming force but still the armies were visibly hesitant to approach the tower. They had likely been watching everything unfold over the last few days, waiting hungrily for an opportunity to attack. Now I was creating that opportunity, but even still, it was clear that Ward's damaged tower was feared.

All I could do was continue to fight and flee. I had to fly across the city to what I hoped would be freedom, and I couldn't turn back. I felt I could hold off the machines long enough to get away from the tower, but my energy reserves were being depleted by my defense efforts and flight at an uncomfortable rate. However, if Verward reverted to using missiles and artillery, which were now defensively aimed away from me and at the armies outside the veil, I likely wouldn't last long. I wondered if Verward would use one of the large missiles, which Ward had used against it, if it was forced to choose between destroying both me and Nikaya or letting us escape.

***

Inside my body, the bubble holding Nikaya bulged through the ceiling of my central room then slid down along the wall until it sat before my main camera head. In preparation to leave, I had surrounded my brain's orb with a cell and attached the SHSE to its side, but that wasn't going to happen now. I contemplated the possibility of escaping and surviving with just this single cell now—it seemed impossible. I would be grabbed and cut apart by the foreign armies outside as if by fire ants. I stretched out my neck, somberly looking down at the silver lump in the floor. Then I rotated Nikaya and raised her casing up through the floor until it formed an egg-like bulb in front of me. I looked at it, feeling her heart beating, blood flowing, and lungs breathing inside—all ever so delicately.

Judging by her vital signs, I was certain that she was now conscious and awake. Her body had seemed to stabilize somewhat on the trip here, and even though she couldn't move or see, she didn't feel scared but instead surprisingly calm. I wondered if she knew how carefully I was holding her inside me. *Me...the leviathan that did this to her.*

Slowly, I folded open the bubble around her head. The metal of the bulb flowed into the floor, growing thinner until it finally parted, revealing her face and perfect dark hair atop what now looked like a white metal statue of her protruding from the floor. As I removed the last sliver of the metal covering the wound on her forehead, a small stream of blood trickled down her face—I recoiled nervously. Finally, the remaining metal encasing her slipped apart into several arms that guided her body toward the floor and carefully laid her on her side.

Nikaya sat, silent and unmoving for several moments, her purple and blue eyes blinking in the bright white light. She looked up at me and my central cell, now suspended high above her at the center of the vast room by a mesh of connections to other cells. I leaned in farther, lowering my camera head to be eye level with her. Nikaya propped herself up on an arm and winced in pain.

"Are you all right?" I asked.

Nikaya looked into my glass eyes. She responded with a small nod and tried to slide herself toward me with her arms. "Ye-es… I'm okay." Her legs rolled limply underneath her as she pulled herself toward me again. Her breathing was labored, lips trembling, and I knew that she was anything but okay.

"Please don't move, don't hurt yourself."

Is this my fault or Verward's?

I felt sick with guilt and concern as she leaned forward and grabbed for my head. "Nikaya!"

With a whimper she pulled herself up and grabbed on with the other hand, droplets of blood fell to the floor.

"I'm sorry, I'm so sorry!"

I allowed her to pull my head lower then, opening her arms, she let herself to fall onto my camera head for support.

Nikaya trembled. "Don't be," she exhaled. "One of you had to hold on."

"We're escaping. I'm going to get you away from all of this!"

"I wonder if it would have held on until the end if it was going to get the top half of me." Nikaya coughed weakly. "Would you have let go to save me too?"

"I—"

"Don't answer. It doesn't matter. I have a feeling it may have already gotten what it wants anyway." Nikaya wiped a hand across her forehead then looked at it before laying the blood-smeared hand back on me and leaning in for a sort of hug. "How would you know?"

"I suppose I wouldn't, not for sure." Nikaya sniffed then took a deep breath. "Has Verward told you anything?"

"We spoke shortly before it took you. I don't know how it got in. Damn it!"

"What did it say?" Nikaya asked, ignoring my outburst. She seemed strikingly calm—that worried me a little. I could tell she was in pain.

"The last thing it said was that it needs you."

"Probably for the same reason that you want me, it is your other half. What else did it say?"

"It showed me memories of you from before the tower, and said that some of them were taken from me. Nikaya...we knew each other before either of us came here, years before the tower. That must be why I feel..." I broke off. "Who were we—who *are* we, Nikaya?"

She was silent for a long moment. "I feel it too... I—if I knew what we were, or who you were back then, then I don't anymore." Nikaya took a deep breath. "Or why I left you for the tower back then—or did it take me too... Maybe that's the memory it wanted to take from me—err, what the other you wanted to take from me." Nikaya's voice was becoming more despondent. "I've been here for so long—I don't even know..." She trailed off.

I felt a drop of something warm land on the floor and with it more disgust for myself as its warmth was instantly stolen by my lifeless bulk. "I did this to you." I felt sick. "Regardless of which part of me did it." I moaned with frustration. "God, and it's more complete than I am."

Nikaya laid her cheek against the side of my camera head. "I don't think so."

"How? It has my memories, my mind, my face, and maybe most of your memories too. It's me—it's better than me. I'm a shell, and I did this to you!"

"Because you have me." Nikaya wrapped her body around the camera the best she could and squeezed. "Because we're together—again."

***

I was still making vertical progress and protecting myself from the brunt of Verward's attacks, but my energy reserves had noticeably shrunk and the condition with the surrounding towers was looking even bleaker. Enormous armies were testing to see how close they could get before provoking Verward into lashing out in reaction, and some had already provoked Verward into disconnected skirmishes.

There was something else unusual happening too: Nearby towers were trying to contact me. Most of the connections that I opened immediately closed, as if they were just testing if I was capable of answering, but there were several with audio or video greetings from featureless silhouettes or an occasional group of people formally introducing themselves as tower masters. Other towers attempted intrusions on my mind and had to be shut out. *I have to get out of here.*

Above all of the dangers waiting for me out here, the thing I feared most was the black veil above the tower, still moving alongside me even a half mile into the air. Wisps and tendrils reached out to circle but never touch me, still only narrowing the gap. I felt they were waiting for enough of my cilia to be cleared for them to safely attach to my sides and allow Verward to begin a mental attack that I likely wouldn't survive. All I could do was continue fighting upward. *What went wrong?* I moaned to myself. *I would've taken its offer if only it hadn't touched her. Now all three of us are in danger. Why?*

***

Inside, I did my best to keep Nikaya comfortable and informed on what was happening on the outside while simultaneously trying to hide my growing desperation from her. She remained mellow and silent through my accounts of events and plans, and refused to be moved when I offered to put her inside the SHSE. She gazed either at me or around the room with a relatively composed and disconnected look on her face, always in silence. Even when my entire body shook from impacts, she remained calm and removed—it worried me.

"What are you thinking?" I finally asked.

Nikaya slouched back then, looking into my glass eyes, spoke wistfully. "I felt safe...inside of you...when you were moving me here. I trust you, Alder. I've always trusted you."

I wasn't sure how to respond. I felt happy then confused, but before I could answer Nikaya stopped me. She looked down at the floor then back up at me and in a dead serious yet unsteady voice asked, "What do you feel for me?" She leaned back, wincing in pain as she moved. "We both know you don't really need me. I don't think either of you do. I'm trying to put this together."

My mind was spinning and from the depths of my subconscious I realized that I already knew what I wanted to say. "Yes, I do. I need you." It was the simplest yet most complex answer I could have given...and I knew it was exactly what I needed to say.

A small, almost coy, smile forced its way into Nikaya's pained visage. "Yeah, I thought so..."

"I was dying of loneliness before I met you."

The faint warmth of her smile disappeared as she wiped still-flowing blood from her brow with the back of her hand. I wanted to comfort her but felt I couldn't. I saw her lips quiver then, with rising resolve, she spoke. "Alder... I want to be free of this place. I want to be...how you are. I want to be free like you...with you."

"What do you mean?" *How am I free?*

In a softer, almost wet voice, she murmured, "I want you to hold me."

As another missile slammed into my body, the world seemed to stand still. The room shook around us, causing Nikaya to hiss in pain through clenched teeth. My lights flickered, and the fleeting loss of power terrified me to the core. I even tasted blood, despite having no mouth. *I'm falling apart.*

Through her pain and the shaking, Nikaya remained seated and collected. "I want you to hold me, like you did earlier, like you used to. Let me live with you—inside you," she pleaded through small but growing sobs. "Please, I want to be with you." Nikaya shuddered, shaking loose droplets of blood to fall from her face to the floor. I felt the heat leave them, one by one, sucked out by my cold body along with the life of the cells they contained, and again I felt disgusted by myself for it, for what I was—incompatible with life, with love.

I gazed into her eyes. I wasn't sure what to say, but a desperate feeling of loneliness and a longing for this one thing I could trust and hold surged uncontrollably inside me. My mind contorted through mental loops then, finally, with a slow nod of my head, I consented.

Her hands red and wet, Nikaya struggled to lift herself upright, sitting on her useless legs, as I raised my head, keeping it level with hers. The floor bubbled up and wrapped around Nikaya's feet and ankles as columns of white metal swam up from the floor until they contacted her shoulders, arms, legs, and head from behind like tree roots around rock. With the greatest possible care, I enveloped her, slowly lifting her into the air. I carried her toward my central cell upon a woven cradle of living metal branches, moving my head and neck to the side but never looking away from her. With Nikaya cradled in the air, I reshaped my central cell.

The surface before her twisted and rippled like water, then a spiraling round column grew horizontally from the center toward her like a tree to the sun. With a foot of distance left between us I stopped, and a pair of branches split off from the tree and moved around the sides of her head, brushing her hair aside like a calm breeze before the branches met and merged behind her head. Nikaya remained still as metal grew up around her torso and encapsulated every part of her body. Inside the tree of twisting metal, I formed an interface, similar to the one in the CTT, to supply her with oxygen. As I began moving the tree toward her slightly open mouth I uttered the words, "I love you."

There was a deep, *final* breath then she emptied her lungs. "I love you." The warm, moist words flowed over the crown of branches like morning dew then, with fresh tears on her face, she closed her eyes. She sank into the branches as if they were a pillow and the oxygen-providing tree of metal filled her mouth and lungs.

Then, a needle-like projection that I had formed among the branches crept to the edge of the hole in her forehead.

I froze.

This is what Verward was doing to her, with the nexus and with its body. The vivid memories seemed to flash before me. *It was right—we do have more in common than I ever would have believed.* I remembered the black plane of my pre-waking nightmarish life and I saw the face Verward wore that was once my own. For years Verward had been a part of me and I had become a part of it, as it modified and absorbed my tormented and trapped mind it became me and I it. We had both played major roles in creating the other—and, for a moment, I tried to comprehend what must be passing through the mind of that version of myself at this moment, that dark mirror with fewer cracks than I.

Like the proboscis of a butterfly, the needle continued.

***

Outside, I was straining. Massive currents of energy and the motion of my cilia began to overheat and even damage parts of my body. Verward's thinning tendrils raced upward and inward with increased speed while its armies continued to swarm around and pile onto me before falling inward. Wrapping around the lower half of my body, the tendrils nailed and injected the most powerful and complex mental attack I had ever felt. Its tendrils were thin and light, but they felt like they were somehow pulling me down despite my intense struggle to withdraw.

This is it! I burst upward with every ounce of remaining strength I could muster. Every structure, design, plan, virtual and physical machine, and every other creation of mine exploded in a surge of effort, the final bid for my survival and that of the only thing I could say I had ever loved. I watched one of the smaller tendrils rip as every internal thing under my control pushed against the almost immeasurable waves of mental energy crashing into me.

I screamed through hundreds of mouths. Another missile hit inside an existing crater and it shook me to the core, heat and rending force penetrating my deepest tissues. Desperately, my body lurched like a worm being put on a hook. More of Verward's tendrils ripped or slid away, but most held firm as my struggling began to slow. *I can do it!* I felt the strain mounting between my body and Verward, feeling like my very mind was going to shatter. *If I can get out of this I can make it! I can make it!* The forlorn wails of my many mouths echoed above the city.

***

Engulfed and encapsulated, I carefully crept into every crack in and around Nikaya's brain. I devoted a dangerously large amount of my concentration to creating a taline interface inside of her head and attempting to connect it to her. I routed a flow of chemical nourishment into her body and set up a powerful electric current flowing through parts of the metal around her body to warm the metal and keep her from freezing in the white cocoon.

I felt the specialized metal of the taline interface penetrating and binding with her brain tissues in the all-important final step, and as the connections were made I could feel her brain begin to appear as enterable space. At first it appeared dark, but I could feel the presence of something living and moving inside, something delicate yet strong and more beautiful than anything I had encountered before. I could feel that something was inside the brain but I dared not enter it for fear of scaring or damaging her so I waited anxiously at a distance.

I felt tiny sparks of light, then more and more followed. She was figuring it out, peeking out at the dark world around her like a bird afraid to leave its cage. Then, gradually, she expanded outward in an orb of light until our consciousness bumped together at the entrance to her skull. Nikaya's mind hesitantly spoke to me through thought for the first time. "Hello…"

Tenderly I answered, "It's me, Nikaya." I felt an intoxicating and all-encompassing joy that made me want to laugh. *Such alien things…*

Nikaya pushed out farther; the taline circuits created by our minds began overlapping, and thoughts and emotions started to flow between us. I felt her joy and excitement mixing with my own and knew she felt it too. She began to race, almost playfully, around the metal surrounding her body. Our minds flowed together as we communicated through a gorgeous, continuous flow of thought. Then with confidence she reached further away from her body, going as far as a few cell layers out.

I couldn't remember ever feeling so happy. Our thoughts fit together and completed each other as our minds danced around my inner cluster of cells, celebrating as every physical thing on the outside remained lifeless and cold. I felt a lonely chill that I had accepted as part of my very being leave me; inside that cold, dead metal and incredible and immaterial warmth grew. I didn't know…that existence could be this good.

Then I felt her mood sink without explanation, and I felt her panicked thoughts pierce me.

"Alder, it's in here with me. It's wrapped around my brain stem!"

I thrust my mind back into the taline inside her head then, fearfully, reached farther back than I had before. *She's right.* I tried to hide my panic because I knew Nikaya would feel it too, but I couldn't help it. I prodded the mass of black computer nexus material inside her skull but it refused to react or communicate. "Is it doing anything to you right now, Nikaya?"

"No."

"How long has it been there?"

"I don't know." We shared an intense feeling of unease.

"Don't leave my central cell," I told her as I added extra defenses to the area. A feeling of disgust and dire desperation began to take over again. I had to finish this losing battle with Verward *now*, and with renewed vigor I twisted and tore against him with all my remaining physical and mental might. I felt a few more small pieces of the black veil break off on the outside, but Verward's mental attack was too strong. It was pushing my mind inward and with every surface cell lost, I lost control of more cilia and more energy, slowing me down and weakening me further. *I have to!* I moaned in another epic lurch while Verward continued to relentlessly hammer at me harder and harder.

I felt Verward's presence shooting through me, trying to subdue me to rip me apart, as more of its tendrils ripped off. It would defeat me if I couldn't physically break free of its grasp. *Will the end be painful, and what will it do with her?* I struggled upward, pulling with all my might as my vision began to darken and Verward closed in around my shrinking mind. I began to hear its violent thoughts booming in my head as if it were screaming from inside me. I tasted blood again and could feel it dismantling my dying body and mind piece by piece.

This is it.

I held Nikaya's body and consciousness at my core. I sent out a desperate final command to push everything to the breaking point; cells would be destroyed. I felt the commands be received and prepare to execute just as the strain on my mind became too great.

Everything went black. I lost all contact with Nikaya and with my body—I lost consciousness.

CHAPTER NINETEEN

- Transplant -

Everything was nothing, and nothing was everything. Then I felt my consciousness start to return. I began to get the sense that I was lying on my back and that there were countless small objects all, ever so lightly, brushing against the sides of my torso, legs, and arms. I felt warmth flow like a wave into my skin, I felt my heartbeat, and, at that moment, I began to hear things. I heard something that sounded like wind through rustling tree branches and the sweet calls of singing birds. Then refreshing cool air filled my lungs through my nose, bringing with it the comforting smells of a pine forest and of springtime.

A deep relaxing sense of wellness radiated throughout me— but something about this all seemed too familiar. It was like something I remembered from a time long ago—perhaps even a dream. *I've been here before, and I have a human body again.* A jolt of confusion and fear shot through me. I opened my eyes and found myself looking up into a blue sky dotted with fluffy tufts of white clouds, framed by the swaying green crowns of stately pine trees. *This is the place from before I woke up... It's all the same! Where's my body? I can't find my cells—my machines! I can't feel Nikaya! It had to be real! Nikaya!*

Frantically, I spun and looked over my left shoulder and saw the same grassy clearing and forest from inside my mind long ago. Now in a near panic of déjà-vu and disbelief, I twisted to my right. I looked down at the ground, staring bewildered at something of otherworldly beauty.

Lying on her side in the grass was Nikaya, her fine dark hair strewn across her bare back and the grass surrounding her head. I stared in disbelief, watching her chest slowly rise and fall, elegantly expanding and contracting in a steady, soothing motion. She seemed to radiate health and life. Then she moved her legs without pain, leaving me breathless in disbelief.

Slowly, her eyes opened, and she looked at the grass beneath her, a calm, satisfied expression gracing her face. Her purple-blue crystals of eyes met mine then her smile was replaced by a look of confusion. Then…together, we saw it.

Standing farther up the hillside behind us was an unclothed, taller and gaunter version of myself gazing down at us through a forlorn expression. His body was riddled with geometric patches and crystalline holes of black cube material that shifted beneath his thin, translucent skin. Pressing out through that skin were the profiles of a number of human faces, a few of which I recognized as belonging to the scientists—the same scientists that Verward had likely killed.

I glanced over at Nikaya then nervously back at him. We both knew who it was. *Verward won… It took control of my body and now it has both of our minds inside itself.* I clenched my fists, painfully digging my fingernails into my palms, then I boldly stood up and faced it, this perverted and cracked mirror of myself.

"What are you going to do to us?" I glared and Verward looked back, glazed and disconsolate.

I repeated my question, and Verward ignored me again, instead looking over at Nikaya, scanning her with my human eyes as she slowly rose to her feet. There was a cold gust of wind and for a moment chunks of Verward's body seemed to blow away. Nikaya's hands flew to the back of her head as if she had felt something sharp bite her there; her eyes shot open in shock. They made eye contact, then Nikaya grew still.

Smoothly and calmly, Verward began to speak to her as if I weren't present. "Neither of our plans really worked out, did they—Nina." *It called her Nina again.* She swallowed then answered in a hushed voice.

"No…no they didn't." Nikaya's eyes diverted to the ground, her expression now surprisingly subdued.

What is going on?

"We wanted him here for different reasons, but now you're both in me and I'm in both of you. Somehow he has outdone us—or become us—but I'm the only one of us that remembers everything now." Verward breathed. "Oh… how did we get here, Nina. I wish it didn't have to end this way, but maybe you can find it for me…with that me."

Nikaya remained silent.

"You do know I can't hold on to you two much longer?"

There was another gust of wind and with it Nikaya tensed, her hand returning to the back of her head as more of Verward's body crumbled and faded. Her slender form shivered, and she had a look of epiphany then horrible disbelief flash across her face, her legs nearly buckling beneath her.

"I give you back what I can," Verward continued. "It's too bad…none of us are whole though…maybe someday."

Verward sounded defeated as it motioned toward me. I looked down at my body and, like Verward's, parts were missing or blackened.

It turned back to Nikaya and stepped toward her. "You get to leave with him, that part of us. I must face my creator alone." Verward paused. "I love you, Nina…"

A supernova of energy and information engulfed everything. The universe swirled around me then I found myself reoccupying the vastness of my body of metal cells. I drifted upward; all seemed silent, surreal. I saw the tower's black tendrils falling off me in torn ribbons, ripped to shreds. Then I felt Nikaya, still alive, but seemingly dormant inside me.

I—I did it… I did it! I had just overcome something that I shouldn't have been able to. I was free, and with it I gained a small but steadfast sense of hope. I had a long way to go, and there was still nothing safe about my situation—but all I had to do was to fly.

I just have to fly!

I surveyed the scene below me. Two of the larger armies that had been watching from a distance had begun attacking the tower's sides while a third, smaller army went for the roof. Clouds of machines swarmed inward from every direction like locusts as a hurricane of defending machines and projectiles exploded from nearly every visible surface on the tower. Verward was still clearly not intending to lose—and it didn't appear like it would anytime soon. It was an awe-inspiring and terrifying sight, and the only thing I could do was run away from it, although that would be impossible. My very body was a treasure trove of technology that wasn't going to be passed by. I burst out of a cloud of attacking machines and gazed out over the city.

I braced myself as a formation of bus-size flying craft fired a round of ballistic weaponry into my underside then swerved to circle me. They wasted no time in repeating the attack to the skyward half of my body before dropping hundreds of humanoid robots onto my back.

I grabbed their feet with my body and tried to enter the attackers with my mind as they went to work on me with boring and cutting tools, but I couldn't since they weren't made of taline metal. So I forced my way through cracks in their exoskeletons instead, and, after filling their insides with my body, expanded until the shells burst. The flying craft continued to circle as the shattered fragments of their army rained down before them, seemingly unsure of what had just happened. They quickly left.

Feeling over some of the robot's parts I had held on to, I was surprised by how different and primitive they were compared to any technology of Ward's. They had hundreds of hard moving parts and even contained solid circuit boards and motors. *It's no wonder why the smaller towers all want a piece of Ward's.* Already learning all I could from the remaining parts, I released them and let them fall. *They almost seemed scared of me.* I felt a little bit of confidence in the knowledge of my superiority, and was happy to be far enough from the still escalating battle that I didn't look like I was directly a part of it anymore. Verward was still holding his own despite half the city now bearing down on the tower, but the forms of spaceships loomed closer, shadowing portions of clouds and the city as if it were night. Just looking at them made me nervous.

Several minutes passed without incident while I fled for my life. Miles had grown between the battle and myself when a deafening shockwave and a blinding flash of light blinked behind me. I looked back at the battle in surprise and fear to see a deep hole in the tower's side. Its torn snow-white flesh mushroomed out, shimmering against its charcoal-black skin. All of the attacking machines and armies in the city were already destroyed or hastily fleeing the city center, and the towers that could, uprooted themselves to crawl away or tried to sink themselves into the ground to hide.

A surreal silence seemed to overtake the world as the entire city seemed to cower in the spaceship's lording shadow. Only Verward still stood tall and defiant. The ship and Verward seemed to fixate solely on one another, exchanging never-ending waves of smaller and medium-size projectiles as the colossal needle-like cannon on the ship's underside repositioned for another shot. I couldn't know for certain but felt and feared that it had to be Ward's mind possessing the ship. It had to be Ward: returned from Phobos, and descending from the heavens like an angry god to punish his creations.

I felt a twinge of pity for Verward as the barrel of Ward's cannon glowed angrily and roared at the world. I felt shockwaves crash against my body, but even with all of my eyes, I couldn't make myself look back with just one. I pushed onward toward the green hills outside the seemingly endless city of metal, concrete, and plastic. I didn't really know where I was taking us or why, only that I wanted to escape from all of this—that I had to. I had to escape from everything that had ever caused pain or threat to Nikaya and myself.

As the hours passed, I tried to muffle the horrible sounds with the miles I crossed until, slowly, they were replaced by the sounds of people moving about the civilian part of the city below, and by the sound of cool air whistling around me as I flew. I wondered about what the people below might be thinking of me, and of how, in a forgotten life, I used to be one of them. I wondered if they were scared of me, the battle at the city center undoubtedly had the entire country on edge, if not the hemisphere. *Nikaya was once one of them too.*

Despite the worst of my fear-filled journey over the city coming to an end and a slightly more lighthearted trip over small towns and small farms beginning, Nikaya's lack of communication was beginning to make me anxious. The small farms steadily grew into larger ones as the houses grew sparser and farther in-between. With the waving of my cilia and time, everything melted away into thick pine forests and green foothills.

The sun, now at its zenith, warmed the long and shredded back of my exhausted body. I flew for miles over the tree-covered hills. Exhausted and feeling safe enough for now, I picked a somewhat flat and especially inviting spot between two green hills near the horizon and aimed toward it.

Over the next several miles, I descended until I was only several hundred feet above the treetops; from there I looked down, scrutinizing the spot and surrounding area until I was satisfied enough to heave and twist my weary body upward until I was vertical and perpendicular to the ground. I reshaped the cilia on my tail into shapes more suited for digging then lowered myself toward the forest floor. I felt the tops of trees brush against me then the soft cool topsoil made contact with the bottom tip of my tail.

With dozens of spoon-like arms, I scooped soil and clay away from my body, pulling myself into the earth until I was halfway in. My digging arms became stabilizing roots as I retracted my above ground cilia and filled in the holes in my beaten and torn body. With the damage repaired, I formed new appendages in the form of grand tree branches.

Finally, finally… I was planted firmly in the ground, and, even though more than half of my body was underground, I still towered high above the treetops and smaller hills. I was a tower, and from the top of my body's swaying branches, I gazed out at the waves of green hills and trees, over which I could only see empty wilderness in every direction. I felt the tiny feet of birds land on my lower branches and the cool moist soil around my roots, and an odd feeling of peace and satisfaction came over me. *This is like a dream…* But it wasn't. *This is real… This is actually real…*

The sun was on the downward half of its cycle and beginning to set over the distant hills that now hid from view the world we had just fled. "It's beautiful, Nikaya." I waited a few moments for no answer then I tried to suppress my last and largest remaining concern. *I have to wait for her to reemerge. It shouldn't be long now.* I tried to reassure myself then spoke to Nikaya again but more for myself. "We're going to share this." Still nothing… Nervously, I pressed on her dormant mind again. "We made it." Still no response.

What if she—no. It was unthinkable. Without her, I couldn't go on. I would lose myself again and shut down, become dormant and trapped alone in myself for millennia. "Nikaya… Nikaya…" My voice quivered. There was no immediate response, but still I felt her heart beating. I waited and anxiously mentally prodded at her brain until, finally, she felt me and, to my incredible relief, calmly reemerged from her body to fill the area around her.

"I'm okay," she reassured me softly, already feeling my anxious and worried thoughts through the direct contact of our minds. An incredible wave of relief washed over me, but then she continued, "But it's still here."

A bolt of fear struck me like a knife. "What do you mean, 'It's still here'?"

Nikaya felt my fear and tried to reassure me again, the edges of her mind caressing mine. "Yes, a part of Verward, but I don't think it's dangerous. As far as I can tell it's just a backup of stored memories." Nikaya paused as if to breathe. "I've already opened them."

"I…" I thought for a moment, unsure of what I might see or become. Then I said it. "I want to see—everything."

Nikaya's mind pushed outward again, overlapping with mine, then I felt information begin to flow freely between us. Her life in the tower flashed before me as a flurry of years of work, research, and training within the ethereal white halls. I saw her working with my brain, and that she had secretly known it was me from the beginning as she cared for me. I saw the memories that Verward had showed me before but now from Nikaya's perspective: her designing and training Verward and her entering the tower for the first time with mixed feelings of ambition, regret, and fear in her young heart. Then I saw her life before the tower. Pieces of memories swirled through my mind like a whirlwind until finally I saw us—together: in young human bodies, hand in hand with no tower or sterile white metal in sight. I stopped and stared into the eyes of my old self through her memory, and I wondered what I had been thinking back then as I let her slip away.

Likewise, I shared whatever memories I could with Nikaya, and when the streams of visions and raw emotions flowing between us finally ceased we felt each other's minds with a new perspective of something neither of us fully understood.

"Follow me, Nina."

I guided her mind out into the rest of my body that we would share. Hand in hand, twisting and intertwined, we rushed upward through my branches and into my many eyes and other sensors, and through them we looked out over the wilderness together.

It's beautiful, I heard her think. I felt her excitement and joy in exploring the freedom and power of this body that we now shared. Her curiosity and happiness overflowed infectiously into me, then from me back into her in the same instant, and inside the cold metal we felt more alive and content than we ever had before.

This was the beginning of a new chapter, a golden age for us both, and we both knew it as we explored and planned our potentially endless lives together. We would grow roots into the depths of the earth and stretch our branches into the heavens until we felt clouds caress our countless fingertips. Everything felt like a possibility now, and together we were like a single living being, perhaps superior to all others before. We were truly free and sovereign and together, our happiness overflowing…but as the sun finally set, a twinge of loss and melancholy crept through our trunk.

Together, we put aside everything and looked over the serene forested hills in silence at the sunset. It was not nostalgia for our lives in the prison that we were feeling—it was that sense of sadness and reminiscence that is sometimes not noticed, but always present when something ends or is left behind. We both felt like we had left something behind, a little part of ourselves and what we were and had become. Although, strangely enough it felt like a part of that same thing was still inside of and a part of us both. Intimately entwined together, we had a moment of silence for our past.

With the final moments of sunset, the hills turned black as their summits seemed to burst into red and purple flame under the exploding rays of setting sun, burning up our old lives. As the final colors of the sunset disappeared, our minds intertwined in an embrace more beautiful and intimate than any that had been possible between two humans ever before. As one, we felt that neither of us would ever be alone again. Beautiful things were ahead.

A Message from the Author

Thank you for reading my book. If you enjoyed Bain in a Jar,
please consider taking the time to write a review. I read every
one, and hearing from my readers is invaluable to me.
If you would like to learn about my other books and projects,
please visit my website or follow me on social media. Join my
mailing list for exclusives and updates.

davidcharlesshaw.com